JUNGLE JANE

THE DIAMOND CAVE OF THE NAKED PYGMIES

CHAP HARPER

This is a work of fiction, and is produced from the author's imagination. People, places and things mentioned in this novel are used in a fictional manner.

ISBN: 978-0-578-52963-9

Dedication

Jungle Jane is dedicated to the creative geniuses of Don Moore and Alex Raymond. Moore's words and Raymond's artwork made both their original Jungle Jim and Flash Gordon stories come to life. I created Jungle Jane in the same 1930s-time frame, but beyond that there is very little in common with the creative efforts of Mr. Moore and Mr. Raymond. However, if they were alive today, I would hope they would enjoy this good old rollicking African story.

Award Winning Novel

Ozark Creative Writer, Inc.
Publish Your Book Award
First Place
Jungle Jane:
The Diamond Cave of the Naked Pygmies
October 14, 2017

Books by Chap Harper

Once Upon a Reef - 2012
Once Upon the Congo - 2015
Beer, Bait, and Ammo - 2016
Under Cuba - 2017
Shortcut - 2018
Jungle Jane - 2019

Lapsley II, Congo River, early 1900's.

Chapter One

French Equatorial Africa, July 1933

It wasn't an ordinary tramp steamer, and it wasn't an ordinary storm. The huge and newly launched British trawler *HMS Victoria II* had left Gibraltar four days earlier. She was bound for New York City on a mission vital to the economies of the United States and Great Britain. New oil discoveries in the Middle East had presented a chance for lucrative concessions for both countries which, if secured, would ease the ills of a worldwide Depression. It would also foil Hitler's plan to use the oil to rebuild the war machine held in check by the Treaty of Versailles. The officials sent to broker the arrangement now feared the fierce hurricane winds would drive the *Victoria II* onto the shoals of the coast of West Africa.

A seasoned British diplomat, Sam Goode, had brought his wife Rachael and their thirteen-year-old daughter Jane Ann along for the adventure. The trip commenced in July, so Jane Ann would have plenty of time to see the world and be back in London in time for the fall school term.

There was also the added benefit of her parents being able to keep an eye on a blossoming young blonde beauty who could easily pass for sixteen or seventeen, as she regularly convinced the boys. There wasn't a shy bone in her body, and given the least provocation, she would skinny dip anyplace there was enough water around. A river, ocean, pond, or swimming pool might find her naked, floating face up, exposing a very attractive young body for everybody to see.

Her dad had worried a great deal about her antics. In an effort to protect her from aggressive males, he had trained her to shoot and fight in the most unfair way possible for a girl being attacked.

"Kick him right in his nut sack!" Mr. Goode would tell his daughter. Then he demonstrated punches to the throat, eye jabs, and then it was back to nut kicking.

Jane loved the fighting and gun shooting and was exceptional at both. If ever there was a tomboy, she fit the description. However, she liked the way boys made her feel. Her sense of adventure not only included going hunting with her dad, but exploring the sensations of making out with boys and the excitement that brought. Chastity belts had long been out of style, but Sam Goode kept his eyes open for one nonetheless. He wished he could just lock her up for a few years; then she could marry, have kids, and put to rest her parents' constant concerns for her well-being. He didn't see how she could keep from getting pregnant, even during the voyage. Her mother, Rachael, had secretly given her daughter a package of condoms, and in what was probably her most embarrassing moment on planet Earth, Mrs. Goode had pulled one over a small banana to demonstrate how they worked. Jane laughed until she cried.

Jane had cornered one cabin boy in a utility closet until he yelled for help as she pulled his pants down to his knees. Not only did she not apologize for her action, she accused him of being a homo for squealing like a little girl. At present, everyone was safe from sexual escapades as bulky life jackets and intense rocking of the boat required everyone to just hold on for their lives.

It was no longer a question of what kind of storm they were in. The captain declared it a full hurricane and ordered everyone to gather by the lifeboats. Jane and her parents stood on the deck as it rolled and pitched, while sheets of stinging rain blasted their bodies. The lifeboats were covered with canvas and stretched tight and tied through grommets.

Jane had taken all the waiting she could tolerate and ran up to the waiting lifeboat and untied enough of the canvas for her to squeeze inside the boat and get out of the rain. She pulled her small piece of luggage in after her and then found a dry place in the boat, away from the blowing storm. Her parents didn't try to stop her since they assumed they would be loaded in the same boat in a matter of minutes—that is, until they saw the wave.

Several times higher than the ship, the wave rose from the water on the starboard side of the vessel where Jane's parents were. Few mariners see a wave like that during their lifetime and rarely does anyone live to describe it. It immediately flipped the freighter on her side and drove her to the bottom.

There was only one survivor. Jane's lifeboat was torn from its moorings, detaching the pulleys and ropes and sucking it in the opposite direction from the doomed ship. It would have sunk as well, except for the tightly stretched canvas that kept it from filling with water. As the wave slammed into the lifeboat, Jane struck her head on one of the wooden seats and was knocked unconscious for several hours. She awoke with a tremendous headache and only a faint memory of what happened to the ship or her parents.

Jane began untying the canvas covering. Once it was partly done, she looked out over the sides. A large quantity of debris had drifted along with her lifeboat. She grabbed one of the paddles and began moving the boat towards items she might need. Food items were high on her list, so she plucked the few canned foods that floated and large glass water bottles from the rubble.

There were bodies as well. One was a soldier whom Jane had remembered flirting with several times. He was face down and she rowed next him, reached over and turned him face up, unbuckled his utility belt, took his wallet, and pushed him away. She was glad his eyes were closed. A pistol and knife were a part of his belt along with a compass and extra ammunition.

There were many other bodies, and she took their wallets for money and any clothing articles she felt she might need. Sharks were starting to feed on the carcasses, but Jane refused to give in to them. She would strike them on their noses with her paddle to make them release their grip on the bodies.

Male bodies seemed more helpful than females since they carried lighters, pocket knives, small pistols and money. The dead women provided clothes she might need and jewelry that could be sold later. A few had purses still strapped around their bodies, and even though most of the items found in the purses were soaked, some items would prove useful. One lady had a zippered rubber pouch that held her medications, an unused journal, and a supply of Hartmann sanitary sheets that had miraculously remained dry. Seeing the product made Jane smile. The pharmacy near her home in London sold the sanitary napkins by allowing women to take them from the counter and drop money in a box so the feminine hygiene product didn't have to be discussed with a male clerk. Jane loved to pick them up and ask the clerks how to use them and then watch the young men disintegrate in front of her.

She was surprised by how detached she became from the horror of so much death around her. Floating luggage was like recovered treasure. Inside were clothes that would be laid on the canvas to dry and useful tools such as scissors, eating utensils, and nail clippers. Women had snacks wrapped in tinfoil, while men had boxes of ammunition, knives, and magazines. She dried out any paper products to use as toilet paper. Although there was some toilet paper in the lifeboat kit, there was no reason to waste anything that could be used later.

As she went through her own luggage, she found a pouch that wasn't hers. When she opened it, she started crying. Her mother had placed all her jewelry inside Jane's luggage in case they were not allowed on the lifeboat. She wished she could thank her and tell her she loved her. Jane wanted to apologize to both of her parents for being such a horrible child. She cried until there were no more tears.

If her parents were among the floating dead, she didn't want to find them, especially if they had been dismembered by sharks. Their deaths would mean she was completely alone with no close source of income or support. If she survived and returned home, her parents' entire estate would be hers, but it was no help to her now.

One of the rings taken off an elderly woman was at least a five-carat diamond. The woman's finger was swollen, so Jane had to cut it off with the soldier's knife, while two large sharks pulled on the body from the other side. One shark removed a leg, and another took an arm, while Jane worked to free the ring. She struck them with a paddle and they released the body but only for a few seconds. A large ruby necklace came off easily just as the sharks pulled her body out of reach.

Jane vomited over the side of the boat after completing the tasks but knew that if she could sell the ring and necklace to the right person, she could live off the proceeds for a few years. She was in full survivor mode, and that meant staying alive now and living without starving in the future after she got ashore. Even though she was only thirteen, she had never been meek and knew she would always go down kicking and screaming.

Before long, she could see land off the port side of her little craft, but it was just a small rise above the horizon and was probably twenty or thirty miles away. She had heard her parents say they were off the coast of Central Africa, but she knew nothing about the country. Her dad had taken her to Egypt, in Northern Africa, to see the pyramids a couple of years back. Also, earlier in the summer, she and her parents had taken a trip from Gibraltar on a ferry and had landed back in Northern Africa for a day trip to the hot and crowded Moroccan tourist city of Algiers. She hated it.

The ocean current seemed to be pulling her south and no closer to the land mass. Each day she would row for several hours toward land, but progress was painfully slow. After five days, she could see a distant outline of trees. Two more days and she was close enough to make a move. The waves were now pulling her boat in toward shore and she was drifting in the direction of a sharp, rocky outcropping. She cursed at the predicament in a characteristically adult manner. "Goddamn it, I must get this fucking boat past those rocks."

Jane thrust the paddle deep and hard until she had blisters on her hand and was totally out of breath. Her little craft just narrowly missed the shoals and skidded onto the sand at a beautiful golden-hued beach. The edge of the jungle was only one hundred yards away. In the area between the ocean and the trees was a flat, grassy meadow teeming with wildlife. Most of the animals stopped their feeding to stare at the girl and her boat. A forest elephant mother bellowed and pulled her young calf closer for protection. Some water buffalo snorted and pawed the ground. A couple of hippos played in the surf just south, completely ignoring the landing craft and its crew member.

In the growing darkness, the animals retreated into the jungle, and a wave of fear washed over Jane for the first time since the freighter sunk. There wasn't anything to attack her at night on the water, but now big animals could reach in the boat and harm her—even eat her alive. The tarp would slow them down until they ripped it and found a tasty thirteen-year-old girl to eat. She had several pistols, ranging from a .45 automatic she took from a soldier to small revolvers that were as small as a .22 caliber. The .45 would protect her if she hit an animal's vital organs, but the .22 would just anger a large animal.

Jane made a bed for herself in the boat with clothing she had taken off the dead women and dried by laying them on the canvas. She tied the canvas tightly to the sides, making the air in the boat dense, stuffy, and intolerable. The stern of the lifeboat was still in the water, so she untied some of the canvas there to let in some fresh air. After opening a can of peaches and eating the whole container, she lay down and went to sleep. It had been an exhausting day and her hands stung from the ferocious paddling.

The gentle rolling and splashing of the waves against the boat had been peaceful and comforting during the night. Monkeys could be heard at times. However, what woke her early in the morning before sunrise was disturbing. It was loud, scratching on the boat and a guttural rumbling sound. Next was the thump of the animal as it jumped on the canvas cover and began walking towards the rear of the boat, heading directly for the opening in the canvas.

The moon was bright and illuminated the opening in the boat. Jane grabbed her pistol and readied it to take on the creature. She wouldn't wait long, as a young leopard squeezed through the hole and turned toward its prey. Jane pushed the safety down and rested her thumb on the checkered surface as her dad had instructed her many times in the past. She waited as the big cat walked a few steps closer. Without hesitation, she began firing—hitting her target several times as it ran to the stern and fled through the hole. There was a thrashing sound not far from the boat—then silence. Most likely she had killed it, but the investigation wouldn't take place until sunup.

After the magazine was ejected, she used a flashlight and discovered that five rounds had been spent. She had checked several times and knew there were seven rounds in the magazine and one extra in the chamber. This left her with three usable bullets. Two more full magazines and a box of shells were in the soldier's belt, so she quickly reloaded. She had carefully dried the cartridges during her long time on the water and wiped them with oil from a can she found with the debris. Looking over her inventory of other pistols, she knew the weapon she just used on the leopard had been the best one for the job.

The sun rose, burning off mist that hung between the ocean and the forest. Birds and animals made noises so loud that her ears couldn't identify the source. Jane cautiously untied the canvas and eased her head above the boat gunnel to see if the leopard was dead. The spotted creature was lying only a few yards away, very still, in a sea of circling green flies. On the other side of the dead leopard, sitting in a straight line, were five small natives—maybe pygmies. She ducked under the canvas, shocked at what she had seen. From that initial glance, it appeared they all had spears or bows and arrows with shields.

She came up again to look at them and found them laughing at her. At this point, she hadn't talked to another human in over a week, maybe two weeks as time was elusive and blurry. Maybe it was all right to make contact. She put on a large woman's belt and attached the pistol holster; the utility belt was much too large for her. She had two large knapsacks she had pulled from floating dead men and slung one over her back. Grabbing six cans of sardines to share, she crawled over the side of the boat and walked to the natives. They stood up and she shook hands with each one and handed out sardine cans.

Jane was tall, and the pygmies came up to just above her waistline. Once she had greeted them all, she demonstrated how to use the key to open the cans. They learned quickly and drank the soybean oil and ate the sardines with joy. Jane had a small fork, but once she had eaten the little fish, she drank the juice as well. From a canteen in her knapsack, she poured water into paper cups for them. They were thrilled and tried to give the cups back to her, but she signaled that they were theirs to keep.

Now it was time to try to communicate. Jane took a seat in the grass across from the natives. A few animals had come from the jungle but stayed a safe distance. Having seen pictures of pygmies before, Jane was sure she now faced them. She had also seen pictures of seven-foot Watutsis in magazines such as *National Geographic* and had fantasies about their large man parts. The same parts of these naked natives were not extremely large but surprisingly adequate for their body sizes and on full view for the young girl.

Jane was wearing a pair of boy's khaki pants with lots of pockets that she had found and that fit her perfectly. They were tight in all the right places and her long, silky, blonde hair hung almost to her waist. Her gorgeous blue eyes fascinated the little people, and the pygmies had no doubt she was a female, but not like any they had seen.

She pointed to herself and said, "Jane." They repeated it with sounds somewhat close to her name.

Holding a pen and a notepad, she pointed at the first native to give his name.

He said "Lamia." Then the others gave names as "Nestor," "Beli," "Padi," and "Azima." She tried to find facial references on each one to tell the tiny natives apart.

As she spoke to them, trying to put together words they could share, she sounded more American than British. Sam Goode had been attached to the British Embassy in Washington, DC for five years. So Jane had completed her first through the fifth grades in Maryland at a private school. She even picked up a little southern drawl from some of the Deep-South kids in her classes.

After the pygmies picked up words for food, travel, and jungle, they became fascinated with her blonde hair. They asked to touch it and then pointed to her crotch and chest to ask if they could see her hidden hair. They pointed to their chests and pubic hair and then back to her. Although she was not shy, she wondered if she would have to use up five more rounds if they got too frisky. Losing her virginity to some of Snow White's woodland dwarfs wasn't what she wanted.

If, however, they had been Watutsi, maybe she would have considered it. From the pictures she had seen, they were some of the tallest people on earth, with soft features and exceptionally large man parts. She lowered her pants enough to briefly show her light brown pubic hair. No one in Europe or America would have ever asked her to expose such a private area. The natives gasped, and she wasn't sure it was a good gasp. When she unbuttoned her shirt and showed them the white skin of her chest, without completely exposing her large breasts, they again gasped and laughed. The puzzled look on her face gave them all a reason to try to explain, and she wouldn't understand it all until she had learned their language. Apparently, their women had a great deal of pubic hair and actually had hair on their chest as well. More abundant hair was considered sexy, and obviously Jane didn't make the grade.

She recovered from her lack of sex appeal and directed them to the boat, so each could carry a load of supplies, which none of them needed, into the jungle. She went with the five pygmies into the jungle, neither knowing nor caring where they were going. They smelled terrible but she felt safe with them. Intuitively, she knew these little people would give up their lives to save hers.

Chapter Two

Jane and Her Merry Men

They worked on language skills during their trek through the jungle. As she walked, Jane would write a new word in her journal and translate it to English. The native terms and expressions were repeated often as they continued through the jungle.

Nestor was the leader. He made all the important decisions and was the one who explained such things as how they shot monkeys, found grubs and safe water to drink, and started fires. They really didn't know how to start a fire so one of the natives would carry embers in a pouch. If they lost them or got them wet, they had to borrow embers from a neighboring tribe. Every so often, Nestor would stop them, and they would slice little slivers of wood, and feed it to the embers stored in the pouch. Some of the men had found tinfoil and put it to good use around the embers. Jane had several cigarette lighters but didn't interfere with their fire ritual.

At night, Nestor would sleep near Jane. The first night out, Padi, a young muscular pygmy, showed Jane an erection and moved toward her sleeping spot. Nestor jumped up like he was flying and struck him with the handle of a spear. He yelped and never bothered her again.

Nestor was another matter. Being the leader, he felt that Jane was his property and would try to mount her during the night. Twice, Jane stuck the muzzle of the .45 in his gut with one hand and pressed a knife at his throat with the other. He would grunt and move to the big leaves he slept on and on occasion, masturbate. Jane saw or heard all of them pounding away at one time or another. It was as though they were a bunch of teenagers. After a while, she realized they were just primitive beings who had little or no possessions and got little joy out of life, except for sex, food, their families, and tribal bonds.

Jane was a teenager and very much wanted to pleasure herself as well but knew the natives might notice, prompting an attack on her and resulting in the shooting deaths of five pygmies. She had attempted to talk to her doctor about masturbation and was told it wasn't a healthy or normal activity for a young lady. "Wait for sex until marriage." There was no one willing to talk to her about sex, and there was little to read on the subject, except anatomy books, which she devoured and memorized.

They spent fifteen days in the deep jungle, stopping at times to eat and hunt for food. The pygmies were excellent hunters, shooting monkeys and a small antelope. Jane helped them one day when she shot a wild pig that ran through their camp. She would help them cook and eat some of the meat, but she drew the line at monkeys. One night, a leopard came to the edge of the camp, walking near the circle of natives sleeping close to the fire. Jane fired one shot above its head sending it into the jungle for good.

As they got deeper into the jungle, Jane had learned enough language to ask some questions of Nestor.

"Why are you on this trip?"

In his language, he explained, "We were told by a healer in the village to walk to the big water with waves and bring back someone to help drive the witches from our village. Two of my tribal members died on this journey; one was killed by a hippo, and the other passed away from sickness." Although he tried to describe the length of his trip, he could only say it had lasted so many days he couldn't count them.

He and his four surviving companions had walked and paddled in dugouts from the Ituri Forest above the Congo River almost 2,000 miles, traveling in jungles so thick, only pygmies could have penetrated them without machetes. They had paddled on rivers with crocodiles, hippos, and deadly rapids. Until now, Jane didn't realize how treacherous their journey had been. Had she known what lay before her, she might never have decided to go with them.

Jane didn't want to offend Nestor by dismissing what she considered mythological creatures so she asked, "What do these witches look like?"

Nestor said, "You couldn't see them, but many people in my villages have died from the witches."

"Did the people have spots on their bodies before they died?"

He said, "Yes, they did."

"On your way here did you pass a big town?"

Nestor answered, "Yes, and it is about five days ahead."

Jane knew that Dr. Jenner in England had developed a vaccine for smallpox and her father had her go through the vaccination process. She had a round scar on her arm to prove it. The United States had not adopted it yet, but if there was a British doctor in this large town then he might help. She would have the doctor question the natives to see if it was that disease.

"What is the name of this country?" she asked.

"Congo."

"And the big town?"

He said they didn't know and had gone around it.

She wondered if she could hold her own in a big African town. At age thirteen, most girls would be ill-equipped to handle themselves as adults. She, however, had refused to act her age. Although she created trouble for her parents, they acknowledged she was brilliant beyond her years. School was always too easy for her, and frustrated education staffers had no idea how to handle her. She had already skipped two grades and was still bored with school. Her fourteenth birthday was coming up in September, only a few weeks away. She was to be propelled to the eleventh grade at her private school in London. Her parents and teachers expected her to complete high school by age fifteen and then enter college.

Applying her abilities to learning a complex Central-Sudanic language called Mangbutu-Lese, she was now constructing long sentences and added to her vocabulary each day. In school, she had mastered French so quickly that the instructor gave her boring French poetry and novels to read while he labored with the rest of the class. This was a starting point for her dislike of everything French. The arrogance of many of the French people she met added to her disdain for the language. However, Jane's mind absorbed these subjects and everything else she read or heard.

The trail widened as they neared the city and they passed many villages and other travelers. Most spoke a form of Swahili, which the pygmies partially understood. When there was time, Jane would sit down and work her way through that language. She learned it was a somewhat universal trading language, so she really concentrated on it every chance she got, but to further complicate matters, Bantu was the local tribal language used in most of the villages. Now she had three languages to conquer.

She learned that the big city was Brazzaville, and as they neared it, they stayed in and around native villages. Jane would exhaust villagers with her quest to learn their languages. In the back of her mind, she wanted to learn the Watutsi language and wanted to meet one for her own perverse reasons. Maybe she would hire a couple of them to be her guards on her trip. The thought made her hot and she would dream about having sex with a seven-foot-tall Watutsi.

After a few days of easy travel on wide and unobstructed trails and roads, they entered the outskirts of the Brazzaville, named for a French explorer who left the language as a gift to the country and all who came after him. Despite her loathing of the language, Jane knew French very well, so this wasn't a concern.

After walking several hours in the city, they began to find Europeans who were shop owners and business men. She popped her head into a small market and asked, "Do you speak English?"

An aged, white-haired man with a large gut spoke to her. "Français seulement, madame," he said, which because he answered the question so quickly, meant he understood it and probably spoke English but preferred not to.

"Old man, I have money to spend in your store if you will speak English to me," Jane said. She felt more at ease with English and wanted to force the issue with the old man.

"How may I help you—my name is Marcel," he said, smiling and offering his hand to her. She refused the handshake since he had lied to her like so many other French people had done before.

"My native friends and I need food and supplies. Will you take either British or US money?"

"I will take either—US dollars will buy you more. Your native friends will have to stay outside."

She was used to the policy of white store owners, so she didn't argue.

"Do you have some boys' short pants I could purchase for them? I'm afraid their nakedness will cause some issues in town."

The old man walked over to his dry goods section and came back with boys' shorts in various bland, navy, charcoal, and khaki colors. They were school uniform designs with an extra pocket on the outside legs. He had done an excellent job of guessing their sizes. The pygmies put them on without a problem, buttoning them in the front, and then explored the pockets.

"Now, do you have some sandwiches, or can you make some? Simple meat on bread would be fine. Something to drink, like a Coca-Cola."

"No problem. Would you like a bunch of bananas? Got some fresh ones."

"Yes, that would be great!"

After he came back with the food, Jane added some snacks and crackers to the order. The total was a little over eighteen dollars. She gave him a US twenty, and he gave her Congolese francs as change. She then asked about hotels where the natives could stay outside.

"There's a big rest house about a quarter mile up the road. Better than a hotel. Your natives can stay in the yard—on the porch if it rains. Do it all the time since they stage expeditions out of there. Husband and wife run it—name's Rhodes. They call it a comfort house."

"Thanks. If I send the natives down later with a note and money, can you fill the order?"

"No problem, madam. I will treat them fairly. Thanks for the business."

Jane still didn't shake his hand or thank him as he was still on probation with her because of the lie...and because he was French.

She and the natives ate the sandwiches outside the store and then walked to the comfort house. It was a large, colonial-style house with large, white, wooden columns and a wraparound porch. She told the natives to wait in the yard under the shade of a huge mahogany tree.

She marched up the steps and knocked on the front door. She heard a voice from inside in French.

"Quit banging on the goddamn door! Come on in!"

"English?"

"A little," the female voice said. Jane was determined to stomp out French anyplace she could. She opened the door and faced a middle-aged woman, devoid of make-up and sporting a mat of tangled hair untouched by a hairdresser for one, maybe two decades.

"Hattie Rhodes. Who are you, young lady?"

"Jane Ann Goode, ma'am. I am the only survivor of the shipwreck *HMS Victoria II*. Met up with those pygmies in your yard, and they led me here."

"Great balls of monkey shit! Francis, get your ass in here!"

Francis rounded the corner with a dead chicken in his hand, and after Hattie introduced the young girl, extended the free one to Jane.

"We heard about the shipwreck—in all the papers—even in Brazzaville. How did you survive?" Francis asked incredulously.

"Don't pester the girl now. She wants to clean up before dinner and then she can tell us of all her adventures."

"I have money to pay for the room and for the natives in the yard. Is there a latrine or outhouse for them? I will provide their food later. They just ate and have some bananas to hold them a while."

"Tell them to use the big wooden latrine and to throw lime on their shit," Hattie said. "Need to piss there, too, as I don't want it on my grass. But they'll be fine in the yard unless it rains, and then they can sleep on the porch. If you speak their lingo, go tell 'em what I said."

Jane went out in the yard and gave the instructions to Nestor. She also gave him a $5 bill and a note to the grocery store owner to fix sandwiches, Coca-Cola, and fruit. She asked Hattie what time the old man closed his store, and if $5 was enough for five sandwiches, soft drinks, and fruit.

"God in Himmel! I can make them sandwiches for half that and they can pick fruit around the yard. I got plenty of Coca-Cola and water. That old man will rob you blind."

Jane told them to stay around the yard, and she would make sure they got food that evening. They seemed pleased and at any rate, were not hungry now.

Jane handed Hattie the $5 bill she had retrieved from Nestor and told her there was more if needed. Hattie opened her room, demonstrated the pump for her bath, clicked on her ceiling fan, and handed her a big brass room key. After she closed the door and left, Jane got a chance to look around. It wasn't a luxurious room, but it was homey and lovely for someone who had been sleeping on banana leaves and fighting off little African guys' penises for almost two weeks.

Three pictures hung on the wall. One was of a large boat on a river, which Jane assumed was the Congo. Another was of a young couple standing in front of a native hut; they were smiling and appeared happy. She looked closer and realized it was Hattie and Francis.

"*What a wonderful and inspiring photograph of a young couple on a great adventure, and here they are, still at it,*" she thought.

In the picture, Mr. Rhodes had on a nice suit, and Hattie wore a proper long dress and held a parasol. She was extremely pretty.

The third picture was of Albert Schweitzer, who was famous in Europe and operated a medical facility somewhere in the French Congo.

Moving her focus around the room, she saw there was only one draped window. A ceiling fan pushed the hot, humid air around in the room. There were two lamps, one by the bed on a table and another next to a rocking chair. The dresser, bedposts, headboard, rocker and tables were made of beautiful, reddish African mahogany. She ran her hand along the dresser and opened a drawer. It was empty, except for a package of moth balls. One of the rugs on the floor was a leopard skin. She smiled when she stepped on it.

The bathroom was a big surprise, as there was a sink next to a big bathtub. A toilet with a water tank near the ceiling had a rope and chain dangling down. The iron clawed white porcelain bathtub had a hand pump at one end and a big stopper to drain it. She stripped off her filthy pants, shirt, and underwear and started vigorously pumping water into the tub. At first the water was brown colored but quickly cleared up. It wasn't long before she found a bar of soap and dug in her pack for a small bottle of shampoo and eased into the cool water. She appreciated this bath more than all the others she had taken in her life. She really wanted to sleep but was afraid of drowning. She fell asleep anyway. After a while, she was awakened by Hattie knocking on her door and realized she had been sleeping with water up to her chin for a long time.

Chapter Three

The Comfort House—Brazzaville

Hattie asked if she could come in, and Jane quickly wrapped herself in a towel and opened the door.

"Girl, I bet you feel much better after a bath. Might need to treat the tub with lye now," Hattie said, laughing.

"I'm sorry to take so long, but I fell asleep. What is the dress code around here?" Jane asked.

"During the day just cover the parts that make the men crazy, and at night, you can put on a dress for dinner if you have one. Right now, we will have some drinks in the great room. Shorts are fine. There's some other guests I want you to meet," Hattie said as she turned to leave the room.

"Will I meet Albert Schweitzer?"

"Heavens, no! He does have a clinic several hundred miles from here, though. I read in the local paper that he went back to Strasbourg last year and may come back in a year or so. He comes and goes," Hattie said. She left the room and closed the door behind her.

Jane did have a dress and a couple pairs of shorts even though they were considered somewhat inappropriate for upper British society. Within the last few years, it was common to find shorts sold in English department stores, but older British women tended to frown upon the practice of wearing them—the exact response Jane wanted to provoke. She put on a white denim pair with cuffs and a blue sleeveless blouse. Her body was tan from sunbathing on the ship—in the nude when she found a private place onboard. She dried her hair with fresh towels and brushed the long blonde strands. She had a pair of shoes in her pack that had about a three-inch heel which helped accent her long perfectly shaped legs. Jane was tall for her age at about 5'7", and with the heels, she was a stately and domineering 5'10". Her face was quite beautiful in its natural state. She was reluctant to put on the makeup she had rescued from the dead women's purses. She decided to simply apply a little lipstick, eyebrow liner, and some highlighter around her brilliant blue eyes. Then she took a last minute to observe her reflection in the standing mirror. She was ready.

As she left her room, she spotted Hattie down a long hallway, signaling her to come on. Once next to her, Jane was led into a room filled with big game trophies mounted on the wall. The rugs seemed to be everywhere, and they featured lions, leopards, zebras, and cheetahs. Most of the furniture was leather or rattan with ample mahogany as well. There were card tables and an enormous bar made of an especially dark wood—possibly ironwood or ebony. Then she noticed the people in the room—mostly men wearing khaki hunting garb. Besides Hattie, there was one other woman who was sitting next to a middle-aged gentleman in a business suit. Hattie took Jane by the hand and presented her to the court.

"I would like you to meet Miss Jane Ann Goode. She is from London and is the only known survivor of the recent shipwreck off our shores."

Suddenly all the men rose to their feet to acknowledge and introduce themselves. She first went to the lady who was still seated.

"Ma'am, I am so glad to meet you."

"Jane, I am Lillian Simpson from Belgium. I must hear your remarkable story. But before I do, I just wanted to say I'm so sorry about your parents if they are indeed lost in the storm." Lillian was an attractive, slender but well-built lady who appeared to be in her forties. She had brown hair with streaks of gray and was dressed fashionably in a long, fitted, sleeveless dress that showed an adequate amount of cleavage—enough to say to the men, "Yes, I have big tits, but I'm only going to show you enough to get you interested." Her English was excellent and spoken with a beautiful French accent.

"Thank you, Mrs. Simpson. I fear they are lost as a wave as tall as a mountain drove the ship to the bottom. Being impatient, I crawled into a lifeboat before anyone else. As the wave crashed down on the ship, my boat was ripped from its moorings and was thrown free. I was knocked out by the wave. After I came to, I searched the debris field for quite a while. I didn't see any other survivors. I collected things floating around to help me survive including a few pistols and ammunition. My dad taught me how to shoot, which came in handy."

The men then started to come by and kiss her hand, introducing themselves and telling her how lovely she was. Jane thought she could see a few erections bulging in their khaki pants. They had also been in the jungle too long.

"Girl, what would you like to drink? Got Tusker beer from Kenya, some wine from Europe, or hard liquor, if you want a mixed drink," Hattie said.

"If someone could fix me a Bees Knees? It's gin, honey or sweet syrup, and lemon juice."

"Can do!" Hattie headed over to the large bar and let Jane be swallowed by the crowd. She could hold her own with just about anyone but chose a seat next to Lillian on a large leather sofa.

"So, Mrs. Simpson, what brings you to Africa?"

"Oh, please call me Lillian, dear. My husband is a liaison to the office of domestic and native affairs in Brussels. We are staying here instead of Leopoldville because we love this rest house, and of course, Hattie and Francis. The officials in Brussels always throw a fit when we stay on the French Congo side of the river, but it's so much quieter and peaceful here. The government calms down when they notice that the expenses are about a third of the charges for a hotel in Leopoldville. Paul comes here every few months and sometimes takes me with him. This is a new position for him. Previously, we were in the Foreign Service posted in San Francisco for ten years. I'm afraid my kids are more American than Belgian. They are now in college except for one who should start this year. I'm free to travel a little."

Helen was intrigued by Jane. "You are so beautiful. How old are you?"

Jane was going to have to lie. If she told them she was thirteen, they would immediately find a way to have her shipped home. Sixteen might do the trick—she added a year to be sure.

"I'm seventeen. A senior in Oxford upper school. I hope to go to

Christ's Church College after this year, but probably will sit out a year, as I have some things to do here," Jane said as Lillian handed her the drink.

"In London, you might be too young to drink, but here—who gives a shit!" Hattie said.

Lillian's husband Paul introduced himself. "Jane, you are quite the adventurous gal. Two or three weeks in the jungle with wild savages—sleeping on banana leaves, I gather. Probably fighting off the advances of primitive natives," Paul said, probing beyond the bounds of propriety.

"Paul! Don't you dare ask her such questions!" Lillian said sternly.

"It's fine, it's fine," Jane said. "I have a forty-five automatic and a knife with an eight-inch blade. The leader, Nestor, got randy a couple times but backed off when a gun was in his gut and a knife blade to his throat. He later protected me from the others. They saw I had killed a leopard the night before they showed up, so they knew I could shoot. It had found its way into my lifeboat at night while I was on shore. The next morning the natives were on the other side of the dead leopard and laughed at me when I stuck my head out of the lifeboat."

"Wait! What in hell have I missed of this story?" asked a young man entering the room, who appeared to be college aged. He leaned over and kissed Lillian on the forehead.

"Jane Ann Goode, I would like you to meet my youngest son, Turner. He could start his first year at Yale in the States either in the fall or spring but is bumming around for a while trying to decide," Lillian said.

Jane was impressed. He stood over six feet tall, muscular, lean and movie-star handsome. Turner had intriguing deep-green eyes, a smile that produced dimples, and streaked, light blond hair. From someplace in her brain, she imagined what their babies would look like…and the size of his penis. She wondered if she would ever get over her obsession with male body parts. She had looked at five naked pygmies for two weeks and had to admit, in their erect state, they were impressive for their short stature. She had now seen more men with the lower body parts at attention than most women do in a lifetime. Since she hadn't yet enjoyed an intimate encounter with a man, she was curious what it would be like.

Turner was looking at the most beautiful girl he had ever seen. He eyed her legs, soft feminine shoulders, breasts, dark tan skin, and captivating blue eyes without appearing to stare at any of those parts. He saw them, though, and couldn't believe the total package. A more gorgeous girl couldn't have been ordered from a catalogue. Without knowing how, he vowed to have this girl for his own.

The three other men in the room came over to listen to Jane tell her story. She repeated it and added she had been learning three languages. Her listeners were amazed since they had lived in Africa for years and had only been able to master a few words.

"Languages have always been easy for me. Let me ask you: which is the most important one to learn—Swahili or Bantu?"

An older man in threadbare khakis spoke up. "My dear young lady." He paused to take a sip of what looked like whiskey on the rocks. "If you plan on traveling about Africa and dealing with various African tribes, then Swahili of course. If you're staying in one place for a while, then learn the language of the locals. Bantu comes in many forms, but some words are the same," he said. He introduced himself as Roger Janssen from Antwerp, Belgium.

"Thank you, sir. What do you do back in Antwerp?" Jane asked.

"I am a diamond buyer," he said and looked closely at the diamond earrings and necklace Jane was wearing. "You, my dear, have very good taste in jewelry."

"My mother's. She put them in my luggage in case the adults were not allowed in the lifeboats. I didn't even know she had done it until I was adrift for a few days," Jane said. She didn't mention the other jewelry she took off dead women.

"The mine owners bring their rough gems to me, and I buy them and take them back to Belgium or Amsterdam to resell them to the diamond merchants who assign them to cutters. Ninety percent of diamonds from this country are industrial grade. Very few are gem quality," Roger said and took another gulp of his drink.

"I stay on the French side of the river, so I'm not bothered with business after hours," Roger said.

"Are there a lot of diamond mines around here?" Jane asked.

"Not in this area, but they can be found above the Congo and along some of the tributaries. God-awful places and most of the mines are found in jungles that have only recently been explored. Your pygmy friends live smack dab in the middle of diamond country and in areas where white men have never set foot," Roger explained.

Turner had tired of the diamond discussion. "Jane Ann, would you like to walk out on the porch with me and watch a great African sunset?" he asked and reached for her hand. She obliged and took his hand and they walked out of the great room to the tune of disappointed old men accusing Turner of stealing her from the group.

His hand felt like it was plugged into her body somehow. She loved the feeling and would have followed him anywhere. They walked the wraparound porch until they faced west and watched the orange ball rest on the horizon with a base of date palms. As they looked briefly at the sunset and then at each other, Turner let go of her hand and put his arm around her waist.

"Jane Ann, you are an amazing lady, and I hope to get to know you better."

"You could start by telling me about your life history, Turner."

"Not a lot to tell. Big game hunter, war hero, multi-millionaire, supporter of the oppressed, and God's gift to women," he said, laughing, and Jane joined him.

"Can you add world's biggest liar to the list?"

"Well, only if you choose to be skeptical. How do you feel about the 'God's gift to women' part?"

"Well, you look good, but who knows? Maybe you have multiple personalities or you beat your girlfriends." She was now facing him and moving closer.

"What are your views on spanking?" he asked.

"My parents rarely did that, and I turned out perfect. As to whether they spanked each other—I never asked."

They looked into each other's eyes. Turner's eyes were sea-green, and Jane was transfixed by them. She wanted to kiss him, but he would have to make that move. The light was dimming now as the sun settled into the palm trees. Turner put his hands on her cheeks very gently and pulled her to his lips. He let them touch briefly and then took in her breath. He breathed with her for what she thought was an eternity. Then he kissed her and used his tongue. He pulled away and bit her bottom lip softly. She was breathing hard, as if she had run a race. She kissed him hard like a wild animal, then stopped abruptly.

"We've got to stop this! I'm beginning to believe the God's gift part."

"You are God's gift. Let's go back inside before we cause a scene. Do I have lipstick all over me?"

"Just your entire head and down your throat." Jane took her handkerchief and wiped his mouth. Satisfied that she'd removed the evidence, she took out a compact with a mirror and reapplied some lipstick.

They held hands and walked into the great room with huge smiles, signaling to the group that their relationship was a progressing relationship. Turner sat across from her at a card table where a deck of cards lay.

"Do you play gin rummy?"

"Yes. Deal them and prepare to be slaughtered."

Chapter Four

Travel Plans

"If we were playing strip gin, you would be buck naked," Jane said as she tossed down another gin.

"How do you put those hands together so fast?" Turner asked.

"Economics of waste, my dear boy. Don't throw away anything that has promise. Build on the cards you were dealt. Does it sound like a philosophy lesson?"

"Sounds like a life lesson—don't play cards with Jane—she'll whip your ass."

Hattie entered the room, clapping her hands as though recess was over in the schoolyard. "Dinner in an hour if anyone wants to go freshen up. We're having chicken on noodles with a cream sauce," she announced.

Once Jane was back in her room, she looked at her dress options. She laid out four dresses: one was an old flapper design still popular with the young, two were classy dresses her mother had bought for her to wear at daytime events, and the last one was a sleeveless, low cut, indigo blue evening dress with fabric flowing on one side to the floor and a cut that would show a little leg showing on the other side. The evening dress appeared to be silk but lighter in texture. She had found it undamaged in some floating luggage and tried it on in the lifeboat. She loved it and knew the men would also. She clearly was over-dressed for a comfort house in the middle of the jungle but didn't care. There was just one person she wanted to impress, and he was already smitten. She might as well devastate him.

Hattie greeted Jane as she left her room and turned toward the dining room. It was a grandiose chamber and featured what had to be one of the largest mahogany tables in Africa. Turner was already there and pulled a chair out for her. The table would accommodate thirty or forty, but tonight there were only ten—seven men and three ladies. As Jane walked in, everyone at the table gasped at how beautiful she was. To those living full time in Africa and those there on work assignments, Jane was a welcome diversion. For Turner, Jane was much more than a novelty—she had put his poorly constructed plans on hold.

"This room, table, and decorations are so grand, Hattie," said Jane. "I can't believe I was walking through the jungle yesterday with five naked pygmies. I forgot to tell you to fix them sandwiches, but I'm guessing you took care of them."

"Yes, dear. They are fine. We may hook up a hose and wash them down tomorrow," Hattie chuckled.

After Jane and Lillian were seated, the men took their places. Hattie was directing the servers, so she didn't take her place next to Francis until she was certain they were performing adequately.

Once seated, she asked George De Smit, a missionary from Belgium, to say grace. He did so eloquently and kept his sermon short. Jane was not fond of religion but was wise enough to keep her mouth shut. Sitting to the left of Turner, she felt his hand touch hers under the table and squeeze it gently. It was such a nice feeling. She let go of his hand to grasp her fork as she started working on a beautiful fruit salad. Since she was the focus of the dinner party, the questions came hot and heavy.

"Dear Jane Ann, with your parents deceased, are you going to go home and help settle their estate?" asked Lillian.

"My Uncle Basil is a solicitor and doesn't live but a mile from my home. I intend to wire him tomorrow. I believe one of your local newspaper people came by today and talked to Hattie, so the word will be out soon that I'm alive."

"Indeed, they did come by, and I sent them on their way until you have some rest," Hattie said.

"What are your plans here in Brazzaville? Do you intend to stay a while?" Paul Simpson asked.

"I need to know if there is a British doctor here or in Leopoldville. If so, I will take the natives by for smallpox vaccination. Then I plan to make sure they get back to their villages and help treat the ones who are sick. They saved my life, and I want to return the favor. We will take the ferry to Stanleyville and then go west to their village. I don't underestimate the danger and will need to hire safari guides and other personnel. From what I've been told, the ferry is as dangerous as the jungle at times." Jane looked around the table at mouths all at full gape. It was as if she had told them she was planning to blow her brains out right after dessert.

A man at the table whom Jane hadn't yet met spoke. "Uhhhh—Jane, my lovely lady. I'm Maximillian Kruger from The Republic of Baden, outside of Germany. You may call me Max. I am an expedition leader for hire, but I must bore you with a story before we get into that further."

He stood up and was only slighter taller than when he was sitting. Adjusting his handlebar mustache by twisting the end of it, he produced a pipe and inserted it in his mouth without lighting it. Middle-aged and sun scorched, he was redheaded, with eyes that were a faded hazel color. He stood behind his chair as though shielding himself from gunplay.

"Henry Stanley went through that region in 1887. He was the greatest explorer of our time, and he lost 511 men going through the area where these natives live. His rear column never even made it up river. He started at the Aruwimi River, and then the Ituri, the natives, the animals, the lack of food, the diseases all took their toll. It is probably the most inhospitable place on earth. I'm telling you this not to scare you, but to let you know that the best were defeated there," Max said, quite proud of the history lesson he was teaching. He was about to meet his match.

"Thank you, Mr. Kruger. You are right to challenge anyone who would take such a foolhardy journey. However, let me correct a few points about Mr. Stanley's expedition to save the Emin Pasha in Equatoria, Africa. First, he should have never taken his expedition through the Congo. He only did it because Leopold II wanted him to blaze a trail through his country as an advertisement for the Congo lands he bought while he was King. I'm sorry if I'm being harsh on Belgium at that time, but it wasn't the country's finest moment." Jane pulled a small piece of orange from her salad and looked at it, smiled, and popped it in her mouth.

"You see, Stanley was in the employ of Leopold II at the time the expedition was being planned, and the only way he could get out of the arrangement was to run the expedition through the Congo. Had Stanley chosen to rescue the Emin Pasha from the Kenyan side of the continent, he would have crossed open savannas with ample game and waterholes and would have arrived in a few weeks and possibly not lost a single man." Jane wiped the juice from the orange from her lips and continued.

"Stanley's newspaper and other backers wanted drama and adventure at the expense of over five hundred lives. Henry Stanley had bearers carry a thousand-pound maxi-gun and a steel boat that came in sections. Many of his men were gun bearers only and didn't share in the labor of transporting supplies. His food rations consisted of big tins of biscuits and improper rations for the porters, whom he used up like firewood." Jane took a breath and looked over at Turner to gauge his reaction to her speech. His mouth was open, and his eyes were huge. He knew she was smart but had not seen it on display before.

"Even though slavery was illegal, that didn't stop Stanley from renting slaves from the biggest slave trader in the world, Tippu Tip in Zanzibar, and recommending him as governor of the Stanley Falls region in the Congo Free State. Later, Stanley would accuse Tippu Tip of being responsible for the near annihilation of his rear guard. If Henry Stanley made a good decision on this fiasco of a trip, I have failed to see it, and I've read both volumes of his *In Darkest Africa*." She looked directly at Max as she spoke.

"The British government was so unimpressed that directly after the news of how many souls Stanley lost on the expedition, they outlawed expeditions to Africa unless it was purely military in nature. And, for those who still think he might have been unjustly maligned and not personally responsible for these losses, he hung natives that displeased him without a hint of a trial. This celebrated explorer watched while men dropped from heat and starvation as he went back to a tent set up by his boys. He found his change of clothes laid out for him by his man servant, who was with him the whole time, but rarely mentioned in his books. I do apologize for rambling on, but I didn't want you to worry that I didn't know the history of the region." Jane dove back into her salad and heard murmurs and gulps from the other dinners.

"Jane Ann, I bet you are the kid that always raised her hand in class because you knew the answer to all the questions," Turner said, trying to lighten the mood.

"I was Miss Smarty Pants," Jane said, with a laugh. Everyone else laughed as well. No one cared to challenge her on anything since few felt her intellectual equal—unless it was Turner, who was also exceptionally bright. She knew dummies didn't get into Yale.

The talk at dinner was tame after Jane exposed Belgium as an evil empire and Stanley as a cold-blooded killer. No one could top her speech, so jokes and current events took center stage. After dinner, the great room became the place for a smoke and the clinking of glasses filled with spirits. Jane got her usual drink. Turner asked her to walk under the stars with him when she finished, so she drank quickly.

He took her by the hand, absorbing the jeers of the other men, and led her to the dark street in front of the comfort house. The stars seemed to have multiplied since the last time she stared up at them. It was warm, and the insects and tree frogs were actively seeking mates, making sounds only insects and frogs would find sexy.

Once they stood in the center of the gravel and dirt road, Turner placed his hand under her chin and raised it to an angle best suited for kissing. They kissed passionately for a long time, and he gently placed his hand on her breast. It felt wonderful to her, and sensations went wild in the rest of her body. He pulled her closer, so she would feel the hard member in his pants. It scared her because she wasn't controlling the events—he was. She removed his hand and suggested they go back inside. He took her hand and walked her up onto the porch. They stopped and kissed again. She wanted to take him into her room and devour him but knew Hattie was always aware of her whereabouts— her protector—her substitute mother.

"Let's go in and talk to Max. He will tell us what we need for the trip. You know I'm going with you wherever you go—don't try to stop me." Turner knew whatever time either of them had on planet Earth, he was going to spend it with Jane if she would let him. Once on the porch Jane stopped and wiped the lipstick from his mouth and applied more to her own lips with her compact and mirror.

Then she reached down and patted his crotch.

"Just wanted to see if you were back to normal," she said even though the real reason was she simply wanted to sate her curiosity. He wasn't completely normal, and the touching caused a quick response.

"Hold up. Let's give it a minute to recover from the pat down," Turner said as he led her to the steps of the porch. "Let's sit here a minute and discuss something totally boring, so it will go down." He brought up the subject of smallpox.

"Do you think there is an outbreak of the disease in the natives' village?"

"You felt bigger than I thought you would. Have you been circumcised?"

"What? We're talking deadly smallpox here!"

"The natives climax after about one minute when they masturbate. How long does it take you?"

"Do you believe in life after death? Do you pray?" Turner asked, trying to be serious but holding back laughter.

"Do you squirt a lot? Nestor shot out the most of all the natives. About a quart, I think."

"At your funeral, do you want flowers, and if so, what kind? This is important because I am about to kill you right here on the porch."

"Is it a sin that I dream about Watutsi penises? I bet they're a foot long. Do you know any Watutsis or even Zulus?"

"Yesterday, a crocodile killed and ate a kid in a nearby village. Can I take you there tomorrow? Maybe the croc is still around."

"Let's go back in, Turner. I've enjoyed our little talk. Hope it helped to calm you down."

Turner stood up. A full-blown erection bulged from his pants, which could easily be seen from a distance. "Now look what you've done," he said.

"Are you two lovebirds going to join us for a drink or just smooch on the porch all night?" Hattie said, as she signaled them to join the party.

"Be right there, Hattie," Jane said. Almost getting caught by Hattie started the shrinkage process, and by the time Jane and Turner reached the great room, normalcy reigned.

The couple had Francis mix them drinks and found Max sitting by himself, smoking his burl pipe. Sitting across from him on a small sofa, Turner started to question him.

"Max, how many men would Jane need to accompany her and those five pygmies back to the Ituri region?"

"Getting there would not be as big of a problem as coming back. The natives know how to get home and survive in the jungle. They smell bad and most of the insects leave them alone. They're small and move well in the bush—require less oxygen to breathe. They can sleep on banana leaves or even in trees. They move fast and aren't burdened with packs, tents, and guns. We'll slow them down and be a source of irritation.

"Actually, fewer people would be best. Here's what I recommend: one hunter or gun bearer—professional, and he should have a native bearer with him, one expedition leader with a gun and his armed assistant, one medical aide since this is a humanitarian mission, and you two, since I doubt anyone could separate you at this point. The guide will know Swahili, and you, dear, already understand the pygmy's spoken words. I don't have to tell you the dangers. Get hurt or sick in the jungle, you die, unless someone can carry you out. You'll be about one hundred miles from a good road and almost two hundred miles from Stanleyville and a doctor, and most of them are missionary doctors. So, six people, plus about three porters and a gun bearer for the professional hunter—ten souls, to answer your question."

Max used a special type of mathematics that didn't count the black natives as "people," but he did take their souls into consideration.

"The ferry boat will be back here tomorrow, and I would like to tour it with you and Turner," Max said, as he looked up and locked eyes with Jane.

"Okay—yes that would be great. I want to see a doctor tomorrow with Nestor and also an attorney to contact my uncle. Possibly a bank as well," Jane said. "Turner, can you show me around tomorrow?"

"I'd love to. Max, how long will it take you to contact these people we will need?"

"A few days. I am free to go as an expedition leader and know others to ask. Let me tell you the prices. The hunter will get a two-hundred-dollar fee as well as I. The medical person is usually a student working here from Belgium and he and the assistant guide normally charges a hundred dollars. Everyone gets ten dollars a day in addition to the other fees, all ferry passages, and meals. Do you have these funds available?"

"I believe I do, but I'll let you know for sure after I meet with the bank."

Turner and Jane thanked him and moved over to the bar for another drink. Jane quietly asked Turner a question.

"I want to sell some jewelry. Do you think it would be wise to ask Mr. Janssen if he was interested in them?"

"If not, I would guess he would tell you where to sell them."

"My mother did leave me a lot of jewelry, but I must confess something to you. As sharks tore at the legs of dead women floating from the wreck, I was able to retrieve some of their jewelry before they were totally consumed. I did it so I had something to sell in order to survive. One lady...I...I...had to cut a ring off while two big sharks were eating the rest of her body. I can't get it out of my mind," Jane said. She began to cry. "It was horrible."

Turner held her until she stopped crying. He told her to stay by the bar, and he walked over to question Roger Janssen. Francis saw her crying and came over to ask her if she was okay. She told him she was sorry but had relived part of the shipwreck. He refilled her drink and said he understood.

"I would only look at larger, well-cut stones," Janssen told Turner. "If they are good quality, I would have the bank make a transfer here. I assure you I would give the young lady a fair price."

"She has a large stone that she wants to give you tomorrow. She wants you to come to her room tomorrow to pick it up," Turner said.

Turner gave Jane the information, and she asked him to walk her to her room. She told everyone goodnight, but as she passed Hattie, who was playing cards with the Simpsons, she spoke.

"Hattie, if Turner doesn't come back in a few minutes, come rescue me," she said laughing.

"I worry that Turner may need to be saved," Lillian chuckled.

At Jane's door, Turner kissed her goodnight.

"Thanks for being my friend, Turner."

"It's pretty easy duty. Goodnight, and let's have breakfast in the morning," Turner said and walked back to the great room.

Chapter Five

The Doctor

Jane was awake early, took a quick bath, and put on some white pants with a sailor button arrangement on the front. They were a modern style and unlikely to have been seen on anyone else in Brazzaville. However, many of the women shopped in Paris before doing their tours in the area. Jane's top was a blue, horizontal-stripe blouse, set off by a white jacket with buttons to match the pants. She recalled that the natives had helped carry some of her luggage through the jungle and went immediately to check on them.

Hattie had already passed out food to the natives when Jane met them on the lawn. Jane told them of her plans to return with them and said they would ride most of the way on a river ferry. Nestor was informed he would accompany her to the doctor to describe the sickness with his people. Hattie asked Jane to explain that they were getting baths with a water hose and soap. On the rare occasions the pygmies had soap, they used it to wash what little clothes they possessed, which were usually for the women in their villages. Pygmies were skin-to-skin people. Clothes interfered with that special contact.

Turner was waiting for Jane on the porch and held her hand on the walk to breakfast, which was served in the great room, buffet style. They filled their plates, poured some orange juice and found a table in front of an empty sofa.

Today she was meeting with a banker, a lawyer, a doctor, and briefly with Mr. Janssen to get a stone appraised and maybe sold. Francis had called the offices and made appointments, and in a few minutes, Roger Janssen was coming by to pick up the stone. Jane had removed it from the ring in case he had questions about the ring's origin. The proper thing to do was to run an ad in every major newspaper and ask if anyone recognized the stone so it could be given back to the family. However, she had risked her life getting it. Without her efforts, it would have been in the belly of a shark. In her mind, she had earned it and needed the revenue it might bring. Turner agreed but after doing some research found that salvage claims almost always awarded the French Congo a percentage of the recovery. It was also possible that the ship sank outside the territorial limits and was free of any country's jurisdiction. This scenario would give her complete ownership of any salvage. Even though the salvage regulations based on French law would probably allow Jane some rights, she didn't want to share the proceeds. Otherwise, this was the wilds of the French Congo, and it was unlikely there was an official who cared enough to investigate this shipwreck. According to Jane's story, the *HMS Victoria II* sank outside of their waters and their authority. Who and why would anyone ask Jane what she pulled off the dead bodies? Since her act of submitting a claim would be putting her rescued jewelry at risk, she decided to take her chances no one would complicate her life. If it went to court later, her uncle was a great lawyer.

"Good morning to you, kids," Roger Janssen said. "I trust you slept well. I saw Hattie washing down your pygmies just now—they didn't seem pleased. Do you have the stone on you?" he asked.

Jane had planned on meeting him in her room but had placed the stone in her purse just in case. She started exploring the contents by unceremoniously laying items on the coffee table in front of her. Tissues, lipstick, a small .22 revolver, a folding buck knife, and a sanitary napkin, which caused Turner to blush and squirm and suddenly find something of interest outside a nearby window. She finally located one of her mother's small jewelry boxes containing the large gem. Turner gasped when he saw the stone. It was a white diamond in a traditional miner's cut, about five carats in size. Roger pulled out a loop and started examining it.

"Excellent quality and clarity. Some small imperfections, as you would expect with a stone this size. The cut is an old style, so it must have been around for years. Maybe a family heirloom. It should bring a nice price. I'm guessing you're opening a bank account today? If so, I will have the money transferred when Brussels gives me a price. We'll wire the money to your bank," Roger said. He wrote her a receipt for the stone and put the estimated value at $8,000. He never asked her where she acquired the stone. He didn't care.

Jane and Turner finished their breakfast and went over their list for the day. The doctor was the first one they needed to see. His office was nearby, and they decided to take the natives, so they could get the smallpox vaccination. After taking care of the pygmies, the couple had an appointment at Barclays Bank, followed by a meeting with a solicitor.

"Turner, what is today's date?"

"It's the seventh of August. Why do you ask?"

"I lost track of time on the lifeboat and in the jungle. It was the second week of July when the ship went down. Gosh, it's been about three weeks since then."

"Are you ready to get started?" Turner asked as he stood up over the remains of their breakfast.

"Yes, do we need to drive today? I saw you pull up in a truck."

"Yeah, we'll put the natives in the back."

Jane told the natives to get in the back bed, and she climbed into the cab of the Renault diesel-powered truck. Turner started navigating the narrow and crowded streets, dodging pedestrians as best he could. After a few minutes, he stopped in front of a large medical clinic attached to the area's only hospital. There were two British doctors, who worked with primarily French-speaking faculty. Jane directed the natives to follow her into the clinic.

It was crowded and smelled of sickness and bad body hygiene. Turner asked for Dr. Jacks and was shown right in. Jane walked behind Turner and told Nestor to follow, holding back the others until they were called. Inside Dr. Jacks' office, a nurse met them and asked them to be seated in simple folding chairs.

There were notices on the walls in French and English describing symptoms of sleeping sickness. Nothing was written in any of the native languages since few would have been able to read it. There were several metal containers for patients to throw up in if needed. The nurse took information from Jane, who explained she needed to have Dr. Jacks interview Nestor about the illness in his village. The nurse spoke some English, but French was what she preferred. The door to an inside office opened, and an elderly white-haired man in a white jacket emerged, using a beautifully carved cane which depicted jungle animals to steady himself.

"Countrymen, come in. I hate speaking French!" Dr. Jacks said, laughing.

"So do I," Jane said and shook his hand.

"God almighty, if you aren't the prettiest thing I've ever seen," he said, looking Jane up and down. "Tell me about this outbreak in the pygmies' village." Francis had given him this information when he called for the appointment.

"Several have died of a disease which had spots and sores. I would like to have them vaccinated for smallpox, even if the outbreak there is another disease—if you will take care of it. If you will ask Nestor the questions, I will be your translator," Jane said. She smiled at Nestor and told him what was about to happen.

The doctor asked Nestor to describe the sores and asked if there was a rash. After getting this initial information, he asked about the size and distribution of the spots at one week, two weeks and so on. Next, he wanted to know when they started scabbing and about any scarring, Finally, he asked how many had died.

After documenting the information, the doctor brought out photographs of people infected with the disease. Nestor identified smallpox without hesitation. Dr. Jacks learned that Jane and Turner had been vaccinated and looked at their scars. He vaccinated all the natives, and Jane asked them to wait outside for her.

Jane thanked Dr. Jacks and paid all the fees. She told Turner to go on outside with the natives as she had a question for the doctor. Once they were alone in his offices she began the questions.

"Doctor, this is a bizarre question, but I'm just curious and would not ask this of anyone else," Jane stuttered and hung her head.

"What do you want to know? You can ask me anything."

"I have never had relations with a man, and I'm curious about something: how much bigger is a Watutsi's penis than a normal man—say, like Turner?" She blushed, especially when she saw the shocked look on his face.

He paused briefly, and then said, "I understand that at your young age you have lots of questions about sex. I have examined a few Zulus and Watutsis and of all the natives the seven-foot Watutsis generally have longer penises. But—only a few inches and not as wide around usually as—say your friend Turner. Young lady, someday you will have a relationship with a man and find the good feeling you will experience during sex occurs not so much deep inside of you—but much closer to the surface. That, my dear, is just science," Doctor Jacks said. He shook Jane's hand as she left.

Outside, she found Turner standing with the natives next to the truck. She got in and motioned for the natives to climb in the bed. Turner fired up the smoky diesel and headed back to the comfort house to let the natives out.

As he drove, Jane spoke. "I asked him how big the Watutsi man parts are."

"What! Tell me you're kidding!"

"He was very 'doctor-like' in his answer. And you'll be pleased to know that he said your parts would do just fine."

"I can never face that doctor again. People don't ask doctors about the relative size of another race's genitals."

"Then how would they ever know if they were missing something important?"

"Would you have relations with a Watutsi?"

"They are not Negroes, you know. They're a separate race, maybe from North Africa."

"Still, do you think you could sleep with one just because he had a big wanger?"

"I'm a virgin and want my first experience to be great, but according to the doctor you might be wider and feel better. See, it's better to study these things."

"Jane Ann, you are so smart and so inquisitive, but having strong feelings for someone and sharing things that are extremely intimate—you won't find that in those textbooks that you probably memorize. Do you remember most things you read? I mean like a photographic memory?"

"Yes. At the beginning of every new course, I read all the textbooks all the way through and memorize the entire book. Then I go crazy sitting in class while the teacher goes over all the stuff I already know. Most teachers don't know what to do with me, so they send me to the library or give me extra reading assignments. The tests are really easy, and sometimes I find mistakes the instructors have made on the tests. That drives them crazy."

"Do you think you're a genius?"

"Maybe, but I think of geniuses as those who have creative thoughts along with some of the abilities I have. I'm not sure I'm very creative."

"College may bore you as well unless you really challenge yourself."

"Maybe, but I'm looking forward to it anyway. Can I go to Yale with you?"

"I think there's a fine arts department for women, but you can't go to the main college—men only."

"Those bastards!"

"Why don't you go to an all-girls college?"

"I do believe I like boys—some of them anyway."

"Watutsi boys?"

"Maybe not—if you work out."

After dropping off the natives at the comfort house, the next stop was the solicitor's office. They drove down dirt roads into the heart of the congested town and found a two-story, tan brick office with a few parking spaces in front. Fritz Vanderslice met them in his front office and ushered them into a nice office with a big fan turned on high. Behind Mr. Vanderslice was a floor to ceiling case full of law books. He noticed both of them staring at the leather-bound volumes.

"You need to have French law, some English common law, and Belgium Congo law which they seem to make up as they go along. Lots of expensive law books.

"I talked to Hattie on the phone, and she said you survived a ship wreck and your parents are now deceased. You want me to correspond with your uncle in London about your inherited estate. Is that correct?" Vanderslice said. He wiped some sweat from his forehead, then leaned in close to an oscillating, bronze-colored electric fan. He was a puffy, overweight, and sloppy-looking man with a red complexion and auburn hair streaked with gray.

"Yes, here is my Uncle Basil Goode's address and the address of the home that will be left to me. Please contact him, first by wire, then by letter to give permission for him to process the will or whatever they call it," Jane said. She noticed that Fritz had a picture on his desk of a pretty lady and two young boys.

"Gladly, gladly. My fee will be twenty-five pounds for all the back and forth needed," he said, wiping his face again and looking as though he might die any minute from heat exhaustion.

"That's a bit steep for writing a letter," Turner said.

"It won't be one letter; it will be several, plus the cost of the wire service and my time."

"It will be fine. Turner can you give us a minute?" Jane said and watched Turner take a seat in the outer office.

"This is a strange question. What is the age of consent for a female in this country?" Jane asked, with the calm of a sleeping crocodile.

"What...what do you mean? Do you mean for a man and woman to get married or maybe you're asking about having relations?" he stuttered and more sweat formed on his face.

"At what age can a woman consent to having sex with a man without him being charged with statutory rape?"

"Uhhh, it's fourteen for a female and eighteen for a man. Have you been raped?"

"God, no! Why the older age for a male? If a fifteen-year-old girl had relations with a seventeen-year-old boy, would the girl be charged in the rape of the man?"

"Uhh, no—his age is more for his ability to enter into a marriage contract and the fact that women mature quicker and have babies at a younger age, I guess. Also, in this country, the rights of women are far more unequal than in Europe. I certainly didn't write the law; I can only tell you about it. Most natives are exempt since they have kids as soon as they are able—besides no one cares."

"Thanks," Jane said. "Here is ten British pounds as a deposit, and I'll pay the rest when you have the forms from my uncle. Oh, if you took jewelry off a dead person being eaten by a shark after a shipwreck, would it be considered marine salvage? Look that up and let me know on our next visit. Thanks for your help."

Jane looked back at the attorney as she was walking out of his office and felt sure he was having a stroke. She hoped he would live long enough to help her with her estate.

"Did you say something to upset him? God, I hope you didn't ask him about Watutsi dicks," Turner said, as he saw the attorney grab a glass of water in obvious distress.

"Don't be vulgar, Turner. Use the term 'penis,' 'genitalia,' or 'man parts.' And no, it was never mentioned."

"Are you ready for lunch? Hattie should have some sandwiches laid out by now."

"Turner, we can't have sex until September the second. That's my birthday."

"What the hell! Jane, you're just outright crazy! Why on that date?"

"Because of the age of consent. I don't want you charged with statutory rape. I'm always looking out for your best interests, dear."

"How considerate of you. How do you know that I want to have intimate relations with you?"

"Your man part certainly does."

"I can't control that. It has its own brain. Just what is the age of consent for the Congo, and do the natives have to abide by this law?"

"Rarely do they see lawyers and policemen, but if a case came to court, there is a law on the books to go by."

"I will ask this question…but I fear the answer. What is the age of consent?"

"Well, it is eighteen for men and considerably younger for women."

"How much is considerably younger?"

"If I tell you, you must keep it a secret. Will you do that?" Jane asked, unable to hide her shaky voice.

"Okay. Tell me."

"You won't like me anymore."

"Of course, I will."

"I'm very bright and physically mature for my age. I had what the doctors call precocious puberty. Started changing and got my period at age ten. How old do you think I am?"

"You look between sixteen and eighteen. I have a sister in college who is twenty and doesn't look much older than you. She certainly didn't –uhhh—fill out like you did."

"Do you like my body?"

"Of course I do. You are one of the most beautiful girls that I have ever seen—from your toes to the top of your head."

"You haven't seen me naked. Could be all the parts aren't in the right place," she said, delaying the inevitable truth.

"Spill it! You're stalling."

"Turner, I really like you, and I would choose you over a Watutsi anytime."

Turner didn't laugh. He looked at her and back to the road where a goat stood directly in the path of his truck. Swerving wildly, he avoided the animal and almost hit an oxcart to his right. Once he had a clear path for the vehicle on the left side of the road, he turned back to Jane.

"Are you going to tell me or not?"

Jane starting crying, and they were real tears. She knew that he wasn't going to like the answer, but it was time to tell him. "I'll be fourteen on September the second."

"Holy shit! That can't be possible! I could have been arrested for molesting a child."

"You have done a piss-poor job of molesting up to this point. In a couple of weeks, you might step up your efforts—legally."

"You don't seem to be a child, but you are—at least chronologically. I'm crazy about you, Jane, but now it seems perverted."

"If you still like me in two weeks, let me know. Until then, I am what they call in America—jailbait. Remember, though, I will be the same girl in two weeks or two years or twenty years. My body is pretty much done, my mind is better than ninety-nine percent of the world's, and I have experienced more than many ladies much older than me. You're just seventeen, so you are also jailbait for older women. When is your birthday?"

"September the eighth. That makes us both Virgos, if you believe in that stuff," he said.

"Wow. Our birthdays are so close to each other. Do you think four years difference will bother us?" Jane asked.

"All I know is that I will like you when you're seventeen since that was what I had to work with."

"I hope you don't wait until then to like me again," Jane said and reached over and squeezed his hand.

The truck pulled up at the comfort house, and they went to the great room where Hattie had prepared a buffet-style luncheon. There were fish and chips in honor of Jane. A local newspaper on the table displayed a headline that read, "British Girl Survives Jungle Trek to Safety After Shipwreck." The write-up listed her age as seventeen and enrolled in the sixth form of upper school in Oxford, England. *That part is true*, Jane thought, as she filled a plate with fish, fried potatoes, and some sliced fruit.

She and Turner sat next to each other on a sofa that adjoined a large coffee table.

Roger Janssen walked by, said hi, and then met with Turner's parents to eat his lunch. The next person to come by was Hattie.

"Sweetie, have you had a chance to read the newspaper article?" Hattie asked.

"Yes, most of it. Thank you for getting it for me. I'm now famous."

"We don't get the big newspapers here often but have been promised the *London Times* when they write their story of you. They will probably interview you by phone as they have already called wanting to speak to 'Jungle Jane.' I'll let you know when it will be set up, dear."

"I pray it's not this afternoon as I have a bank appointment and a tour of the river ferry to get in if Turner doesn't wear out. He is my driver you know."

"Of course, sweetie. Enjoy your lunch."

"Uhh—Jungle Jane, what are you going to tell the London Times about your age?" Turner asked.

"I'm not sure, dear, but I will come up with something." She leaned over and kissed Turner on the cheek. "Jungle Jane wants you badly," she whispered in his ear just to frustrate him. Turner looked around to see if any policemen were in the room, shook his head, and dove back into his sandwich.

Chapter Six

The Riverboat

The B.A.O. (Banco da África Ocidental), or Bank of West Africa, was glad to have Jane's account and was even more excited when she told them about the transfer from Brussels coming in a few days. She rented a safety deposit box for her jewelry and deposited several hundred pounds and a few American dollars into a checking account. It was a lot of money to have in the middle of a worldwide depression. The money's origin was not discussed. Jane had stripped wallets, purses, and luggage off dead bodies and from the jaws of sharks, but this banker didn't need to know the story. She also owned an estate in London and her parents' bank and investment accounts. Her father had been successful, and both parents had inherited sizable fortunes. She knew her father had life insurance policies but wanted that money to stay in the British account, which would also be hers shortly. She asked the B.A.O. bank manager, "Would you please notify Barclays and my uncle, Basil Goode, who lives in London, about my new account here in Brazzaville, in case transfers need to be made?"

She had her own small account with Barclays, which was set up as her college funding account. Her goal was to be able to transfer funds back and forth with ease. She left with a supply of counter checks, paperwork which included her account number, and her safety deposit key. Now it was time to meet Max at the docks on the Congo River.

Turner parked his truck near the crude loading platform in front of a steam-powered and aged paddle boat with the name *S.N. Lapsley II* in fading paint emblazoned on the stern. Turner had made inquiries with the captain about the history of this old steamer.

Standing on the wooden gangplank, he shared with Jane what the captain had told him.

"This old boat is the second *Lapsley*," he began. "The original *S.N. Lapsley* was severely damaged when her inexperienced captain hit a sand bar during her first run down the Congo. Several natives drowned, and the boat was taken apart at the docks. It had been sent over in boxes donated by the church and mission office in Alabama where Sam Lapsley had received his training. Her design was fine for the sluggish Mississippi River, but no match for the torrent rapids of the Congo. Design changes were made, and a new boat was shipped here, funded by the churches in Alabama. It didn't get launched until 1906, and by then, Sam had passed away from a jungle sickness. The mission managed this hunk of junk until 1931 when they retired it. A new company purchased it, replaced a couple of rotten boards, slapped on some new paint, and remodeled the state rooms. She was and still is a utilitarian vessel, outfitted to accompany missionaries, church officials, and nurses. The engine was held together with parts salvaged from other wrecks, and some of the crew probably had the choice of prison or shoveling wood into a boiler. It looks to me like a vessel looking for a place to sink."

"Isn't she a beauty?" quipped Max, as he walked up the busted and splintered dock to greet the couple.

"Is the boat still afloat or has it settled to the bottom of the river?" Turner asked.

"Do the terms 'used up' and 'tramp boat' have any meaning to you?" Jane asked.

"Give it a closer look, and don't judge the book by the cover," Max said. For some reason, he seemed to be defending the vessel.

They walked up a loading platform and took a gangway to the upper level. The smells were unescapable. Max led them through a maze of supplies stacked on the decks until they reached the aft cabins. The two that adjoined each other by an inside door had been modestly remodeled and were still spartan by any standards. On the walls were two pictures of flowers; neither species grew in the Congo. The beds were singles, with one bedside table in the middle and headboards that were attached to the bulkhead. A marine head was in a small water closet with a sink and a pump to bring in cold water only. The small metal tub required water to be poured in and drained directly into the Congo afterwards. There was no toilet paper, and Jane made a note of that omission. A small mirrored dresser, lamp, and chair completed the furnishings. It would do, especially compared to the horror she had heard occurred on the lower deck. There was a reserved, outside, upper-deck sleeping area that featured cots under a tarp with a communal toilet. She would put the natives there and would make sure they were taken care of. She was ready to meet the captain. Max showed her the way to the bridge of the thirty-year-old ferry.

Captain Rudy Pistorius, an Afrikaaner, appeared to be blended into the boat. He was old, dirty, unshaven, and wore clothes that at one time had been a uniform. Somehow, he appeared to be perfect for the beat-up control center of an antique craft that was seeking a home at the bottom of the Congo River. He seemed quite capable of finishing the *Lapsley* off in spectacular fashion.

"What in the hell is a pretty girl like you doing on this godforsaken boat?" Rudy Pistorius asked. He took out a cigar that had been chewed into a slimy dark stub.

"I'm going to Stanleyville on your next trip upriver, which I understand will be in about four or five weeks. I'll need three state rooms and passage for five adults. Also, I need to pay for five natives, who will use your cots under the tarps on the upper deck. We will bring aboard our food, but I'll need to hire one of your cooks to prepare our meals. We'll keep the food in our rooms since I understand there are thieves onboard. I will need a price from you, and I'm willing to give you a deposit to secure my accommodations."

"Young girl, this boat is like traveling through hell riding on a wet devil's ass," Captain Pistorius said. "You will wonder what hideous crime you committed to deserve this punishment. The smells alone will poison the air so completely you will find yourself crawling on top of the bridge to catch the occasional whiffs of oxygen that drifts by. You will see men die and women raped. I hope you're not among them. Children will fall overboard and drown but usually scream a lot first. I am the law and usually have to shoot those that commit crimes on every trip. Short trials are conducted by me and then a bullet to the brain and off to be eaten by the river. You must know that every kind of business is done on this boat. I'm the only policeman. It is quiet now, but shortly there will be food cooked and sold, merchants of all sorts, and a full-service bordello. Illegal drugs are everywhere, guns and ammunition can be purchased, and killers for hire are common. If anyone thinks you have money you will find a machete at your throat. They hate white people.

"A full city of evil will be created on the lower deck. Some will hold on to something and shit over the side, other will find a spot on the deck and add to the pile. Sickness and disease is everywhere. Many will not live for the two or three weeks it takes to get to Stanleyville. This steamer will leave a trail of bodies all the way until we dock. Of course, you will be somewhat insulated on the upper deck, but below you is a festering underbelly of a piss-poor country just awaiting the opportunity to rape and kill you, and not necessarily in that order. We use fire hoses to clean up every three weeks, but it really doesn't help much. Still want a ride?" the captain concluded.

Undeterred, Jane replied, "Yes. How much is the deposit?"

"Ten US dollars a person and another ten when we leave. Five dollars each for the natives. Bread, meat, and water will be provided for them. Suggest you provide them some fruit. Our cook can buy them food on the boat. Usually, fresh bananas are brought aboard at each stop. The cabins I will reserve for you at ten each, but the total will be fifty US dollars equivalent. When you board, I will assign our upper galley cook. Twenty dollars should cover his services to you for the trip. You can eat in the officer's galley with us, if you like, or in your rooms. We can offer hot water for your baths brought in by our stewards for one dollar. I think Max told me you may have a medical person onboard. If any of my people get sick, I will pay him five dollars for his services for each person he treats. We may have some spare refrigeration space left, but you need to mark it well for your people and show it to our cooks and stewards when you load it. Any other questions? If not, I'll see you in about four weeks—depends if we have to stop for repairs and such."

Jane took out one of her counter checks and wrote the captain a check for the deposits.

"Baie Dankie," Max said as they left the captain and the bridge.

"Buy a donkey? Why did you say that to him?" Jane asked Max.

"It means 'thank you' in Afrikaans. The language seems to be an offshoot of Germanic languages—sort of a creole for the Dutch," Max, who seemed to be fluid in several languages, said.

"Max, if you have time, will you school me some in Afrikaans? I'm a quick learner," Jane said.

"I would love to, my dear. I may have a translation guide at the comfort house," Max said.

Turner offered Max a ride, but he had a car at his disposal and thanked him for the offer. Jane and Turner drove around the town looking at old buildings. They talked about what they needed to bring to make the trip more comfortable.

"Will you share a room with me?" Jane asked.

"Of course. Can I run naked through the room?"

"I certainly hope so."

"I hope we both have our birthdays by then. Yours is only fourteen days away, and mine is twenty days off. My parents may leave by then, so we need to tell them something more about our relationship before they go." Turner pulled the truck to a stop overlooking the harbor. He took Jane's hand.

"I hope our friendship continues to grow. I'm not scared off by your age since you are more mature than any other girl your age. I just wanted to say that I care for you deeply, and I am committed totally," Turner said and then kissed her passionately, all the while wondering if he might be arrested for the kiss alone.

"I should have you arrested, but I promise not to if you'll continue to be my boyfriend."

They drove back to the comfort house and had drinks in the great room. Soon it would be time to get cleaned up and dress for dinner. Jane loved this place. It was like being in an old movie where people were so civilized and proper. So very different from the paddleboat trip they were about to take, followed by the long jungle trek. She would enjoy this world while she could.

Chapter Seven

Side Trips

The next morning, Francis received a box containing books. He had an ongoing deal with a used book store in London to send him an assortment of used novels and some works of nonfiction every couple of months. The shipping cost was always more than the cost of the books, and it took about two months for one shipment to arrive. Most items of any size came by boat, but some smaller objects of value came by aircraft since there was a small airport for private planes and charters in Brazzaville, and across the river in Leopoldville, a slightly larger airfield owned by the government. Ferries crossed the river between the two capitals several times a day. These books were usually by well-known writers in England and America.

The guests at the comfort house were always excited to get their hands on a best seller, even if it had been on the shelves awhile and was used. Most of the comfort house's library was dog-eared and worn thin, so new books were a godsend. Turner and Jane loved to read and imagined they would have an excess of time on their hands for the next few weeks. Francis brought the heavy box into the great room as the guests were having breakfast, causing quite a stir.

Jane was the fastest person to the books and started calling out titles.

"*Cimarron*—any takers?"

Turner took it and sat back on a sofa with his unfinished breakfast in front of him.

"How about *The Good Earth?*"

Mrs. Simpson raised her hand.

"*Backstreet?*"

Hattie signified by holding outstretched arms.

"Oh, my God—*Brave New World*! This is only a year old. I'll take this if nobody minds," Jane said.

Included with the treasure trove of novels in both English and French was a fresh copy of Joseph Conrad's *Heart of Darkness*, a masterpiece written first in 1902. At least three copies were still in the comfort house library, but all were in bad shape. If one were caught in the Congo without having read the book, there was the chance for immediate ridicule. Both Jane and Turner read it in school and both had discussed how difficult it was to read as a fast-paced piece of literature. It was almost as though the book were written as a textbook on how to write a great novel. The reader expected there was going to be a test on it afterwards. Usually, there was.

Cabin fever had set in and Jane and Turner were taking a ferry today to Leopoldville to explore. They had been locked up reading books for two days as hard rains had trapped most people indoors. The natives were moved onto the porch and were doing well. The couple had begun to stockpile items for the expedition, so a shopping trip was in order. Leopoldville was only thirty minutes and about two miles across the Congo River, but they would be entering another country. Brazzaville was the capital of French Equatorial Africa, which included several territories. The French Congo was the area encompassing Brazzaville and huge land areas west and north. Directly across the river was Leopoldville, the capital of the Belgian Congo, which controlled an enormous country extending both west and south of the city. Much of both countries were largely unexplored. These areas had changed names in the past and undoubtedly would suffer the same fate later on.

Turner parked his truck near the dock, and they walked down to the ferry terminal. As usual, there were several choices of boats available. They could have taken the truck on a small car ferry but opted to leave it. The cleanest ferry was only for passengers and featured a seating area on the second deck. The fee was only twenty-five cents US. Turner paid, and they took a front seat and were told it would leave in ten minutes.

"Here's my plan. See if it's okay with you. We will do some shopping and then have lunch. After that, we'll go to the Ciné Central for a movie, pick up our packages, and head back on the ferry before dark—maybe stop for coffee at one of the cafés," Turner said.

"Holy crap! This will be our first real date. How exciting! But, no matter how much fun we have, you can't stay over at my place tonight. Just way too young for that sort of stuff," Jane said, laughing.

"You're going to really play this up until September the second, aren't you?"

"For your protection, my dear. Just think anticipation and patience."

The boat engines fired up, blowing black and gray smoke into the air. The ferry first headed upstream into the current. The operator in the pilot house knew exactly how to work against the current, so he would dock at the precise spot on the other side of the river. Once that was done, he tied off and the passengers filed off the boat.

Like many African towns during the colonial periods, there was a white sector and a native or black sector. It would also include Asians, Indians, and other nationalities. Turner and Jane accepted this segregation as a part of life in Africa and didn't complain since they would have been in an almost singular minority.

Once they left the ferry, Turner hailed two single-wheeled carts which somewhat resembled the Chinese rickshaw versions, except they had no cover on the top and there was a native who pulled in the front and another who pushed in the back. They were called pousser-pousser carts, which is "pusher-pusher" in French but translates to "rickshaw" in English. They were only singles, so they hired two and told them in French to take them to the nice shopping area near the cinema. Even though it was a hot day, the air moved over them like a breeze while being moved along briskly on the carts.

The pushers stopped in front of the *Photo Zagourski* shop since many tourists wanted their pictures made by one of the few professional photographers in the city.

"Turner, can we get our pictures made?"

"If we can do it in a hurry. I don't want to spend all day posing in this heat."

Jane was wearing trendy white slacks and Turner wore Khaki shorts for this occasion. Pants for girls were just coming into style so people noticed them, but shorts on a white girl in an African city was taking it a step too far unless they were worn around their hotels—never on a shopping trip in public.

Mr. Zagourski was working through a pile of paperwork at a desk that featured a wall full of guns and knives behind him. He smiled and greeted the young couple in French and quickly shifted to English when he found they preferred it. After hearing that they just wanted a keepsake picture of them together and not a long, expensive photo shoot, he reverted to French for a while.

Using a jungle backdrop with live potted plants and a scene that featured the Congo River, he had Jane sitting in a rattan chair with Turner standing next to her. He took five or six shots and then took their money, adding a small fee to have the photos delivered to the comfort house. He recommended a place for lunch and some shops that had honest owners.

Jane did the most shopping. She tried on several things but bought very few items. Turner tried to be patient but had been through this agony with his sisters many times. The main item that she needed were hiking boots—serious boots for the jungle. The clerk in the clothing store where Jane had exhausted most of the sales staff recommended a men's boot store since women's fashion didn't lend itself to equipment for actually going into the bush. Some of the styles might help in tall weeds, yet were mostly designed for cocktail parties on the lawn. She did buy a pair of leather fashion boots to cover that possibility. She also bought some sneakers and sandals for lounging around the comfort house and the decks of the steamer. They left them with the store to pick up later and found the boots she really needed at a men's store nearby.

The couple had spotted the movie theater and found out the next feature, *Shanghai Express,* would start about the time they arrived. It would be in English with French subtitles, but that was fine with them. One of the clerks told them the theater might close down because it wasn't making enough money. It was in the middle of the Great

Depression, and businesses started up and closed at an alarming rate. The movie was a dime, and the popcorn and the Coca-Cola were a nickel apiece. They found a couple seats in the center of the theater with Turner taking his favorite seat next to the aisle.

"You sit there so you can go pee?"

"I have more room in the aisle. You can have it if you want it."

"I'm fine, thank you. Do you want to make out when the lights go down?" Jane giggled.

"I like making out with you anytime, but I don't think this is the place," Turner said nervously.

At that time, the movie started, and Marlene Dietrich appeared on the screen wearing a black veil. Later, she removed it and exposed her beautiful face.

"Do you think she's pretty?" Jane whispered.

Knowing a loaded question when he heard one, Turner answered, "Of course she's beautiful, or she wouldn't be a giant movie star. You are much more beautiful, and I'm glad you aren't a movie star, or I'd have to stand in line to speak to you."

"You're full of it, Turner, but thanks for saying that."

After the movie about civil unrest on a train to Shanghai, Jane had questions about their planned trip on a river steamer.

"Will we have trouble with revolutionaries or military types on our trip up the Congo, Turner?"

"There hasn't been an insurrection since 1931 when the Pende tribesmen killed a tax collector after one of their tribesmen was killed by government forces," Turner explained "As a result, between three hundred and five hundred Pende tribesmen were killed. They didn't stand a chance against the well-armed government military. It's been calm since then, except for some revolts from forced labor at some of the mines. The only reason I know this is because my dad worked the case for the government."

"I'll bet all sorts of things occurred here several years ago," Jane said.

"Conrad's book influenced public opinion around the turn of the century and many believe that's why the Belgium Government took over the country in 1908," Turner said.

"Has it been better since then?"

"Compared to massacres of millions of people before that, I guess it's better. Do you want to get a cup of coffee before we head back—maybe some dessert? We really didn't have lunch, except for the popcorn at the movies."

"Sure."

Turner led Jane to a small café with tables under a blue-striped awning on the sidewalk. The little tables were wrought iron with chairs made to look as though it was a French sidewalk café. It was a beautiful day, but hot and sticky from all the rains. They ordered coffee and a pastry in French from an attractive girl who wrote down the order, while an older man brought out a tall fan and turned it on for the couple.

"I love being with you, Turner. Do you think our relationship will last or after you sleep with me, will you leave me for an older girl?" Jane said as she reached over and grasped his hand.

"When we have slept together one hundred times, I will discuss age, but not until then," Turner said.

"When are your parents leaving?"

"In a few weeks—why?"

"This is crazy—never mind."

"I love crazy ideas. What is it?"

"We're going to be aboard a boat, maybe sleeping in the same room, Turner. Together for weeks—maybe months in the jungle in the same tent. So—I'm not the person to ask this, but I'm willing to marry you if have any feelings—like that."

Turner was shocked—speechless. He took her hand and looked into her eyes. He then kissed her deeply and had to pull away when coffee and French pastries arrived at their table. The girl smiled and hurried off so that she didn't interrupt a developing romantic encounter.

"I could easily spend the rest of my life with you. I can't breathe unless you are around, but do you want to get married for the appearance of propriety aboard a Congo steamer that will have a bordello on the first level? The tent may not lend itself to great lovemaking anyway. We need to talk about college—and even kids— and where are we going to live? What am I going to do for employment? We've talked about college in California, but Jesus Christ, marriage is such a big, big deal. This is why you asked about my parents?"

"Drink your coffee and eat your roll. Just think about it," Jane said. She was clearly enjoying watching him self-destruct.

Turner burned his lips on his coffee. He was undoubtedly panicked. The pastry disappeared from his plate in a couple of bites. He pulled some money from his pants and laid it on the table.

"I'll go get our packages, and you drink your coffee." He kissed her on the cheek and scurried off to pick up their purchases at the shops.

Walking to the shops he was thinking, *"I have just had a thirteen-year-old girl propose marriage to me, and I'm actually considering it. How could I get into a quickie marriage in the middle of the Congo without my sisters being there? They would kill me if they couldn't dive in and help plan it. What will my parents think when I tell them her actual age? They might disown me. Marriage before all the fun in college? Isn't marriage what ruins all the fun in people's lives—isn't that the reason they put it off so long? Kids—hell I'm still a kid—Jane is a baby—I'm marrying a baby!"*

Jane was smiling and calm when he met her at the outdoor café.

"It was just a thought, Turner. We'll talk about it later."

"Okay. It's just such a shock. I know I want to marry you sometime—when, I'm just not sure," he said in a shaky voice.

They found a couple of pushers and arrived at the dock as a ferry was about ready to cast off. They ran and jumped on before it left the terminal. Turner didn't say much on the way home. When they arrived at the comfort house, the natives were back in the yard. Roger and Max were trying to talk to Nestor and were showing him something Roger had in his hand. When they saw Jane approaching, they broke off the attempted conversation, and Roger put the object back in his pocket, as though he had been caught doing something wrong.

"Boys, what were you talking to Nestor about?"

"Those pygmies live right in the middle of diamond country, and I was just asking them if there were any mines in his area. He could understand what I said but shook his head when I showed him some stones," Roger said. "Oh, there's been an eleven-thousand-dollar deposit made in your bank account for the gem stone you had me sell—came in today."

Jane was furious. "Max and Roger, I'm paying for this expedition, and it's not a goddamn diamond hunt. We're going to help a sick tribe. Do you understand?"

The two men apologized and went back into the comfort house. Turner had parked the truck and was now by her side as she went to talk to Nestor.

"What did they ask you about the diamonds?" Jane asked.

"All white men want to know about diamonds. I shook my head that I didn't know about them."

"Good. Let me know if they bother you again. I told him our expedition was to help your village with their sickness."

"Thank you, Jane," Nestor said in his native tongue.

Jane looked at Turner. "It worries me that once we get in the jungle, part of our expedition is going to be on a different mission than ours. I would start all over and get new men if I thought there was time."

"As long as there are men, there is greed, Jane. We must be prepared to shoot anyone that turns on us in the jungle."

"I hope it doesn't come to that! Maybe we need a highly paid bodyguard for this trip."

"One that hates diamonds? You and I like diamonds. But two bodyguards would be better, so they can watch each other."

Jane laughed and took Turner's free hand as he carried her packages. As they walked up the steps, Jane looked at Turner, smiled and said, "Maybe we can have a combination birthday and marriage party."

Chapter Eight

Youth and Truth

Turner took the packages to Jane's room and turned to leave when she shut the door, pressed him against the wall, and kissed him intensely. He recovered and opened the door, peered out, and headed for the great room looking for a sandwich. He found a tray of small finger sandwiches left over from lunch and gobbled down a few.

"Turner, those are old! You'll die of food poisoning. Let me fix you some fresh ones," Hattie said as she grabbed the tray and headed to the kitchen.

"I'm fine, but Jane might want some to hold her over until dinner. We went to a movie and had some snacks but never got around to a proper lunch."

"I know you two are in love—anyone could see that. Have you thought about marrying her?" Hattie asked.

"Hattie, we're both so young. How old were you and Francis when you married?"

Hattie had quickly made a few fresh bologna sandwiches and was cutting them into four pieces each. "I was fifteen and Francis was seventeen. I was pregnant with our only son, so it was a rushed-up affair. Our son is thirty-two now, and we have four grandkids. It worked out just fine. Francis worked for a British mining operation and made some good money. He was a part owner and sold his interest and we settled here. We can speak several languages and love meeting and caring for people. So, Turner, young people get married all the time. My mother was thirteen."

"I worry my parents won't approve. Hattie, Jane is much younger than she told us initially."

"Oh, they know now. *The London Times* came this morning with Jungle Jane's story. There was an interview with Jane's uncle, the barrister. He reported that she wouldn't be fourteen until next week on the second of September, but she looked much older and had skipped several grades because of her superior intelligence. Our local attorney, for some reason, was interviewed and reported that the age of consent in both the French Congo and the Belgium Congo was fourteen. He said she would be free to marry then and had a boyfriend who was slated to go to Yale next year. Why he reported that, we don't know," Hattie said.

"Crap, I know why—because she asked him—I'm sure. You won't believe what she asked the doctor—but I'll never tell you."

"The truth is that the lawyer is quoting Belgian Law, which is usually applied on both sides of the river for convenience sake," Hattie said. "The French here, if they so choose, can use French European Law which states the age of consent for women is thirteen. I know that because my mother was told that when she married. The French like to get an early start on their hankie-pankie," Hattie said, laughing out loud.

Jane walked in on the end of the conversation. "What are you guys laughing about?" she asked. She saw the sandwiches and picked one up and bit into it.

"Honey, let me show you the *Times* that just arrived here this morning. The *Daily Telegraph* should be here in a few days." Hattie pulled the paper from the top of a desk that was in the kitchen.

Jane sat down at the desk and stared at the headlines. "Jungle girl found safe in the Congo." She began to turn red, then pale, when she read the account of her fighting off savages and wild animals in the jungle. The paper reported she was only thirteen but looked like she was a college co-ed who was so smart that universities were fighting over her for admission to their schools. A school picture of her was included at the top of the article with lions and elephants placed strategically around the borders.

"Where do they get this crap?" Jane said as she slammed the paper on the desk.

"Turner, we need to talk," she said as she grabbed his arm and pulled him into the hallway. "Do we have a plan?"

In a way, Turner was enjoying seeing her out of control. She had always appeared to be so self-assured—unfazed and ready to challenge anything that came along. Now it was his turn to be the one in charge.

"We're going to seek out my parents and tell them that we want to get married before they leave and before the boat casts off. Are you okay with that, and do you love me?"

"Of course, I love you—remember it was me who proposed."

"Jane, I'm just a recent upper school graduate with just some assets set aside for college in America. Can you help me get past that problem? I can't get you a proper ring or wedding dress."

"My mother's engagement and wedding ring is in the safety box at the bank. I have enough money for us to have a nice wedding, pull off this safari, and still go to the US for college. I just got a wire explaining the admission requirements for Stanford Medical School in California. They're mailing paperwork by the fastest carriers. Mostly air, they said. Stanford allows women and married students. We need to tell your parents that we have plans, or they will think we're getting married out of desperation."

"I agree we need to have answers for them," Turner said. "What do you plan to do with your house and estate in England?"

"Keep it. I have a cousin who is going to college nearby and living in a dormitory. She could live there as a caretaker while she finishes college. I need to send her a wire and one to my uncle, instructing him to use my parents' funds to maintain the estate."

"What will we tell them about children—they'll want to be grandparents. My sisters are still in school and not married. However, one is engaged to an American on the East Coast," Turner explained.

"We'll tell them we'd love to make them grandparents. How many kids do you want, Turner? I'll have as many as you want."

"Really—I have never heard you talk much about kids. How about four—two of each?"

"Done—I was an only child and was bored to death—needed someone to fight with."

"Normally, the girl's parents provide most of the expenses for the wedding, but I don't think that rule will apply since they are deceased. It shouldn't be that expensive if we have it here at the comfort house or in one of the big hotels in Leopoldville."

"I vote for here. I absolutely love this place," Jane said.

"Guests? I wonder if I can get my sisters to fly in. How about your uncle and some cousins?"

"Maybe. Can your sisters be bridesmaids? I have some cousins whose parents are rich enough to fly them here. No scheduled flight, so they'll need to do charters—very expensive."

"When or how can we get this put together before the boat gets here and my parents leave? The flights will take almost two weeks or at least eight to ten days." Turner said. "Can we run to the bank and get the ring before we tell them, so I will have an engagement ring to wear?" Jane asked.

Before Turner could answer, Jane grabbed her purse with the deposit box key in it, and the two were out the door. They only had thirty minutes before the bank closed, and while Jane was getting the ring, Turner went next door and sent a couple of wires for himself and two for Jane.

After retrieving the ring, they rushed back to the comfort house but stopped to check on the natives, who were sitting in the grass in the shade. She ran up to Nestor and told him she was marrying Turner. He relayed the news to the others, and they all jumped up and cheered.

"All of you will be invited to the wedding if you wish to attend," she told them in their language. "Many people will stare at you and ask you questions, but I will translate for you. You will be honored for saving my life in the jungle. Will you honor me by coming to my wedding?"

Nestor signified that they would if they could stand by the back wall. She agreed and gave each one a hug which produced a few erections which they tried to hide by turning away.

"Please tell them to sit in a row," Turner said.

She told them to sit and they obeyed. Turner dropped to one knee and pulled the ring from his pocket. It was a marquise-shaped stone about two carats and lit up as the rays of the African afternoon sun bounced off the facets. She was smiling, but the natives looked perplexed as they had never seen such a ceremony.

"In front of your adopted native friends, I wish to ask for your hand in marriage. I want to be beside you for the rest of our lives," he said. Jane translated as best she could in one of the most difficult and ancient languages in Africa. "I want you to have our babies when it is time. I want to share your life until we die. Will you make me the happiest man alive by being my wife?" Jane translated the last of Turner's proposal as Turner placed the ring on her finger. It fit almost perfectly.

"Yes—yes, I will!" Jane then pulled him up from his kneeling position and kissed him.

The natives stood up and jumped up and down. She showed them the ring. They looked pleased and then looked at each other and then back to the ring.

As the couple was about to leave, Nestor asked Jane if he could speak to her. He then asked if they could give her a wedding gift once they got to his village. She said yes, as she didn't want to offend them by saying it wasn't necessary. She explained to Turner what they discussed, and they went inside the comfort house.

"I sent a wire to one of my sisters," Turner said. "I also contacted your uncle asking for your hand in marriage. It was the proper thing to do. I hope that's all right?"

"Of course. If he comes, I'll have him give me away."

Once they were on the porch and about to head down the long hallway, Turner stopped her and looked into her eyes.

"Jane, do you know why I'm really marrying you?"

"Because you love me, I hope?"

"Nope! It's because you have a shitload of money and I'm broke!"

They both were laughing as they walked into the great room and watched as Turner's parents, Lillian and Paul Simpson, stood up at the couch. The looks on their faces were grim. Turner walked towards them. Fear crept up his body. Jane clenched his arm and dug into his flesh with her fingernails.

"Mom and Dad, I want you to know that Jane and I are getting married. We ask for your blessing." That's what he wanted to say and pictured himself saying, but it didn't happen that way.

Before he could say a word, Lilly Simpson walked toward Turner and tried to separate him from Jane, so she could talk to him privately. Turner and Jane would have no part of it. Both turned and faced her and told her if she had something to say she should speak to them both. Paul Simpson walked over and took Mrs. Simpson's arm and led her back to on the couch. She was visibly upset.

Turner began addressing them both. His voice trembled at first, but as he went on, a power deep inside lit a vocal flame, and he talked with an authority that shocked both parents.

"Mom and Dad, I plan to marry Jane Ann Goode, with or without your blessing. I was hoping you would accept this announcement with joy, as that is the feeling I have being with her. Obviously, we are young. That isn't exactly a bad thing since for me, as it means we'll be together longer. The date of the wedding will be Jane's fourteenth birthday, the second of September. There is time for relatives to be flown in, and I would like my sisters to be here.

"I would also like to have my parents here as well. I love you both a great deal, and I know you're concerned for me. We have thought this through and wish to be married before you leave. We'll depart for the trip upriver a few days after the wedding. When we return, we both will be applying for entrance to Stanford Medical School in Palo Alto, California. We will split our time between there and Jane's estate in London. We currently have the funds for school and living expenses. The wedding will be here at the comfort house, if Francis and Hattie approve, and we'll be happy to pick up the cost.

"I love Jane more than anything in the world. She will make a great daughter-in-law and wants to have four grandkids for you after med school. I know our young ages are still an issue for you. We're still kids—but smart and capable kids that want to start and will start a life together. We know the age of consent, so we'll enter into marriage without having broken that law. It would please us greatly if you would accept this marriage. Oh, by the way, Hattie's mother was thirteen when she was married, and there aren't many people on earth as kind and good as Hattie Rhodes."

Turner spoke with such a powerful and professional voice that even Jane's mouth gaped. Lillian Simpson was crying, and Hattie, who had been listening from the kitchen, ran out and hugged him. The other guests clapped. Finally Turner's parents stood and smiled, giving in to what they knew would be a losing battle.

Chapter Nine

Relatives

Lillian apologized to both of them and took Jane's hand to admire the ring.

"It was my mother's. I'll always be grateful she hid it in my luggage," Jane said as she hugged Mrs. Simpson again. Lillian Simpson didn't dislike Jane but believed that her son was being robbed of some of the best free times in his life. The truth was that Lillian had been pregnant with Turner's older sister Carole when she was sixteen and had just turned seventeen when she and Paul married. She had experienced the issue for which she was so opposed.

After listening to the engaged couple explain their plans, the Simpsons committed to being all in on the wedding. Lillian would help with the planning and remarked that it would be good practice for her daughter's wedding that was taking place next summer. She had her address book with her and began composing the wires to be sent to many of the same people listed for her daughter's wedding.

Paul pulled his son aside. "Son, I hate to always be the practical one, but how are you two going to pull all this off without some money coming in? You don't have a job. Stanford is an expensive school unless you have scholarships. Then the costs of the flights back and forth. How do you feel about using Jane's inheritance for all this? Don't get me wrong about her. I've been impressed by that young lady since she explained Henry Stanley's fiasco to Max. The truth is this: if I were in your shoes, I would turn the world upside down to win that girl over. There couldn't be anyone that beautiful and smart anywhere else in the universe, and if you waited until she was fifteen or sixteen, she would be gone. My concerns are purely financial," Paul said as he put his arm around his son.

"Thanks for your concern, Dad. The money we're using isn't really her inheritance but from jewelry she sold," said Turner "Mainly one big stone that Roger sold for her. That and some more jewelry will get us through the expedition and for a couple years at Stanford. She wants to use her inheritance as a backup and to maintain her estate in London. I believe you put some funds away to help me at Yale, even though I do have a nice scholarship. Of course, we'll both apply for scholarships at Stanford and have already sent for the paperwork. Jane is only a few credits shy of her upper school completion and has been told that she can test out of that if she wishes. We are searching to get those books. We are hoping someone coming from England can bring them. She reads a book and can memorize it word-for-word. Back to the money: it's after the first two years that concerns us at this point. We'll have to do some undergraduate work first, then four years of medical school, and then time as a resident. It's a long commitment."

"Long, but worth it," Paul Simpson replied. "You were lukewarm on med school because of the time required before. As smart as you and Jane are, it is proper that you challenge yourselves with the hardest courses and positions, so you can contribute to society and make the money that comes along with the profession. We'll help you kids as much as we can and with the wedding. When Stanford finds out what they have with you two, they will find a way to keep you." Paul walked Turner back next to Jane.

Jane had asked Hattie and Lilly if they would help plan the wedding. They were pleased to help. They went to a table and started making lists of Jane's invitees, as she had Turner's relatives list started. All the invitations would need to be by wire service. Jane informed them that she had invited the pygmies to attend and they were going to stand in the back against the wall. Hattie said she could get folding chairs for them, but Jane said they asked to stand. Mrs. Simpson looked shocked but didn't comment.

After Jane had done her best to write down the names of her aunts, uncles, cousins, and friends from her memory, she went over to where Turner, his dad, and Francis were at a coffee table, also compiling names from his line of relatives. All had to be coordinated with the boss of all lists—Lillian Simpson.

At first, there were two separate lists of invitees, one created by Jane, and another done by Turner, his dad, and Lillian for his family. They started with relatives and best friends, but after a while, Lillian had a list of government officials to add on.

Jane listed her Uncle Basil and Aunt Abbie Goode from London first. Then she placed their two sons, her favorite cousins, George and Peter Goode, on the notepad. Afterwards, lesser aunts and uncles and cousins—the ones that received Christmas cards each year but not presents.

Lillian listed her two daughters, Carole and Lauren, and one of Turner's cousins from Belgium, Petra Simpson. Turner also requested an invitation be sent to his best friend, Jim Wimberly, in California. Lillian also saw to it that all embassies and government offices would receive invitations.

The flights for the guests would require them to fly either to Brazzaville or Leopoldville, which were more like makeshift airfields with some fuel and a couple of mechanics. Both had sheds for going through a primitive customs office. A few hotels were listed on the wire, along with the phone number of the comfort house. Calls between large towns in West Africa were possible, but phone calls to Europe were rare and difficult. When it had occurred in the past, it required calling Johannesburg, while an operator called Europe and relayed the conversation back and forth. The caller never actually talked to their connection, just a relay from the operator.

Almost immediately after the wires were sent, they began to get replies. Since Jane seemed to be famous in Europe, there was a good response. Some relatives and friends of both were also coming from the States. After a few days, the hotels listed on the wires were getting reservations. Maybe thirty or forty altogether. It would be a nicely attended affair.

Hattie had an upright piano that was rarely used and pushed against a wall. She knew a singer and a jazz trio from a local club. Francis did some leg work and talked to government leaders on both sides to make up brochures of things to do in both cities for the guests. A botanical park had just opened earlier that year and was nice, with pretty art deco gates. There was limited time, and Jane didn't want people to come all the way from Europe and America and not have a good time. But this was the Congo—people don't go on Safari or vacation in the Congo. They came there to work in the mines or as government officials on both sides of the river. Copper, gold, and diamonds brought in the money. Life was hard and dangerous. There was disease and sickness. Natives typically died in their forties. Jane wanted to meet everyone at the airport and give them shots. Hopefully, they would ask their doctors about malaria—at the very least, malaria. Her parents made her get shots before they left England.

Maybe someone can rent an elephant for the party, she thought, as she had heard about parties in the area that had them. She decided to ask Francis.

"Francis, can you get us an elephant to ride at the wedding?" she asked as he headed out the door to run more errands.

"Yes, I can. There's this guy who has work elephants and rents them out for parties, but you have to guarantee him a certain amount of rides. I'll book it for you, my dear," he said. He walked to the truck, list in hand.

Jane thought to herself how easy that was to set up, but she knew most of the items left would be harder. It couldn't all be done all in one day, so she pulled Turner to the side and whispered to him.

"Sweetheart, can we have a few minutes alone from this madness?"

"Certainly. Let's go by the bar and get a cold drink and then sit under the ceiling fan on the back porch," Turner said.

There was a small sofa—more like a love seat adjoined with a small coffee table and directly under an old ceiling fan. It made a squeaking sound if the speed was set on any setting that would actually move the air. It was a hot, sticky day so they endured the sound and turned it to full-propeller mode. Turner and Jane were sipping on bottles of Coca-Cola and looking at Hattie's jungle garden in the back that melted in to the real jungle a few hundred yards out. It was not unusual to see monkeys at the edge of the forest. Leopards had been seen at night along the outer part of the jungle. Small antelopes, deer, and forest buffaloes loved Hattie's little clearing, rich with tall grass. At present, there were a couple of peafowls and a small wild hog using the space.

"This is really a paradise, isn't it, baby?" Jane said.

"It's a paradise because you're in it," Turner said, pulling her close and kissing her.

"Do you realize that in the last few minutes we've planned our whole lives together? Do you think they believed we had been planning everything for weeks?" Jane asked.

"Well, we had touched on most of those subjects during the last couple weeks, and I think it all came together quickly. I still don't feel good having you pay for so much. I just feel I should be providing for you."

"Look, Turner, after med school, I'll start having babies, and you'll be working to keep food on the table for me and the kids. You'll get your turn, and besides, that money came from me fighting sharks over people's dead bodies. I still have I lot of jewelry left, not counting my mother's, which I would rather not sell. There is a monstrous ruby neckless that I would hate to part with. We have talked to big jewelry stores across the river, and they'll buy some of the dead body jewelry—maybe three or four thousand more. It will be enough to pay for the wedding and most of the expedition, with about ten or twelve thousand left over. I have no idea how much my parents left me, but they also had started a college fund—probably not a large sum. Anyway, we're probably far better off than ninety percent of students starting school and newlyweds starting their lives together. I'm not worried, are you?"

"I'm really more excited than anything. Where are we going to spend our honeymoon—here at the comfort house, a hotel in town, a steamer full of smelly natives, or a private train car? There is a train here, you know, but it doesn't go where we want to go." Turner rattled on.

"Yeah, the Congo-Ocean Railway is nothing for the French to brag about. They're using forced labor—killing off natives every day. I have read every paper Hattie receives from here and abroad. Local news covers it up, but European papers tell it like it is. I believe I'll pass on the train ride. Just place me in a room with a bed that has you dead center in it. I'm so ready to pounce on you." She grabbed his cheek and directed his lips in her direction. Her hand gently drifted over his pants. "You get hard so quickly," Jane said, grinning.

"That also means I will explode all over you quickly as well until I get used to you. I hope you will have patience."

"Explode all you want, dear, but after that you will be put to the test with all your athletic abilities," Jane said, laughing.

"Should I be running a few miles every day before the marriage?"

"You'll be fine."

After about eight days, some guests began to show up early. The fastest way to fly to the Congo from London required chartering a plane across Central Africa from Nairobi. British Imperial Airways had passenger service to both Nairobi and Cape Town, but once at either city, a charter would still have to be booked since the airfields at Brazzaville and Leopoldville were very primitive. Jane's Uncle Basil Goode took the shortest flight possible. He was the first to arrive to represent the family and to go through the paperwork of the inheritance of her parents. His wife, Abbie, came along as well. Abbie was French, a free spirit, and several years younger than Basil, who was Jane's dad's younger brother. Jane had other aunts, but none were like Abbie. She was like a wild kid who never grew up. Jane adored her. She was in her late thirties and totally out of the control of her serious husband. She would always sneak a drink or a cigarette to Jane and helped corrupt her any way she could.

Abbie was pretty and sexy. All the men loved to be around her and she certainly didn't fight them off. There were rumors in the family that she was not above the occasional affair. It wasn't that she was too much woman for Basil—she was too much woman for any man. Untamable—unpredictable—exciting. However, she was a mother at seventeen of twin boys, now nineteen years old, who were in their second year at Oxford's Christ the Church College. They had always loved to pester Jane when she was little, but she liked them anyway. George and Peter Goode were coming in a few days for the wedding and then would be stalking any pretty girls who showed up. They were so much like their mother, it was scary.

As soon as Abbie saw Jane, she picked her up, hugged her, and kissed her on the lips. "My God, girl, you have grown up to be prettier and sexier than me. I am so proud. My training paid off. Where is this stud that thinks he can keep up with your insatiable carnal needs?"

Turner extended his hand to Abbie. "I'm that lucky guy, and I agree it will be a challenge and one I will exhaust myself in the attempt," Turner said.

She wouldn't take his hand. Instead she walked up to him and kissed him on the mouth with such passion that Turner was gasping for air when it was over. "That's the way Jane has been instructed to kiss. Kiss like you want the clothes to come off next," Abbie said, laughing and reaching out for Basil as he walked up.

"I want you to meet my husband, the great barrister, Basil Goode. I married him so he could help keep me out of jail for molesting men." She laughed again. Basil merely shook his head. He was used to her antics.

"Turner, I'm glad to meet you. May I suggest that you never have these two at the same party without calling the police first," Basil said, smiling. He was a tall, handsome man, with impeccable taste in clothing. His temples were graying nicely and his hair appeared as though his barber must be a part of the household staff. Jane saw him as a younger version of her now-deceased dad.

Basil set up a time in a couple days to go with Jane and Turner to both her local lawyer and her banker to start in motion her desires for the settlement of the estate. Later, Abbie wanted to go to Leopoldville to a jazz club and a movie, and as Basil said, "To see how much trouble she can get into."

The wedding was now just a few days off and the boat would be in not long after the ceremony. As soon as it was unloaded, cleaned (hosed down), and reloaded it would be off again with a newlywed couple onboard. For now, it was time to put the finishing touches on the wedding. A wire was just received that Turner's sisters, Carole and Lauren, would be there the next afternoon. Everything was falling in place.

Chapter Ten

Parties

Turner met his sisters as they arrived by plane at about noon two days before the wedding. He and Jane had driven to the Leopoldville Airport in Francis's old Ford sedan and had waited by the gate. Carole Goode came through first, hugged her brother and then grabbed Jane and tried to twirl her around but found Jane was more than she could handle, so she hugged her instead. She saw Jane's ring and placed her own engagement ring beside Jane's marquise stone.

"Wow, Jane, what a beautiful ring!"

"So is yours, Carole," Jane said as she peered down at the carat and a half round sparkling gem on Carole's finger.

"I'm sorry that nobody likes me, and I'm ringless," said Lauren, as she hugged her brother and Jane.

Both sisters looked like their mother but had blonde hair and flawless, beautiful faces.

"Have you girls ever passed for twins?" Jane asked.

"Yes, a few times. We even switched dates at the movies once. The guys were so wrapped up in the movie they didn't notice. We even kissed them during the show, and they still didn't get it until we walked out of the theater. Under the lights, they figured it out. Personally, I thought Carole's date was a better kisser," Lauren laughed.

"You don't know how excited I am to have the two sisters I never had growing up. Turner talks about you guys all the time and refused to get married unless you were here. Your mother is getting practice in for your wedding next summer, Carole," Jane said.

"Has she calmed down about your age and all?" asked Carole.

"Yes. We've had some long conversations, and I hope we're getting close. She only has Turner's best interests at heart. I'll tell you this: if I had a girl and she was my age, there's no way I would let her run off and get married," Jane said. She punched Turner in the side. "Cradle robber!"

"You don't look fourteen, Jane, and you're drop-dead gorgeous," Carole and Lauren said, almost in unison. "Our brother did well," Carole said.

They walked to the car arm-in-arm. Jane actually looked older than the sisters since she was three-or-four inches taller.

They loaded into the sedan with two suitcases each and let Turner give them a quick tour of the city and some of the Art Deco construction going on. A new sports facility with a swimming pool had just been completed. He drove them by the new botanical park, then the movie theater, jazz club, and bars.

"I see we won't be too bored while we are here," said Lauren.

"Lots of eligible boys from Belgium here. Some right out of college and posted for the government here," Jane said to Lauren.

"I'll keep an eye open," Lauren said.

Turner knew the time for the next car ferry across the Congo and timed it beautifully. He drove on and parked at the far end, so he would be the first off. Everyone got out of the car and took the gangway to the upper observation deck where they sold soft drinks. Turner treated, and they all enjoyed the breeze coming off the river. However, the smells of the city and the open latrines along the waterfront caused the two sisters to cover their noses.

"Do you get used to these smells?" Carole asked.

"We realize it won't go away and treat it like a small wound that won't heal, but you know you can't die from it," Jane said. "You also need to be prepared for the five pygmies at the comfort house. They have a reason to smell—it wards off the insects in the jungle. Hattie keeps hosing them down, but it doesn't help much."

"Tell us about Hattie and Francis—Mother seems to love them," Lauren said.

"Hard not to. They stood up for me and Jane and they treat everyone great—even the natives," Turner said.

After landing in Brazzaville, Turner became the tour guide for the town, even though there wasn't as much to see on that side of the Congo.

"Economically, the tourism industry doesn't support the population as it does across the river. Rubber, wood, and agricultural products supplement the limited mining done in French Equatorial Africa. As with most colonial towns and cities, there's a segregated white section, which is always nicer than the native sectors. The comfort house makes up for the lack of other activities."

Turner's sisters made a dead run for her parents who had just come down the steps from the porch. After catching up with them on most everything, Jane asked if they would like to meet the natives. She introduced the sisters, and they shook hands with each native and tried to talk to them. Jane translated with a fluid understanding of their language. Lauren and Carole were fascinated, especially Lauren who was an anthropology major at Princeton—a great place for language study since the college turned out well-educated Presbyterian missionaries and sent them all over the world. Immediately, Lauren wanted Jane to teach her their language.

"I'll give you my notebook first. Learn what's there and then I'll teach you more," Jane said.

"You need to know that Jane has a photographic memory, so you may learn a little slower than her," Turner said.

"Great! I'm excited. What other languages do you know?" Carole asked.

"French, Spanish, some German and Dutch. I'm learning Afrikaans, and two more native dialects, Bantu and Swahili, which is sort of the national language of the natives. The slave traders used it all over Africa."

"Wow, that's a bunch of languages! It's really easy for you, isn't it?" Carole asked.

"All studies are pretty easy for me. Math and science challenge me some. I just don't think I'm very creative, and I feel that's a weakness," Jane said.

"You were creative when you told all of us that you were seventeen," Turner said.

"I'm not sure lying counts as being creative," Jane said.

"Well, it's certainly making stuff up. Good writers do that," Lauren said.

"Then a writer I shall be," Jane said, laughing.

Hattie and Francis were now coaxing everyone up the steps and into the house. Introductions were made, and then they were led to the great room for drinks and more introductions.

Abbie had been drinking for a while, and in her usual high-spirited way, promised to corrupt Turner's sisters to the bone.

No sooner had the luggage been set down than Turner had to go pick up Basil and Abbie's two sons, who had flown in to the Brazzaville airport. It was only about fifteen minutes out, and Basil elected to go with Turner since they had some things to discuss.

There were only a couple of spare rooms available at Hattie's place, but she had a lot of cots and rollaway-beds. Abbie and Basil took one, and the two girls took the last one. George and Peter had reservations at De Ville Brazzaville and had wired ahead for a driver and car. They were determined to hit the action wherever it was.

"Turner, I think you and Jane Ann will make a marvelous couple," Basil said as they sped along the gravel road that led to the small Brazzaville airport. "She seems crazy about you, and I feel you will be the one that tames that wild animal in her. She about drove her parents crazy. She is beautiful, with a tremendous and very adult figure, and smarter than anyone around her, including her teachers. No one knew how to handle her and my brother, Sam, was extremely concerned. He would be more than pleased that she is settling down with you. Medical school will give her a little challenge, and later she will be a very fussy mother.

"Let me warn you about my boys before we pick them up. They will go after Lauren like a moth to a flame and will probably fight each other over her. She's just their type."

"Ha! Trust me, Lauren can take care of herself. She is pretty and knows it. Many a handsome guy has been felled by her charms. I just hope your boys don't get their feelings hurt too easily. She loves 'em and leaves 'em. The guy that captures her will really be something."

"Remember, they've been trained by Abbie."

"Well, that's not playing fair," Turner said, and both laughed, knowing Abbie had all the answers.

The boys were off the twin prop Boeing 221A which had just started service from London a few months before and then added a flight to Nairobi on to Johannesburg, and finally one to Brazzaville. Basil motioned he would meet them after they cleared customs. Turner and Basil took seats in the small airline terminal and waited for the inevitable long period of checking suitcases and passports.

Basil looked at Turner. "We need to sit down with Jane's attorney and banker here and talk about her inheritance, Turner. She wired me to put it all in an account to maintain the house and to let one of her cousins live there while she's at Oxford. That cousin is one of my nieces, and I'm fine with it, unless drunken orgies happen to break out there."

"Be sure to invite me when that happens."

"My brother Sam left her sizeable amounts of cash, life insurance proceeds, and a recovering portfolio of investments that was severely decimated by the market crash in twenty-nine. By far, the most valuable were his and Rachael's land and property holdings. A small farm in the Cotswolds, rental units in London, a beautiful home and grounds in Oxford. And I was surprised to learn that they had kept their home in Maryland from the time he was stationed in DC."

"Wow! Does she know about all of this?"

"She's been to the farm, and I'm sure she has listened into conversation about their rental units, but I'm not sure they ever told her they kept the home in the States. I didn't know about it. I did their wills and trusts way before they left to go to America and never updated that part."

"You're aware that she has over ten thousand in the bank here?"

"I knew she opened an account, but where in the hell did she get that much money?"

"As the sharks were eating the floating bodies of the victims, she fought with them to get the jewelry from the women. She knew she would need something to sell so she could survive."

"Thirteen years old and fighting sharks. She is something else," Basil said.

The twins were headed towards them with their luggage in hand. After Turner was introduced to the twins, they were to be taken to their hotel to drop off their luggage and get room keys. Turner drove them and waited until they had checked in.

"Room okay?" their dad asked.

"Lots of rattan furniture and pictures of wild animals. The room will do nicely," Peter said as they took the back seat of the car and headed for the comfort house.

"What is this comfort house?" George asked.

"Officially, I think they are called rest houses, but the Rhodes took it up a notch," Turner said. "It's a big house with several guest rooms—some with baths and others have shared facilities. There is a great room for drinks, card games, and just visiting. The dining room is mainly for dinner and you sort of dress up for that—it's all at one long table. The place reminds me of a place out of the movies. I really think you'll like it."

"Turner, what's the girl situation—any singles around?" George asked.

"I will have one unattached sister there and one or two cousins from Belgium. There will be a bunch of girls there from London. Some I believe that may not be related to you. Petra from Amsterdam looks like a model and a movie star all rolled into one. I'll see that one of you gets to pick her up at the airport."

Turner hit a pothole, jolting everyone out of their seats, then swerved to miss a cart being pulled by a water buffalo.

"Tell us about your sister," Peter said.

"She's incredibly pretty and tough on guys. Two years of college at Princeton has made her a hard woman. If you know anything about anthropology, she might speak to you, but don't count on it."

"Boys, you are here for your cousin's wedding, not to start a war with the Simpson family. Remember that and be civil."

The boys erupted in laughter. "Yes, Dad, we'll be good boys."

After parking in front of the comfort house, they climbed the steps and were met by Hattie, who hugged the boys and personally walked them into the great room. The boys took in the trophies mounted on the wall, along with African shields and spears.

Turner's sisters were front and center to meet them. After the introduction, Peter took Lauren's arm and walked her to the bar. He was ambushed by Jane before he got too far.

"Peter, already you have the prettiest girl here on your arm." She kissed him, thanked him for coming. Then she asked about George and went straight to where he stood with Carole.

"George, you know this one is taken—but isn't she gorgeous?" Jane kissed George and promised to find him a girl to party with. Turner's cousin from Belgium was a freshman at a college in Amsterdam and the word was she was beautiful. Her name was Petra and she would be there in about an hour. Turner had arranged for George to pick her up at the airport. He wanted both of Basil and Abbie's boys to have a good time, and of course the girls as well.

"Carole, now that you've met me, don't you think you should re-think this silly engagement idea of yours?" George said, laughing and moving Carole closer to the bar, which was getting crowded.

Francis was helping his regular bartender satisfy the growing throng of invitees. Most everyone would be in by tonight, including Carole's fiancé, Martin, who was in his senior year at Harvard. Shortly, a couple of cars would have to cross the river to get more wedding guests and then return them later. It would take trips in the two vehicles owned by the comfort house and any other cars that could be borrowed or rented. Several people would be staying across the river, but most would find their way to the comfort house. The pusher-pushers would line up for trips back and forth, and the guests would find them fun unless it rained since most didn't have canopies to keep them dry.

A welcome party was planned for the evening, with live entertainment, hors d'oeuvres, and drinks. A jazz trio from Leopold would travel there to entertain, and the pygmies would come inside briefly to let people interview them with Jane translating. They would be carrying spears and bows and arrows, but they would be wearing the shorts that Jane bought them since she doubted any one wanted to inspect their private parts.

Tomorrow would be the night of the rehearsal dinner, but during the day the guests would be free to go shopping and take the elephant rides and tours. Francis had a list of all the native stores that sold spears, shields, and local arts and crafts. And of course, the next day would be the wedding at mid-day. Government officials had been invited from both the French and Belgian offices. The British had embassies on both sides of the river, and a few of the officers would be at the wedding. An offer was extended to these government officials to invite young college-aged sons and daughters who were there for the summer to attend as well. Some had already headed back to class, but others delayed because they wanted to go to a rare wedding in the two cities. The local papers hyped it as "The Jungle Jane Wedding."

It wasn't often that so many people would attend a destination wedding in the Congo. There had never been a greater excuse for a jungle party.

George asked for the keys to the Ford Sedan, so he could pick up Petra Simpson at the airport. He got the phone number for the comfort house before he left in case he got lost. The airport was pretty easy to find since there was only one in town, and it wasn't that crowded. He located a good parking spot in front of the terminal. He found some souvenir shops and bummed a sheet of paper and a large marker to make a sign. Using a bright red color on a white piece of paper, he wrote in large letters "Petra, I am your date for the wedding—George."

After standing at the end of the customs line for what seemed like a half hour, he saw her and wished he had a classier sign. She had a flawless olive complexion and coal black hair that fell below her waist. She was runway-model tall and beautiful. Her eyes were soft deep brown, and her smile was genuine, revealing brilliant white teeth. He had won the ultimate prize at the wedding.

On top of all that beauty, Petra was wearing white shorts and a lavender sleeveless blouse. Her sandals had a slight heel, which accentuated her legs and made them even sexier, if that were possible.

George had been dating for years and wasn't new at the game.

The challenge in front of him would take all his skills and charms. She was laughing as she walked directly to the sign and stuck out her hand. George took it and greeted her with a soft kiss on her cheek. She smelled wonderful.

"So, you are Jane's cousin from London, is that right?" Petra said as she led him to her three bags of luggage.

"Yes, but I go to school at Oxford. And you are in school in Amsterdam?"

"Correct. I love your sign. I guess I'm assigned to you for the duration of the visit?"

"Absolutely! It will be an arduous task, but someone has to do it. In case no one has ever mentioned it, you are very attractive."

"Thank you, George, and you are quite handsome."

"Thank you. With that settled, why don't we just get married too and start having kids? I mean the cake is being baked—all the relatives are here. Let's just get it done."

"Of course! It sounds fun! Now, where are you taking me first before our marriage ceremony?"

"To a rest house, which Hattie and Francis Rhodes call a comfort house. It's like something out of a movie, and you'll love it. I believe they are setting up a rollaway bed for you with Turner's sisters, Carole and Lauren. My brother Peter is trying to convince Lauren to marry him, too, about this time, I'm sure. Knowing him, he'll want to barge in on our plans. It's going to be crowded at the front of the audience in a couple of days." They both laughed as they bounced around on the rough roads leading to the comfort house.

As they pulled up in front of the house, Turner and Jane rushed out to welcome them. Turner hadn't seen his cousin in about two years. Most of the guests had already arrived, and now the party was in full swing.

Chapter Eleven

The Events

As more and more guests arrived for the party, Lillian Simpson put her two girls to work serving hors d'oeuvres. Petra took the hint and grabbed a tray. No one could have possibly been served by more beautiful women. Jane felt guilty that she wasn't helping but knew this was all about her and Turner.

After things had settled down somewhat and people were listening to the jazz trio, with a few even trying to dance to the music, Lauren asked if she could see Jane's notes. They ran down the hall to Jane's room where she found her notebook, then handed it to Lauren with some explanations. It had all the languages she was studying, so she pointed out her notes on the pygmies' dialect.

They ran into Peter as they left Jane's room. Jane walked Peter and Lauren to the back porch, where there was a small sofa and an overhead light built into a ceiling fan. All agreed it was much quieter and more conducive for studying. After Lauren read a while, Peter would read her a word and she would try to translate. It was a difficult task, but she learned a few phrases. Then she and Peter went back inside to find Jane. Interrupting an embarrassing childhood story about one of Jane's early dance recitals actually was a relief, so she was pleased to get away from her aunts and uncles for a while. She accompanied Peter and Lauren to where the natives stood eating a few treats taken from an hors d'oeuvres tray.

"Nestor, Lauren is studying your language. Do you mind if she tries to talk to you?" Jane said in their language.

"Do you miss your family?" Lauren asked.

Nestor replied that he did. Lauren asked a few more simple

questions, and Jane cleared up any words not communicated well. Peter thanked them in their language, and they let the natives go back to sampling treats they would never find in the Congo basin.

"I'm really impressed that you have picked up so much in such a short time," Jane said. "You as well, Peter. Isn't your major pre-law?"

"Pre-law with a minor in German. Not because I like the language—but Hitler has just made himself chancellor, and I smell trouble. I want to help if I'm needed."

"My parents had the same concerns. They were on a mission to secure some oil concessions before Hitler got his paws on them."

"Sad about your parents. I really liked them. You know, we might do some kind of service for them. We had one in England, but of course you were in the jungle," Peter said.

"I agree. Let's talk to Hattie to see if we can sneak in an early morning service," said Lauren as she headed toward Hattie, who had now started picking up empty plates and glasses.

"Hattie, do you think it would be possible for Reverend DeSmit to perform a short memorial service for my parents early tomorrow morning—say around eight a.m.?" Jane asked.

"I'll call him—or check the bar area—he was there talking to your uncle a few minutes ago. Maybe he hasn't gone yet. He's an Episcopal priest, so he'll be less formal than the Catholic ones."

Jane, Lauren, and Peter found the Rev. DeSmit nursing a beer and talking to Basil Goode at the bar. He agreed to hold a short service the next morning and took out a pad to record information from Jane and Basil about the deceased couple. Jane walked around to her relatives and invited them to the service.

The next morning, Rev. DeSmit held a nice but brief memorial service for Sam and Rachael Goode. Various family members told of good memories of them, and Jane relayed how her mother had placed her jewelry in her luggage before the ship sank. As soon as it was over, the last-minute planning for the wedding started taking place.

Turner had to go by a jewelry store in Leopoldville to pick up the wedding bands. Well aware that it was Jane's birthday, he had a special gift for her. Lunch would be a birthday celebration for both of them with cake, finger sandwiches, and elephant rides. In the evening, there would be a rehearsal dinner and a buffet in the great room. There would also be a special dinner in the dining room for the wedding party.

Jane's bridesmaids were Turner's sisters, Petra, and one of her school friends from London. Turner had chosen Peter, George, and a cousin from Belgium to be groomsmen. His best man, Jim Wimberly, was a friend from the States whom he had gone to prep school with in Virginia. Attending school in the states enhanced Turner's mastery of English, even though he had been studying it for years. Jim had been to Brussels to visit Turner, and they had fought over girls and gotten drunk together on many occasions. His flight was due in later in the morning, and Turner would pick him up across the river as he ran his many errands.

Jane really liked Lauren and her commitment to learn the language of the pygmies, and she asked if she would be her maid of honor. Lauren agreed to do it. Basil had agreed to give Jane away. Everything was set—even a little flower girl was found from one of the families of the British Embassy in Leopoldville. Hattie and Francis had invited both embassies' senior staff, and some had attended the party the night before. Jane met one of the ambassadors who knew her dad and had nice things to say about him. Jane also had errands to run but was lucky to find plenty of people to take care of them, so she could be with the guests.

At noon, the outdoor birthday party was set up with a table for gifts; it had been hastily put together from local stores that morning. Jane and Turner opened the gifts with a great deal of laughter since most were local crafts, which were bizarre and comical. One of Jane's gifts was a wooden carving of a native man with what looked like a barrel for clothes. When you pulled on the upper body, he rose above the barrel and out came a huge penis. The native figure was smiling, but the crowd, including Jane, was laughing hysterically. Turner and Jane had spears, masks, shields, and enough wooden carvings to decorate their future house in African motif.

The cake, which had both names on it, was cut, and finger sandwiches were laid out in trays. Hattie had ordered from a local caterer, and Basil picked up the tab. The party was fun, and the elephant rides were a big hit. The mahout, or elephant handler, took two guests at a time up the dirt road about a few hundred yards and then back to the party. He had brought a wood platform with steps going up to the elephant's back. Just as Lauren and Peter climbed out of the basket on the elephant and were standing on the top of the platform, Lauren yelled something that froze the crowd.

"Black panther! Black panther!" She pointed at the yard by the corner of the house. Moving towards them slowly but deliberately was a large black leopard. Jane was standing on the steps to the porch when she spotted the creature. She shouted at the crowd.

"Freeze—do not run! Everyone yell at him!"

The factions of the crowd that still had the ability to speak started yelling at the big cat in a vain attempt to scare it off while Jane rushed to her room. On her way, she yelled "paka!"—a Swahili term she had heard the pygmies use.

It only took her seconds to find her .45 and an extra clip. Nestor and the natives ran to the yard with her. Jane walked directly in the path of the large black cat and stared in his eyes. The party members had moved to the sidelines and behind tables, but no one ran except the elephant and her mahout, who were at full gallop, bellowing, and blowing dust behind them as they retreated at full speed down the dirt road. Jane clicked off the safety and chambered a round. Nestor and Padi were next to her with spears raised; the other three natives had bows drawn.

Francis had retrieved an 8-bore, double-barreled elephant gun. He was on the porch but didn't have a good shot with the crowd between him and the cat. The crowd was silent except for the whine of someone's motion picture camera. The leopard was not going to stop. Jane raised her pistol and fired a round over the cat's head. He hunkered down and almost turned to run, but he was hungry and determined. Jane could see his ribs and realized he had probably not eaten for a while. He was the most beautiful animal she had ever seen: black, powerful, sleek, and his muscles rippled with every small movement. No tissue was wasted on fat, as connections of sinew, cartilage, ligaments, and powerful muscles all coordinated into a primal force ready to find the throat of potential prey—even human prey.

This black leopard was a prime example of a perfect carnivorous creature designed to kill. Greenish–yellow eyes contrasted against his deep black skin and bright large fangs made him even more imposing. Jane didn't want to kill this marvelous creature unless she had to.

Faint spots could be seen on his side as he decided to charge. Jane lowered her weapon and fired, hitting the animal in his neck, through shoulder muscle, and tearing through his lung. The bullet slowed him briefly; yet the big cat recovered and continued. The next shot hit his hindquarters causing him to flip. Regaining his balance, he forced himself to run a few steps and spring into the air. Screams from the crowd filled the yard. Jane fired three shots in rapid succession. The natives engaged their weapons. One of the bullets, spears, or arrows must have struck and penetrated a vital organ because the huge cat landed exactly where Jane had been standing before she moved to dodge the airborne leopard. The beast was still twitching as Jane stood over it and fired two more slugs into its big skull, splattering blood on her white slacks. As she reached down to touch it, she noticed that two spears and three arrows had hit their marks as well. As she examined the dead leopard, she patted it and began to cry. Turner ran over and took her in his arms.

"That was the most beautiful creature I have ever seen in my life, and I killed it. I…I…really didn't want to kill it."

Turner hugged her and consoled her as did her relatives and friends. Because of the pictures and amateur movies taken, Jane would forever be Jungle Jane. In a few weeks, one roll of movie film taken by a newly released Bolex-16 movie camera would hit newsreels at movie theaters all over the world. Soon Jane would become a heroine, a legend even, and an inspiration for young girls all over the planet.

The elephant came back, a little wide-eyed and skittish, but nonetheless back to carry the next guest. The leopard was thrown in the back of a truck and taken to a taxidermist who would process the beautiful hide for Jane to pick up on the way back from her trip. Maybe she would have it mounted for a gift for Hattie and Francis."

~~~~~~

Later that day Basil, Jane, and Turner met with the local attorney and banker at their offices to discuss her estate. Jane was surprised by the assets put back by her parents. Her newly discovered home in Maryland led to a discussion about schools on the East Coast. After reviewing the assets, it was apparent they could buy a small home in California and keep the Maryland house leased.

They all returned to the comfort house after papers were signed and filed and it was decided that Basil would meet with them later in England to finalize any outstanding paperwork. Turner asked to stop by a local jewelry shop where he picked up a couple of items. One was a birthday gift for Jane. She opened it on the way back to the comfort house. She let out a shriek and held up a sterling silver lifeboat neckless with an engraving that read, "You are my lifeboat forever— Love, Turner." As he was driving, she leaned over from the back seat and kissed him, causing the car to swerve dangerously close to a wall covered with purple bougainvillea flowers. Basil helped correct the steering from his shotgun position.

Events at the comfort house had calmed down and people were off on excursions, shopping, and resting back at their hotels. At this point Jane and Turner had rest on their minds as well. They left the door open to her room and both laid on her bed with a ceiling fan turned to full speed above them.

Jane looked over at Turner and said, "Baby, tomorrow we can take a nap buck naked together."

"Yes, dear, we can, but I seriously doubt if the nap part will take place."

Several people passed by their room and saw the couple sleeping, but no one bothered them.

Chapter Twelve

The Wedding

The rehearsal dinner was to be open to everyone. Turner's parents were in charge and had it catered by a large firm across the river. Turner and Jane had spent some time after their nap discussing the status of their souls, choices for a family church, and a question and answer session on their individual beliefs with Rev. DeSmit. He mainly provided the answers. Jane wisely kept her agnostic leanings to herself and just told the priest that she was raised in the Church of England. Turner was Episcopalian, so he was correctly aligned and apparently satisfied the Rev. DeSmit's thirst for worthy believers. They prayed with him. Jane silently asked for forgiveness for killing the leopard, and then selfishly asked for Turner's penis to be large enough to make her happy. Jane wasn't sure that prayers went anywhere, but she gave it a shot. She started to ask forgiveness for the penis request and realized the prayer was over.

The couple had written marriage vows and gave copies to the reverend. He frowned, as they guessed he would, since the traditional and boring "Obey your husband" verse didn't seem to be there. He acquiesced, read them, and muttered something while he shoved them into his robe. They discussed the ring exchange, their entrance to the main room, and all the particulars of the wedding ceremony.

Jane and Turner needed a drink after the heavy praying and headed for the bar. While they were waiting for their drinks, Max came over to tell them he had received a wire from Rudy on the steamer. He would be at the dock in three days and ready to return to Stanleyville in four days. They should have all their supplies on the dock early on the fourth day. They needed a name stamped on their supplies for their expedition. Turner and Jane decided to call it "Simpson-Pygmy Rescue Mission."

Max had found them an explorer-gun bearer. He asked if they had found their medical aide and another guide. Turner told him they had and would tell him about it later. Neither Jane nor Turner trusted Max or anyone he would hire for them. Both felt he was looking for anything that was of value in the jungle.

The couple had found a recent medical school graduate who had earned credit for part of his residency requirement by treating the natives in the jungle and submitting a report on native diseases. The other guide was referred to them by the British Embassy. He was a former lion hunter from Kenya, a medal holder from the Great War and had been appointed as a game warden by Belgium for the Congo region.

Most of the preparatory work for this journey was now finished. This trip would allow the game warden to assess the poaching of wildlife in this remote part of the Congo.

The expedition was set. Jane and Turner were filled with excitement; however, they didn't see danger in the real sense that an experienced soldier faces battle. Their youth didn't allow for a sensible amount of fear or trepidation. It was a big adventure, and they were invincible. They didn't think it was possible for them to die.

The rehearsal and the dinner went off as planned and the party afterwards was fun. All the guests would be a part of the couple's lives for many years and both realized that you don't just marry one person but their entire family. They would be there for them their entire lives, and Jane and Turner believed that the joining of the families was a great match.

Turner's parents would be grandparents to their children, but Jane wouldn't have a set of grandparents for their kids. Basil and Abbie realized this and agreed to take on those positions in the future. Jane loved the idea and knew that her parents, had they lived, would have been wonderful grandparents. Having children was a few years off, but an event they all looked forward to. There were also great-grandparents on both sides, but they were not in a position to make this trip. Turner and Jane would visit them after the trip to the natives' villages.

The natives were having a good time, even though Lauren and Peter spent a great deal of energy working with them on language. They spent most of their time standing at the back of the room as the servers brought them food and drink. Everyone found out that they loved honey, pork, and palm wine, and every effort was made to make sure they had plenty of everything they desired. Jane checked on them all the time and thanked them many times for standing with her to face the leopard. She assured them that they would be headed home soon with medicine for their tribe. On this night, Hattie was washing their shorts for the wedding, so the naked natives were truly going "native." Pygmy secrets were on display and many of the guests would have their pictures taken with them.

~~~~~~

The wedding was set for eleven so that everyone could have lunch at the reception afterwards. Jane had a chance to spend some time with Turner's best man, Jim Wimberly, and liked him. He said he would give his right arm to go on their adventure with them, but had to get back to school in a few days. However, he was going to the University of California at Berkley, so they would have plenty of time to visit in the future since Palo Alto was close by. A new Bay bridge was being built, which would be completed in two or three years, making the journey much easier. Until then, they would use ferries, which were numerous.

Before the wedding started, Jane gave Turner a gift. It was a beautiful gold pocket watch that opened to a compass on one side and a watch on the other. One side said, "Never lose me" and the other said "Always have time for me." It was signed "Your Watutsi woman, Jane "Jungle Jane" Simpson." He loved it, and for the first time, he saw her married name. He gave her a small silver jewelry box with a beautiful strand of pearls. It was engraved, "The real jewels are not in this box but in your heart. I love you and hope I can be the Watutsi of your dreams. Love forever, Turner."

Jane laughed and kissed him and told him she loved him. It was time to get dressed for the wedding, so she went to her room where attendants helped do her hair and makeup. She held the pearls in her hand and decided to wear them during the wedding.

Outside the comfort house, a huge tent had been erected for the reception and the recent rain had cooled things off a bit.

As they worked on her hair and makeup, she began to reflect on what had happened to her in the past few weeks. She was so happy to be alive. So happy to have met Turner. So excited about the future. So sad her mother and father were dead. She had treated them so badly, and now they couldn't be a part of one of the biggest days in her life. She was thankful for Uncle Basil and Aunt Abbie. She had tears in her eyes, but a smile came to her lips when she thought about Abbie. Abbie was in the room, helping her get ready for the wedding. Jane asked her to come closer. She told her she loved her, hugged her, and cried for a minute. Abbie understood the emotions and returned the hug, making her smile again.

Abbie held up the beautiful wedding dress which she had brought from home for her. It was now Jane's as was the ring on her hand, so there was a connection. Everything would be okay and then again, everything would never be okay. She would enjoy this day as much as possible with the absence of her parents.

The time had come, and Jane was led down the aisle by her Uncle Basil. The priest allowed Turner and Jane to read their prepared vows to each other, which they wrote without editing by the priest. Each one's vow was to make the other happy and to devote their lives to helping others by being the best doctors possible. Reverend DeSmit got in a couple of prayers and charged them to keep God in their lives. He tried his best to turn unholy homemade vows into a church-sponsored union that would surely otherwise wallow in ungodliness without the impartation of strict religious rules. Jane and Turner looked at each other and winked while the priest was buried in his dialogue. Jane thought about school during this time instead of the ramblings of the Reverend DeSmit.

Their college acceptance had been wired from Stanford with a strong nudge from the national media and a well-placed call from Turner's uncle, who was a graduate of Stanford Medical School. Jane had taken final exams in the last few days for the courses she needed to graduate from upper school in Oxford. She made a perfect score and found one question which had an error. She corrected it and gave the appropriate answer.

The priest glared at her, sensing her attention was elsewhere.

They exchanged rings, gold bands with tiny elephants and crocodiles carved around the outside. They had found a jeweler in Leopoldville who designed and made the rings on short notice and also agreed to buy a few thousand dollars of Jane's safety box gems. They were worth much more, but the economy was mired deep in the Great Depression so she was lucky to get them sold.

"You may kiss the bride" were the priest's next words, and they both knew now that there were no more barriers of age or any impropriety between them. They could legally wake up together and kiss each other good morning. But for now, they had a honeymoon suite at The Villa Hotel in Brazzaville. They walked down the aisle amid everyone's cheers and then walked back in through a side door a few minutes later for pictures. Mr. "Z" had agreed to be the photographer for the wedding, and Paul and Lillian Simpson had requested to pick up the expenses.

They wanted to change into something more casual for the reception, so they locked themselves in Jane's room. Their new clothes lay in front of them on the bed. As they undressed, they looked into each other's eyes and smiled. In seconds, they were nude, staring at each other.

"Wow! You do have all your parts in the right places," Turner blurted.

"I don't think the Watutsis have anything on you." Jane approached Turner and held the part she had craved in her hand and stared at it.

"Do you mind putting it in me for just a few minutes before we meet the crowd?"

"Well, I guess if you insist. We need to put on a rubber since we aren't ready for kids yet."

Turner put one on and then walked Jane to the bed and moved

their change of clothes to a chair. The excitement for each of them was not measurable, but still there was a slowness and gentleness with which Turner treated her. It would be a simple missionary style for now, and as he placed himself in her, she was not only delighted by how good he felt but understood that having a penis in her wasn't just the act. It was the smiling, handsome face and muscular body and the person she loved placing it in her wet vagina.

Turner used fairly slow thrusts so the lovemaking might last, but it was useless. Remarkably, Jane was climaxing at exactly the same time he was emptying himself into the condom. Although she tried to keep her moaning down, since there was a houseful of people, it was apparent to Turner that she would be a wonderfully noisy lover. She was flushed, excited, and wanted to examine the condom since she had never seen semen up close. In her usual scientific mind, she had to touch it and feel its consistency.

She then looked up at Turner and said, "Sweetheart, can we do this every day of our lives? It felt better than I thought was possible. There are two parts to having sex. One is the connection of the body parts and the other is the physical attraction and love you have for the other person. If I had done it with a Watutsi, I would have missed the second part, and the first part would have probably been repulsive." Jane spoke much like the young teenager she was.

"Sign me up for the everyday part, and I agree with your two-part analysis. Now, we better get dressed and meet everyone for the reception. Also, the part where we climaxed at the same time doesn't happen often. We'll be chasing that little treat for a long time."

"I'm not going to ask you how you know so much about sex at age seventeen."

"Guys talk. They all think they're experts."

"Are we going to be experts, sweetie?"

"You bet your pretty ass, and by the way, it is very pretty!"

Chapter Thirteen

Departures

With her cheeks still flush from the excitement, Jane followed Turner through the door and out onto the porch. Cheers and catcalls filled the yard and tent area. They all knew what had just happened.

Turner grinned and addressed them with, "Hey, we're legal now, and yes it was fun. Now, where is that big cake?"

Jane and Turner cut a beautiful wedding cake and carried a piece to the head table where they picked up their plates and sampled the food on the buffet. After they ate, there were presents to open and toasts to be made. A small band played some dance music and some songs just for background music. It was a great wedding to have been held in the steamy French Congo, and one the guests would talk about for a long time. The reception went on for a few hours. Most of the guests hung around, except for a few who had to catch flights in the afternoon. By the next night most of the people would be gone, and the newlyweds would be putting their gear together for a honeymoon on a paddleboat steamer, preparing to be jungle explorers. The wedding had been fun, and Jane had even started to write thank you notes to be mailed from Brazzaville, French Equatorial Africa. She was sure that the notes with stamps from the Congo would be keepsakes.

She and Turner were pleased at the number of people who made the trip. It was expensive, time consuming, and not a comfortable trip to make, but family ties were strong with both sets of relatives. The flights were makeshift charters from British Imperial Airways, Air France, and private operators. Most took seven to twelve days to complete the trip to their respective homes. There were no scheduled flights from London, Paris, or New York to the Congo and they would have to cut across to Nairobi or connect with a flight from Cape Town. These planes were slow and were required to stop at many small airstrips to refuel and for overnight accommodations. This gave them an extra opportunity to crash either on their landing or taking off. Once in the air, they were cold, noisy, and bumpy, even though the advertisements showed them with bunk beds and great meals served in luxury armchairs. It was not as comfortable as depicted in their brochures. Large bowls were always handy for air sickness.

However, for some of the guests coming from the East Coast of America, their trip to Europe was quite pleasant if they took the Graf Zeppelin airship from New Jersey to Germany. It only took three days and flew nonstop in comfort. Turner and Jane knew that her relatives had spent a fortune on these flights. Yet, a certain reality came over the couple. Even though they rarely thought about it, they accepted that most of their relatives were wealthy, and family ties were strong.

Divorces were rare, and family gatherings were frequent and well-attended. Both Turner and Jane saw the abundance of family love demonstrated when relatives would travel around the world and accept a fourteen-year-old girl marrying a seventeen-year-old boy. Neither had jobs and both needed to finish school, but everyone believed in them and supported them.

Turner sat down next to Jane as she took the first bite from their wedding cake.

"Do you realize how lucky we are to be loved by all these people?" Turner said.

"I do," Jane said. "Just think: a few days ago, I was walking through the jungle with five naked natives, not knowing where I was going or what I was going to do. My parents were dead, and I was lost. Then I met a perfect man who agreed to marry me and walk off into the jungle and risk his life with me."

"You know those natives would have died to protect you. I saw that in their eyes when the leopard attacked the other day. Call it fate, karma, or a religious experience, the arrival of the natives as your lifeboat hit shore was an amazing coincidence. They trust you and couldn't care less how old you are. I very much want to help them too.

I hope we get to their village in time to help some of them, even if we can only vaccinate the ones who are still alive. But—and I don't think Max was just trying to scare me—it's going to be a dangerous trip, from the time we step on the steamer until the time we get back."

Three days later, all the guests who came in for the wedding had gone back home or on to more adventures. The remaining guests threw Turner a small birthday party, which just turned out to be an excuse for everyone to get drunk.

The *S.N. Lapsley II* was docked, and all the equipment for the expedition was stacked and labeled on the docks. The expedition now had a name. The Simpson-Pygmy Rescue Mission was now stenciled on the supplies that sat ready for loading on the steamer. Since Jane had booked all the better cabins, much of their cargo would be stacked in an area to the rear of the aft cabins. It was a perfect place, enclosed by deck rails, and under a portico to protect it from rain. The supplies were to be draped with netting and guarded by the natives who were close by in a fenced area. The loading would go on through the night along with food that would be stored in the refrigeration unit in the main galley.

Jane and Turner had spent two nights at a hotel, then spent the daytime hours back at the comfort house to visit and to see off the guests. Those nights had been wonderful for both. They found exploring each other's bodies exciting and intoxicating. Both worried they couldn't find enough condoms to last them for the trip, but most were made of a new latex material and could be washed and reused. They didn't want a pregnancy at this point.

They made several trips to the boat securing items in their quarters and foodstuff in the galley for the trip. A generous donation of beer, wine, scotch, and imported cigars were presented as a gift... or bribe...to Rudy so that the trip might go a little more smoothly. He grunted, "Thanks ma'am," as Jane handed him enough booze to keep him drunk for two weeks. She noticed on a subsequent trip to the boat, the captain had installed a security gate after the gangway leading to the aft cabins. The area for the natives also had gates on both sides of their outside enclosure. They would be locked only at night, but it sent a signal to the wild passengers on the bottom deck to stay clear. She smiled and realized that the booze and cigars had done the trick. The cost of the scotch alone was almost as much as her fare.

On the day of departure, Francis and Hattie accompanied them to the dock. The couple had backpacks with them and a paper sack of sandwiches and pastries that would last almost a week if they found room for them in the cooler. Hattie had also fixed bags with sandwiches and fruit for the natives. Jane had paid them handsomely for their stay at the comfort house and gave them a huge bonus for helping with the wedding.

Jane hugged Hattie and Francis. "Hattie, we'll be back in a few months with big stories to tell," Jane said. "Please store my wedding presents, dress, and extra clothes for me, and I will pick them up on our way back. We need to get to Stanford right after the Christmas break to catch the second semester, but we hope we can spend a few days with you and Francis before we head to the States."

At the gangplank, their medical officer and the new British expedition guide was waiting for them. Both looked the parts they were playing. The young doctor standing with one foot on the gangplank was actually wearing a white sports coat, white pants, and white buck shoes. Next to him was a rugged man with a large mustache, graying hair by his temples, squared jaw, and wearing a safari jacket. He looked as though he had just stepped off a movie set of some great white hunter film. The doctor, who was on this trip to satisfy part of his residency requirements, introduced himself to Jane and Turner as Nicolas Dubois, and the large hunter gave his name as Alan Chambers. Max was also there to greet them. Later, they would meet Max's expedition companion, a German man by the name of Lutz Holtzman.

"I wish to hold a meeting in my cabin as soon as everyone gets squared away onboard. Say in thirty minutes—say 10:45? See you then," said Max in his most authoritative voice, which failed to reach the profound level he was shooting for due to his comical five-foot-two-inch frame.

Rain blew across the decks as Turner and Jane made their way onboard. The circus of native impromptu markets came to life as they walked past women and men selling food items, baskets, clothing, palm cooking oil, and coconut milk. They were now peering out from under their tarps, yet still hawked their goods as they sought shelter from the rain.

It was quieter on the second deck, with the cabins directly behind the captain's bridge almost void of natives. Jane and Turner had made several trips to unload gear already, so the place was now like a tiny home.

They sensed the rocking of the lumbering vessel as it pulled out against the current of the giant Congo River. It was a river of contrasts. At times, it would be miles across, 700 feet deep, and churning up huge waves. At other times, it was rather narrow with sandbars and snags. The river charts were done in pencil so that on each trip an eraser could take away sandbars that were no longer there, and the captain could then add newly formed ones. Islands formed with deposited sand until the vertical growth looked like sand castles from a fairy tale. An amazing collection of tributaries and smaller rivers flowed together and made the Congo the second largest river in the world by its discharge into the ocean and by far the deepest river on the planet. Zaire was its native name. Turner and Jane stood outside their room sheltered by the overhang from the rain and watched their steamer cut to the middle of Stanley Pool and towards the wilds of the Belgian Congo. It was time to meet Max.

He sat in the dining area on a tall metal stool borrowed from somewhere on the boat. Max was trying to compensate for his vertically-challenged body by having everyone at the meeting sit below him in normal size chairs. There was suspicion he trimmed a few inches off the participants' chair legs. Next to him, on his left, was his second in command, Lutz Holtzman. A short man of five-foot-eight inches, he still towered above Max. He nodded when his boss spoke and in every aspect was a splendid toady. Lutz was not only German, but a member of the new National Socialist German Workers' Party, proudly wearing his Nazi swastika pin on his shirt collar.

"Thank you for your promptness at this meeting. It will be short and to the point," Max said as his thick German accent transitioned to an almost unintelligible form of English.

"Our mission is that of a humanitarian nature and should be simple enough to execute. I have determined it will take us about two weeks to reach the pygmy village after the boats drop us off on the banks of Aruwimi River. How long we stay there will be determined by the extent of the sickness. Maybe a week or two. Once that task is completed, we will walk back to the boats and travel downriver until we pick up the road to Stanleyville. It is my understanding that some will fly back in float planes and others go back on this boat. I figure the total trip will take twelve to fifteen weeks—shorter for those flying home. I am being paid to lead this expedition and keep you safe, and that's what I intend to do."

Turner and Jane visually searched his clothing for his badge of political affiliation. Nothing there, but he did go find a Nazi for partner, and that didn't bode well.

"Lutz Holtzman has worked in Africa for more than twenty years and has led many an expedition and also served honorably in the German military. He will be my second in command. You should feel comfortable to have experienced and capable leadership."

Modesty didn't seem to be taught in German school, and furthermore many people apparently didn't understand the concept. Jane was essentially their employer and had to add her comments.

"Max, I hired you to provide us with competent expedition people, and it's possible Mr. Holtzman may be just that. However, as I can plainly see by his collar pin, he is also a Hitler Nazi. Thank God I'm not a Jew, or my throat would have already been cut. How on God's earth can we trust this man?" Jane asked. Lutz squirmed in his chair.

Speaking with as much conviction as he could muster, Max replied, "What you read in the papers is blown way out of proportion. I assure you that Hitler only wants peace with Belgium and England. I am not a member of the party, but hundreds of thousands—if not millions—of Germans are backing this leader because they want change. Lutz lives in Germany part of each year and certainly cares about the success of his motherland. Don't judge him because he cares about his country."

Jane looked Lutz directly in his eyes, "Did you expect to lose your democracy as soon as this idiot took office?" It was obvious she was not happy to have a Nazi on her payroll.

"Mrs. Simpson, first thank you for hiring Max to be a part of your expedition, and of course, allowing Max to choose his assistant," Lutz said. His English was perfect, and Jane suspected that he spoke other languages equally well. His face had a nice collection of wrinkles caused by being toasted by the African sun. He appeared to be in his early fifties, fit, blond, Aryan and muscular.

Lutz continued. "You know we didn't know really what to expect. Here is a man who cut a deal to be appointed chancellor without earning the majority of the voting public. Adolf Hitler's speeches seem to reach into the hearts of the people and light a fire. We have been punished too much for the big war. I admit that his policies on the Jews are harsh, and we hope popular opinion will stop it. I certainly don't have any problem with the Jewish people and many are my friends. For whatever reason, he has it out for them, as well as homosexuals and gypsies. He has declared a state of emergency since the Reichstag burned to the ground this year about a month after he was appointed. We are nervous because he's doing so much and spending so much money rebuilding the military. What the people like though is the sense that Germany is getting strong again. There is national pride. We have been down so long. I mean you no harm, Mr. and Mrs. Simpson, and I am really good at what I do." Lutz's voice dripped with sincerity.

"You do know that Hitler had the Reichstag burned down so he could declare a state of emergency? Once he did that your democratic form of government came to an end. There will be war eventually. He will rebuild his military because the countries in Europe will not stop him. Those countries—my country—collectively have their head up their ass. When they pull it out, they will find a gun pointed between their eyes. England has reported in the papers that military weapons are being built in defiance of the Treaty of Versailles. Germany itself will never satisfy him. He will spread like a disease. You may find it exciting now, but when your country's young people go off to war, it will be horrible—new machines and awful ways to die. Mr. Holtzman, I truly believe you are naïve to the evil that this man will do, but if you stay in Germany, you will be wrapped up in it. You will not have a choice. Right now, you can't speak up because he has stopped the freedom of speech. I will allow you to be on the expedition but request that you keep your Nazi pins and political beliefs to yourself," Jane said. She later told Turner she felt sorry for him and the millions of people swept up in the hysteria.

"I understand you have some members of the Simpson-Pygmy Rescue Mission you might like to introduce, Jane?" Max said.

She stood and motioned her two expedition members to stand up.

Jane pointed her hand towards a young man of medium height with straw-colored hair and intelligent, blue eyes. He was quick to smile, and his body language suggested he was full of energy.

"This man is Doctor Nicolas or Nick Dubois from Antwerp. He is completing part of his residency program by doing field medicine in the jungle. We are fortunate to have him with us."

The last to be introduced was Jane's hired gun. She went over his background before formally introducing him and explained that he was a veteran of the Great World War, having earned the Victoria Cross for taking out two German machine guns inside concrete bunkers, then carrying five wounded soldiers to safety, being wounded each time he retrieved an injured man. Afterwards, he became a safari guide in Kenya and later in Tanzania, saving many hunters from charging lions and elephants. She continued to explain that he was a tracker, a crack shot, and the very man you wanted in your foxhole. Probably at this time, every man in the room believed they would have preferred to have Jane in their foxhole, but no one spoke up.

Alan Chambers was six-foot-five-inches tall, with broad shoulders, brown, sun-streaked hair , and a deep, dark tan. He was the type of man who shaved and then needed to do it again every hour. He had movie star looks, and although he was almost sixty years old, only had slight graying around his temples. When he stood up to be introduced, some people gasped. This guy was the real deal.

"I would like you to meet Alan Chambers, who was recommended to us by the British Embassy in Leopoldville. We are pleased to have a man with his experience as an extra guide on the trip." Jane explained his background, and Alan didn't need to add much. He did say that he would have a gun bearer along named Muvunanyambo.

"Please call him Yambo—the whole name means 'the defender of noble cows' in Tutsi," Alan explained

"What guns will you bring, Mr. Chambers?" Lutz asked.

"I will carry a Holland and Holland four-bore single with improved powder, and Yambo will have a Browning Automatic Rifle with Belgium Mauser ammo. Twenty-round clip. Holds off unfriendly chaps and smaller animals."

"Fine weapons. I will use a .577 Nitro," Lutz said. Chambers didn't respond to the information; he merely shook his head in affirmation.

"Where is Yambo?" asked Jane. "And what is the difference between Tutsi and Watutsi?

"He is housed with your natives. He may have startled them since he is so much taller. He's of the Tutsi people. Some call them Watutsi, but they are the same, I believe," Alan said.

"My God! Jane, can you contain yourself?" Turner said. He watched as Jane cooled herself with a fan she had found in the room, gasped for air, and held her hand over her chest.

"I'll try to hold myself together," she said, laughing. Since she was fond of calling Turner her "Watutsi Man," everyone was pretty much on to the joke.

Alan looked at them both and then automatically caught on to the humor, as the large penis story was well-known in Africa. "Jane, I've seen him undressed. It's possible what you've heard is true among some of the Tutsi, but frankly I didn't see that much difference."

Max was smiling broadly as he started up again about the trip. He certainly wanted to defer any speculations about penis size since his short stature would likely suggest a miniature appendage. He passed out a map that he had hand drawn. Colors were used as a key for places and objects on the map. Blue was for rivers, brown for roads, and black for towns and villages. He explained that leaving from Stanleyville, the expedition would take trucks to a spot on the road above Banalia where the Bunga river crosses under the road.

Turner looked at his map and saw the river flowing between black dots representing Banalia and another town, Kole, just above where the river went beneath the road. Assuming the bridge hadn't washed out, which apparently was a common occurrence, not only there but all over Africa, they should have easy access to launch the dugouts.

People were always striking off from Cape Town to Cairo on auto trips to see if they could make it. Most didn't, but on one trip, the group had to either build or rebuild over 140 bridges to reach their destination. Most were makeshift affairs and never lasted long.

Max launched back into his map. "We will have military trucks that will take us to the river, thanks to Turner and Jane's well-placed calls on Belgium's governor in Leopoldville. Once he learned it was a humanitarian mission, he was onboard to help. They will be back in six weeks to pick us up, so I suggest we get back by then. Boats will meet us at the river crossing. I called an outfitter, who will have the boats meet us there once he gets notice we have arrived in Stanleyville. They are only boats in the sense that they sometimes float and move with the speed of those using the paddles. Most are dugouts and have been used by the natives for hundreds of years.

"Please look at your maps and notice where the Bunga meets the Lulu River. Here, we will attempt to go upriver and find where it splits. Several miles above that split is the pygmy village. Nestor has told Jane that there are several spots of rapids since the river starts at a high altitude and runs very fast. We will have to do quite a bit of walking, so be prepared for it. Any questions?" Max asked.

Surprisingly, there were few questions, but the actual trek didn't start for two to three weeks. There would be many questions by then. Jane folded her map and carefully stored it in her small knapsack.

"It's lunchtime, Turner. Let's find the galley or mess or dining room or whatever they call the place where food is placed in front of you," Jane said.

Turner smiled and took her hand and led her to a dining room that actually had white tablecloths, along with some eating utensils and glass bottles of water. It wasn't long before the entire group sat down, along with Rudy and his head officers. A couple of Belgian Army military officers joined them. The lunch was sandwiches with some crisps. No one complained, especially Jane and Turner since Hattie had outdone herself with their sandwiches.

After lunch, some of the crew played cards games in the same room. Turner and Jane had other games in mind and found the sanctity of their room to play. With a small fan blowing warm, humid air across their nude bodies, they made love in an increasing variety of positions. All felt wonderful, and it was doubtful they would get around to card games on the trip. Jane loved being on top, so she could control the length of the strokes and also could tease Turner unmercifully by holding his climax at bay until he begged her to finish him off.

They couldn't believe how exciting their lives had become. Both had expected to be in school at this time, yet here they were having incredible sex, in a steamer going up the Congo, and preparing to enter the jungle, where just about anything could kill them. Even the prospect of dying in the jungle didn't weigh on them now. This was a time of unbridled happiness, and they were enjoying every second of it.

Chapter Fourteen

On the Boat

Sore from constant sex, the couple decided to walk around the upper deck and to check on the natives. Nestor let them into the gated and fenced-in enclosure so they could visit for a while. They asked the natives how they were doing and if they had been fed. There were no problems, and sandwiches had been left with them along with water.

Yambo stood up and spoke to Jane in French. She asked what other languages he knew and found he spoke Bantu and some Swahili. His Bantu was of the Kirundi dialect, and Jane had only learned a little of it. She asked if he minded teaching her more of the language, and he agreed.

She was impressed by Yambo's soft, light-brown features. He looked stately—even regal. She had heard that the British had measured their skulls, height, and skin tones and applied the Hamitic Theory to prove that they were more European than their countrymen, the Hutus. The Hutus resented being judged inferior, and the stigma would fester for many years to come.

Suddenly, they heard a gunshot below on the first deck. Rudy rushed past the caged area and flew down the gangway. Turner and Jane followed him down. A man lay dead with a bullet hole in his right temple. A partially clothed young woman stood nearby holding a small pistol. She was crying, but not because she had killed a man. She had injuries to her face, and blood was pouring from her mouth. Rudy had his native workmen question her.

"This man my customer. He not willing to pay me and I ask him to pay. Then beat me—choke me—would kill me for sure," the prostitute said.

"Her killing the man was self-defense," Rudy said, becoming both her defense attorney and her judge.

All the man's possessions, clothing and shoes were put in a canvas bag with his name tagged on the bag. His nearly nude body was then pushed into the Congo where it would bobble a while, then be eaten by crocodiles.

As Rudy walked the gangway with Turner and Jane, he told them, "I usually have several canvas bags by the time we reach Stanleyville. Their meager possessions are turned over to the military who return them to the next of kin. A written report is also stored in the bag, if the authorities wish to investigate further. They never do. Dead passengers are just part of a captain's job."

Beyond the sex, meals in the dining room, and the occasional shooting or stabbing, Jane and Turner were entertained by the frequent encounters and stops made by the steamer. As the big boat neared towns and villages, a flotilla of dugouts would head to the big steamer and tie up alongside. Some of them were swamped and sank out of sight. The ones that successfully secured themselves with ropes began to uncover the goods they had for sale.

On this particular day, Jane pointed out to Turner a dead monkey that was being passed aboard. Next Turner spotted a small antelope that was causing quite a stir due to the amount of money being asked for it. It sold along with several large fish, live chickens, and bottles of homemade palm wine. The dugout people came aboard and purchased or bartered for clothing, cooking utensils, guns and knives. Many of the merchants on the steamer were there on a semi-permanent basis and only got off for a while at large overnight docking facilities.

Rudy would send his cooks down to buy fish and other foodstuffs as needed. He bought a huge catfish for their dinner in the evening. Jane began to gag at the smells drifting up from the bottom deck and asked Turner to take her to their room. Once there, they turned the fan on high, but it was as if the smell had become glued to their nostrils. Jane filled the small bath tub with fresh water and invited Turner to join her. It was crowded—so crowded that she had to sit on top of Turner. He didn't mind, and after soaking for quite a while, the smells didn't seem so bad. They tried having sex in the tiny tub and couldn't find a comfortable position. Still wet, they lay on the bed with Jane on top of Turner and let the fan blow across their damp bodies. It felt great.

They practiced this bath-to-bed technique every day until Rudy complained about the amount of water they were using. At the larger docking facilities, the boat would take on large stores of water, but at times it would be several days before fresh water came aboard.

During these times, the couple washed themselves with wet towels. It was a Sunday. They knew this because they could hear church songs being sung on the lower deck. As Turner rubbed towels all over Jane's body, he marveled at what a beautiful young woman she was. She was tall and slender, with beautiful, tanned, flawless skin. Her soft, round shoulders were cool to the touch. As he looked at her from behind he saw the perfect hourglass, feminine curves and shapely buttocks that reached out and asked to be touched. As he turned and looked at her from the front he could only lock eyes with her and smile. She seemed to get more beautiful every day. Rarely did she use make-up, but when she did it was blush for her cheeks and some dark cosmetics for her eyebrows and eyelashes. She was a true blonde, with ocean blue eyes that Turner believed were one of her most beautiful assets. He stopped applying the wet towel for a minute and kissed her lips and then each eye gently. She laughed and anxiously waited for him to finish. Her breasts were much larger than Turner had expected since she was tall and slender. He loved their shape.

The fan was blowing across their bodies, and Jane had already put him inside her and stared into his eyes with every thrust. How could he have gotten this lucky? He then thought about what they were going to face in a few days. It was going to be dangerous, and he didn't want her hurt in any way. He frowned, and Jane noticed it immediately.

"What wrong, Turner?"

"Just don't want you hurt in the jungle."

"My father said something one time to my mother when I wanted to go horseback riding by myself. She was scared for me and protective. He said to her, 'Boats look beautiful in the harbor, but they are meant to be sailed.' Now, I'm not sure if that really applied to that situation or this one. We can't stay on this boat in this room and have sex forever—even though it would be nice. We have to unfurl our sails and do something in this world. Move out of the harbor and face the whitecaps," she said, laughing at her own statement.

"You're full of crap. I love you so much, and I'm sorry to say something depressing while we make love, but it does have me worried."

"You'd better be concentrating on us going at the same time. Can you do that?"

Not answering the question, Turner's eyes rolled back, he moaned, and responded to Jane's spasms as they enjoyed a rare mutual orgasm.

"Maybe you should be worried about me more often, so we can go together all the time," Jane said.

Jane removed the condom from Turner and held it up to see the amount of semen in it. She was filled with a child-like fascination when she considered that this white liquid made babies and was generated with such pleasure and passion.

"I think I'll wash it and reuse it since we don't have that many left. These latex ones aren't easy to find in Africa. Maybe we'll find a drug store in Stanleyville," Jane said, filling it a few times with water until it looked like a balloon, then draining it and laying it on a washrag to dry.

At dinner, everyone was pleased to have fried African catfish, compliments of the captain. Jane had stopped by and practiced her Afrikaans on him during the day. He was impressed by how much she had learned since they had first met. She learned more as he gave her a few short lessons. Yambo had filled in part of her day by teaching her Bantu as well. She would not forget any of what she learned today from either teacher, but as a backup, she still kept a journal.

Nick sat at their table for dinner and talked about some people he had treated on the boat during the day. First was the prostitute who had eye and mouth injuries from the man she shot. He put stitches in above her eye and treated her dislodged teeth as best he could. Then there was a young child with a fever. It appeared to be malaria, so Nick gave the child an injection of quinine. He told the young boy's mother to look for side effects and call him if he had any of them. In one day he had seen cases of dysentery, measles, food poisoning, and various types of venereal disease. The lower deck was a giant petri dish of disease and sickness.

"Other than all of that, it was a good day," Nick said.

"How old are you, Nick?" Jane asked.

"I'm nineteen. Finished high school at fifteen and finished premed in one year and then Med School in three years., Two years more for residency and then it's on to my specialty."

"Which is?" asked Jane.

"Neurosurgery."

"Holy crap! Where are you going for that specialty?" Turner asked.

"It's still in its infancy, but there are some good schools doing great work. If I stay in Europe, I would probably go to Oxford and study under Dr. Hugh Cairns. Then there's Dr. Naffziger at the University of California, San Francisco. He's great. But probably the best is Dr. Harvey Cushing at Yale School of Medicine. He discovered Cushing's disease and a measurement for high blood pressure."

"I had planned to go to Yale, but Jane and I are going to medical school in Stanford, California," Turner replied. "I don't know what to specialize in. I just recently decided to go to medical school, and it's been a little difficult researching anything from the middle of the Congo."

Jane changed the subject about her and Turner going to Stanford. "I have heard from some doctors from Great Britain I've met here in the Congo, and they say there is work being done on penicillin at Oxford for use as an antibiotic. It comes from mold but doesn't isolate very well. A lot of native remedies include mold as a remedy, so I guess there is something to it," she said.

"Yes, I've read all the reports from Dr. Fleming and Dr. Florey. It is just a matter of time before they find a way to separate the portion that acts as an antibiotic. When they do, it will affect everything we do as surgeons, so that secondary infections don't occur after operations. I did bring quite a bit of some experimental versions to test," Nick said.

"Hey, enough of this medical talk. Don't you think we need to get a card game going tonight? They'll let us play right here in the dining room. The lighting is good, and we can break out some booze," Turner said.

"That would be fun," Jane said. "We haven't played since the comfort house."

"What's a comfort house?" Nick asked.

"It's a rest house, or African boarding house, and a wonderful place. We'll take you there after the trip," Turner said.

"Let's recruit another player. Do you think Alan Chambers plays cards? He's British so he was probably born with cards in his hand. Jane, why don't you ask him since you have more charm than the rest of this table put together," Turner said.

Alan Chambers was sitting with two Belgian military officers, enjoying a drink and a smoke after finishing his meal when Jane approached him. He smiled and stood up as did both of the officers.

"Boys, please sit down. Mr. Chambers, we're putting together a social card game tonight, and we would love to have you join us. We only have three players and desperately need a fourth or we'll have to fold up and go home." Jane had the charm turned up.

"How could I disappoint such a beautiful woman and my employer as well? What game are we playing, or have we decided?"

"Maybe Spades, Four-handed Sergeant Major, or even Oh Hell. However, most have voted for Spades since it's a new American game. We learned it last week from a friend from the States."

"Spades it shall be. Not many people know the game in Africa, but an American at the British Embassy got us all hooked on it about a month ago. Come get me when you are ready. I have some liquor to donate for drinks."

"Great! We'll come fetch you in a little while."

When they finished their cake for dessert, the tables were cleared of the dinner dishes, cards appeared, and drink glasses were filled with ice stolen from the galley. The galley had three large refrigeration units, and one actually worked most of the time and contained an ice maker. All of them were ammonia-based designs that had been around ships for many years. When the *S.N. Lapsley II* was purchased from the missionaries, the first upgrades were the refrigeration units. In the Congo, food spoils quickly, and Rudy didn't want a ship full of barfing passengers.

The four expedition members sat around the table, each with their own cool drink to ward off the hot Congo night as they were each dealt thirteen cards.

"No partners this time. We'll play cutthroat!" Jane said.

The big steamboat had slowed to a crawl since it was difficult to see the floating logs and snags at night. The crew had large spotlights trained on the river in front of them. If they spotted something, they would yell at Rudy or whoever was at the helm. "Big log—starboard at ten o'clock." With the big lights trained on the floating object, the helmsman would make his adjustments. Many nights, it was just too dangerous to move at all, so the boat would lie at anchor and idle her engines for the generators.

So far on this evening, there were pleasant sounds of cards shuffled, drinks clinking in glasses, people laughing, the rumble of the engine and an occasional yell from a crew member. It would be a night Jane would remember fondly.

Chapter Fifteen

Visitors

The morning after the card game, Jane and Turner slept late since both were groggy from the drinks. Even though they might be late for breakfast, they took time to make love first. Jane said she didn't want to take their opportunities for granted and would not waste a morning or an erection. Turner could barely open his eyes but furnished the required engorged member even though Jane did most of the work. She didn't complain, and Turner liked the lazy sex while he laid back and took in the pleasure. He could get used to it. Afterwards they hurried to the dining room in time for pancakes and some bacon, which was part of the supplies they had stored in the refrigeration unit. There was a buzz among the other members of the expedition. There would be several unscheduled passengers coming onboard at their scheduled docking today at Mbandaka. The rumor was that they would be military men.

After breakfast, Jane went to the bridge to see Rudy for a quick language lesson. When she knocked on the glass-paned door, he motioned her to come in. He had a map in his hand and had subrogated the helm to one of his younger officers.

"Good morning, Rudy. Did I see you playing cards last night?"

"Yes, we played a few hands of bridge for a penny a point. We did well but were playing against some greenhorns who didn't know how to bid. It was fun nonetheless. You want a few lessons?"

Rudy liked Jane, not only because she was beautiful and smart, but because she was almost the same age as his fifteen-year-old daughter, who was in school back in Leopoldville. He also had two sons who were eight and twelve. Jane could tell that his daughter, Aziza, had him wrapped around her little finger.

"Did Aziza get the dress she wanted for the school dance?" Jane asked in Afrikaans.

Rudy answered in his native tongue as well. "Yes, of course. She always gets what she wants. Her mother gets mad that I spoil her, but her grandparents are in Cape Town, so it is my job."

Rudy had to translate "spoil" for her.

"Does she look like me?"

"Yes, she looks a lot like you—blonde, with blue eyes, and beautiful, but not as tall and filled out as you."

Rudy explained "filled out" using his hands over his chest. Jane got the message.

"Who are we loading on the boat in Mbandaka?"

Rudy smiled. "You just snuck that one in, didn't you?"

Jane laughed. "It's all part of the lesson," she said.

"Military. Tribal problems upriver. I've been getting Telex communications for the last two days. Hopefully, they'll bring their own food because I can't feed them all."

"Did you hear the name of the tribe?" Jane asked in English.

"I think they said Manyema. They are usually the troublemakers."

"Where will these troops sleep?"

"On the decks and on the roof. Not a problem unless it rains—and it rains almost every day."

"Sorry you have them to deal with. Thanks for the lesson. And I hope I get to meet your daughter someday."

Rudy tipped his dirty ball cap and smiled. There was a crackle from the radio equipment behind him, and he slid his chair back to inspect the new messages.

Jane left the bridge and headed for the natives' compound.

Nestor was asleep on a cot when Jane found him.

"Nestor, I need to ask you something without alarming the other men."

Nestor rubbed his hand up and down his face trying to regain his senses after being in a deep morning nap. He stood up and walked out of the compound and over to the railing and looked down at the muddy Congo rolling underneath them.

"What do you know about the Manyema natives, and do they live close to your village?" Jane asked.

"I know them. They rob villages looking for ivory. They are cannibals. Sometimes they kill and eat pygmies because they think we have magic properties. They do not live close to us, but they travel long distances to get ivory. It has been many years, but we have been attacked before. Killed many of them with poisoned arrows," Nestor said.

"The military will be getting on the boat to go find them and correct the problem. I hope they don't attack us on the trip to your village."

"I would not want that either. Many people would die," Nestor said.

Jane patted him on the back and went back to her room. Turner was cleaning his .45 caliber 1911 pistol when she entered. She had one almost identical.

"What are you doing, dear?"

"If a bunch of drunk military types make advances toward you, I want to protect you."

"I will have my gun strapped on, and if they try anything, it would be better if I shot them. Less likely to hang a pretty lady."

"According to Rudy's first mate, there may be as many as forty or fifty of them. They have the right to take over the boat if they want to, but they're only going as far as Lisala, which is the next stop after Mbandaka. Even so it would be three or four days on the river. So much for our peaceful honeymoon cruise," Turner said with a great deal of disappointment in his voice.

There was a loud whistle from the captain's wheel house, a signal that the boat was docking. Most everyone rushed to the rails to see the boarding party. The Belgian Army troops were scattered on the docks with knapsacks, rifles, and sleeping rolls. The white troops wore boots, shorts and pith helmets. The native troops wore similar uniforms, except they sported fez hats that made them look much like bell boys with guns.

The officers came onboard first, most likely to push people around to get what they wanted. First, they moved Alan Chambers and Nick into the room with Lutz and Max. Two of them would take turns sleeping on the floor. They knocked on Jane's door. She said she was taking a bath and told them come back in a week. She also mentioned she was armed. When the officers learned that she was the now-famous Jungle Jane and that she headed the Simpson-Pygmy Rescue Mission, they gave up on trying to commandeer the room. They climbed a ladder to the roof and saw that there was plenty of room, but the roofing material would only hold a few men. They counted out a few places with strong underlying struts and placed ten men there. The pygmies and Yambo were crowded to one side, and the native soldiers who numbered about ten were placed in the enclosure, but the pygmies and the Tutsi kept their cots.

The rest were scattered around on the decks both downstairs and upstairs. No one was happy with the arrangement. The merchants were crowded out of their makeshift stores, the prostitutes had no privacy, and the criminal element felt pressure to behave. Once everyone was in place and Rudy had negotiated a price from the Belgian Military officials, the lines were cast off and the now overloaded steamer puffed and grunted back into midstream. The troops brought their own cooks and food. Lunch would be the first test.

In the crowded little galley, compromises had to be made. The army cook had decided on salami and cheese sandwiches with a small bottle of milk and a couple of sugar cookies. One person assembled them and the other passed them out to the line that stretched all the way down the gangway to the first deck. The process started early, so that once the soldiers were fed, the officers could eat in the dining room with the others. The dining room had only six small tables, and like most steamers, there was precious little room between them.

So there would be room for the officers, Jane and Turner filled trays and took them to their room to eat. Cold cuts, crisps, and cold Coca-Colas were served. Having any kind of cold drink was a treat. Jane had found the Coca Colas at a market in Leopoldville and bought a couple cases for the trip.

Lunch was filling, and the sex afterwards was quiet and passionate. They always locked their doors and closed the blinds, but there was so much traffic going by their room now. Everyone knew Jane's room since she was recently married, and likely the most beautiful woman they had ever seen. Officers had caught the soldiers with their ears pressed against her door and windows. Jane usually wore shorts on the boat, as did most of the men, but the ogling and catcalls had forced her to put on slacks. She only had two pairs and constantly had to wash them by hand and hang them to dry in the bathroom.

At about three o'clock, Max called for a joint meeting with the expedition and the Belgian military officers in the dining room. The tables were stacked on top of each other and extra chairs were set up. Max started the meeting by explaining the humanitarian mission they were on and briefly described the location of the natives' village. He also mentioned that the military had allotted three trucks to carry them to the portage point on the river. The head officer, Colonel Marcel Rousseau, stood and spoke next. He apologized for displacing people. He said he hoped they realized that this mission was dangerous, and it was possible some of his men on the boat would not come back. He further explained that Manyema natives had killed several hundred villagers in their quest to steal ivory and anything else they could find. After seeing the location of the pygmies' village, he felt it was on the extreme southern range of the Manyemas' territory and felt his military efforts would have them contained before they moved that far. He asked what weapons the expedition had in case they were attacked.

"Our primary anti-personnel weapon is a Browning Automatic Rifle with one hundred rounds of ammo," Alan said.

"A very fine weapon," Colonel Rousseau said. "We have two of them with the Mauser rounds, and I wish I had ten. The three military trucks that were allotted to you may have to be reduced. I think you understand and that parts of the operation are not under my command. We will have over a thousand men in the field in a few days, so this will be a large deployment. We will defeat them and send them back to their villages, but it will take some time. Thank you for your understanding. We will be off the boat as soon as possible. If any of the men get out of line, please let any of my officers know. Do you have any questions?"

Jane wanted to ask what stirred up the natives in the first place but assumed the military probably didn't know anyway. She guessed that it was the result of some bad treatment of the natives by the owner of one of the mines where many of the natives worked as forced labor, but it was unlikely anyone would admit it. Jane invited the colonel to play cards with them after dinner. He graciously declined but said he would join them the next day after the men became more settled. He looked like the perfect commanding officer with strong jaw bones and well-trimmed gray hair at his temples. He was about six feet and had avoided the usual bulging stomach men in their early fifties seem to acquire. He smiled a lot and always bowed and kissed Jane's hand. She liked the attention and was becoming more tolerant of the Army's imposition because of the politeness of their commanding officer. He was doing his job and doing it well.

Jane left the group and went up to the wheelhouse to see Rudy. He was at the helm but gave it up to a shipmate when Jane came in. He started to apologize to Jane about the Army and she stopped him.

"Rudy, none of this is your fault—just a necessary adjustment. I trust the colonel gave you a fair price."

"Standard half-price military rates. I'm okay with it since I get bonuses on any profit we make on the trip. You doing all right?"

"Yes, I'm fine and feel bad I complained so much at first," Jane replied in Afrikaans. "And don't tell your daughter about the bonuses, or she'll want another dress." She smiled.

"I'm worried that your group might be going anywhere near those savages."

Jane asked to translate "savages."

"Alan Chambers makes me feel safer," Jane said.

"He would be right next to me if I was stupid enough to head into the jungle."

Rudy translated "stupid" from "onnosel" and explained.

"I better find Turner to keep him out of trouble."

As usual, Rudy smiled and tipped his hat to her as she left.

She found Turner in the dining room having a beer with Alan, Max, and Lutz. Lutz and Max were smoking cigars, so she decided to sit next to Nick, who was at a table next to them.

"Would you like a Coca-Cola or a beer?" Nick asked.

"A Coca-Cola would be nice. Thank you."

Nick found her one in the cooler, then sat down next to her.

"Jane, you'll be entering med school even younger than me. You know that Turner will not be able to keep up with you. I think you and I are very much alike since we remember everything we read. Not many people can do that."

"Did your school teachers give you special assignments or books to read?" Jane asked.

"Of course, and I kept skipping years in school or they just gave me tests for the whole year at one time. I was not popular with the other kids."

"I had the problem of being fully developed at age ten. I might as well have been from outer space."

"Precocious puberty. Well, I didn't have that problem. I was the opposite as I was in grades I shouldn't have been in for three or four years, so I was smaller than everyone else. Didn't have many friends. It was a rural school in a small town in Belgium. My parents finally sent me to a boarding school in Antwerp. There were others there— not many, but others who were advanced and well ahead of their age. It did help because they had to deal with us as a group. Finally, a professor of science was given the group as a project, and he loved the challenge. He would give us college level subjects to study and then gave us exams that would have been hard for graduate students. We loved it. Slowly, he began to assign us to areas where we excelled. Mine was science and chemistry, so I was scooted off to medical school in Brussels. Some were directed to PhD programs in language, writing, math, and music. I do think most are doing well." Nick looked beyond Jane and out the window at the river as he remembered his misfit classmates.

"Nick, what you said about Turner not being able to keep up with me: please never say that to him. I would never want to hurt his feelings; I love him with all my heart and soul. The only difference in us is that he can't retain things as I do. He's exceptionally smart and was admitted to Yale before I met him.

"I don't know anyone who can do what I do. I can listen to foreign languages and memorize them. I read a book, and I not only know what I read but the page numbers as well. I'll just slow down and enjoy my time with him in med school. I'll have spare time for learning languages, reading, and maybe hobbies. After med school, I want to start having children while Turner is building a practice. Do you think I will be able to stay by his side in medical school without letting on how much I know?"

"You're a very determined young lady, and no one can grasp that you are fourteen years old. I think you can stay by Turner's side in med school by being totally honest with him. He knows how rapidly you learn, and he is smart, so you won't fool him. Simply say that you're going to learn the medical profession at his pace and occupy any leftover time with other pursuits that might be helpful to the profession, such as language studies, so you can practice in other countries if you wish. Or, here's an idea—teach your kids foreign languages while they're young and can absorb them. Chinese is so difficult, but kids pick it up if they hear it all the time."

"What a great idea! Thanks, Nick."

"My problem is I want to get married, but I've never dated and really feel helpless. You're so pretty, and if I didn't know you, I'd be terrified to speak to you." Nick blushed.

"You're a really cute guy, so girls will be attracted to you. I'll help you with what to say to them. Have you seen any pretty girls on this boat?"

"No, not really. One of the prostitutes isn't bad looking, but I'm not that desperate."

"God, I hope not. Maybe a Belgian family will get on at the next port. Anyway, I'll help you when the time comes," Jane said. She finished her Coca-Cola and patted Nick's hand. Turner had finished his beer and stood up and took her arm as they walked to their room.

"Did you guys solve the problems of the world?" Turner asked.

"Most of them—the important ones anyway," Jane said. She kissed him softly and grabbed his rear as they entered the room.

Chapter Sixteen

A Dangerous Port

It had been three nights and part of four days since the military had invaded the *S.N. Lapsley II,* and in a few hours, they would reach the docks at Lisala. During this time, the Simpson Mission had more or less adjusted to the crowded conditions.

A shooting had taken place two days ago between two men who were gambling on the lower deck. Both died of their wounds, even though Nick and an Army medic worked on them almost immediately. Two more canvas bags hung in Rudy's utility room.

Colonel Rousseau had joined them for a game of Spades for a couple of nights. Even though it was a new game to him, he quickly picked it up and won several rounds. Military tactics and card games seem to fit together well. After a while, Turner and Jane would suddenly yawn and excuse themselves as tired travelers. Colonel Rousseau wasn't fooled, but he was gracious in bidding them goodnight.

Jane and Turner had settled in to quiet games of sex. Slow, methodical movements, almost torturous, with constant eye contact and kisses that barely connected, taking in each other's breath. Oral sex became an important part of the lovemaking. Sex was still new, and there was so much to be explored. These silent erotic activities were enjoyable. Even though the freedom of moaning and loud sex might return to their sexual repertoire after the military left in a few days, they knew they could also revert to their new, silent techniques any time they felt like it.

Jane had learned a great deal more language skills working with Rudy and Yambo. She felt fairly fluent in Afrikaans and Bantu. She had to use French and some German onboard since Max and Lutz spoke it most of the time. Most all the army personnel spoke French. The native element of the army spoke several languages but mostly Swahili, so Jane spent a lot of time working on mastering the universal language of Africa. The native soldiers were housed with the pygmies and the lone Tutsi.

Water was conserved on the trip since so many people were onboard, but occasionally the natives would strip down and wash off with water hoses. Jane was walking up to their fenced area a few days earlier just as Yambo was hosing himself off. There it was, hanging proudly between his legs. She froze in her tracks and stared. Yambo wiped the water from his face and noticed she was staring and turned away. She smiled and waved at him awkwardly, blushed, and went back to her room to tell Turner what she had seen.

She was practically giddy as she described the long slender Watutsi appendage.

"Turner, it was really long, but so thin! He hadn't been circumcised, so I'm sure that made it look longer. But I finally saw a Watutsi dick." She was almost breathless with excitement.

Turner started laughing at the ridiculous amount of delight she was experiencing. To Jane, it was as though she had discovered a new planet or an extinct animal walking the earth thousands of years ago.

"Will you be able to stay satisfied with my humble pecker now that you've seen the champion of the world?" Turner said, trying to look sad.

"Of course, dummy. It was just this obsession I had since I didn't know anything about men's penises. I'm fine. Theirs is so skinny. Wide is better, don't you think?"

"I think you are nuts. Very cute—but absolutely nuts!"

Jane ran and locked the door and shut the blinds then began to undress Turner. As she performed oral sex, she would stop and examine Turner's penis, then kiss it and look up and smile at him as if to say, "I'm really happy with what I have."

It was right after lunch when the steamer took the deep channel close to the eastern shore of the Congo. The area was a jungle that had just come into sight after miles with nothing but swamps and marshes on that side of the river. Rudy saw movement in the underbrush and tapped the whistle with several repetitions of three short blasts each time. The military quickly caught on and took their positions as did Alan, Max, and Lutz.

Suddenly, swarms of arrows filled the air along with the sound of shotgun blasts and lead pellets tearing through parts of the boat. Several people were struck. The military immediately returned fire, even though there were few clear targets. Rudy quickly swung the damaged *Lapsley* away from the eastern channel toward the western shore and shallow water. He knew this river well and charted it on each trip as sandbars shifted and deep channels became clogged with debris. Now he was in danger of running aground. The attackers knew exactly what the steamer would do in order to defend itself, but Rudy had some choices. He could stay on the outside of the eastern deep channel where he was relatively safe from running aground and mostly out of the range of the arrows but still in the range of the shotguns and rifles. He took that choice, rather than moving all the way to the shallow edge on the western shores. Besides, he had a gunboat and more of one than he realized.

All of a sudden, automatic gun fire erupted from the roof and second deck. The Army had put two water-cooled machine guns into service and were cutting a swath through the jungle. Occasionally, natives would come into view, and they were either dropping from the sustained firepower or running for their lives. It was assumed that these were the Manyema, and the trouble from them was just beginning.

Two lead buckshot pellets penetrated Turner and Jane's room. Since the shots were aimed upwards, they entered at the upper front wall and into the ceiling where they lodged without exiting through the roof. Outside their stateroom, a few arrows were stuck in the wall. The couple had been in the dining room talking with Nick when they heard the alarm and saw Alan, Max, and Lutz rush to get their weapons. Since their passage was blocked by incoming arrows, they decided to stay put.

Immediately after the machine guns had quelled the attack, Nick and the army medic went to work. Nick had his medical bag and headed downstairs where the majority of the wounded were stationed. Jane and Turner were by his side as he closed the eyes on one dead woman at the bottom of the gangway. She had been struck in the brain with a shotgun pellet and in the chest with an arrow; either shot could have been the fatal one. Several people had been struck with arrows. Most of those wounds weren't serious, but no one knew if there was poison on the tips. Although the natives often rubbed feces on the tips to cause infections, there was no sign of it now.

One army private had been struck in the chest above his heart. Nick decided to leave the arrow in place and have him transported by float plane to a hospital in Leopoldville for surgery. The flight would take three days—maybe two if they flew some in the early morning darkness.

There was only one other death. An elderly native, who sold food in the makeshift market, was struck by pellets in his stomach and chest and died from either shock or heart attack. The wounds were not that serious. By the time all the wounded had been patched up, the steamer was pulling into the docks at Lisala. There was one small float plane there and the colonel quickly put it in service to fly his wounded man to Leopoldville. He ordered the medic to go with him and promoted an assistant to his job.

Normally, this would be an overnight stay, but as soon as firewood for the boilers and fresh water, supplies, and passengers were loaded aboard, Rudy was going to shove off from there. Some Belgian citizens and their families boarded in an attempt to escape the warring in the area. It wasn't clear if they were government officials, mine operators, or consignors. One thing was clear—there were attractive young girls coming aboard. Nick noticed and so did Jane. The plotting began.

Rudy asked Alan, Max, and Lutz if they would keep their arms handy in case of another attack. It didn't seem likely since the military was on the ground and moving inland with other forces that already had landed on the docks.

Colonel Rousseau stood before his men and was waiting to address them with their orders when a captain under his command approached him.

"Sir, may I tend to something on your face, sir?" the captain asked.

"What the hell is it?"

The captain took out a bandana and wiped a lipstick smudge from Colonel Rousseau's cheek, having been placed there by Jane on his departure from the steamer. He laughed as did his men. He then smiled as he addressed them.

With all the excitement, no lunch had been prepared, and it was late afternoon. The cooks began to get to work, and people found tables in the dining room. Jane took Nick's hand and sat him at a table towards the back of the room, so they could observe. Turner was with Alan and the others on the roof keeping guard, even though it wasn't clear they needed to. As a mother and her pretty, dark-haired Belgian daughter entered the dining room, Jane quickly walked up to them and asked if they would like to join her and Nick. She spoke in French, but soon found they spoke English, Dutch, and German, as did many in her country. She introduced herself and Dr. Nicolas Dubois. They accepted the offer as they didn't know anyone aboard. They introduced themselves as Caroline Martens and her daughter Zoë.

Jane started the conversation and invited the mother and daughter to join her for a meal consisting of pork chops, green beans, and fried chips. Jane assured her that it would be better than what the boat would serve them. After they agreed, Jane went to the kitchen to ask for the portions for their guests. As she returned, Zoë was asking Nick about where he lived in Belgium. He told her and inquired about her school. Jane sat down and started a conversation with Caroline since Nick and Zoë seemed to be doing ok. Caroline revealed that her husband was a copper mine co-owner and had asked her to go to Stanleyville until the unrest was over. Jane bit her tongue about the unfair treatment of the forced labor and mistreatment of the natives. She turned the conversation to Zoë.

"How old are you, Zoë?" Jane asked. "By the way, you're very pretty."

"Thank you, but not as pretty as you. I'm seventeen and hope to begin college in the spring semester. How old are you, Jane, if I may ask?"

"Well, this may shock you, but I'm fourteen. I'm married to a wonderful man who is on the roof helping man a machine gun nest. I plan to enter college in America in the spring semester as well."

Zoë and her mother looked shocked.

"Fourteen! You look older than Zoë!" exclaimed Caroline.

"I had a condition that amounted to early onset puberty, and I have the unusual ability to memorize books, so I move a little ahead of the class."

"Nick, you're a doctor? Have you completed your residency? I hope you're little older than me as I'm feeling a little aged here," Zoë laughed.

"I also had the issue of memorizing books, Zoë, and I just finished medical school in Brussels at the University of Louvain. This trip we're going on will count as part of my residency requirement, and the rest will be back at University Hospital in Brussels until I pick a specialty. I'm nineteen. Where are you going to school in the spring?"

"Thank goodness you're older than me. I was beginning to feel like an old spinster! I'm going to the College for Arts and Architecture in Brussels. I plan to study to be one of the few female architects in Belgium."

"Wow! How impressive! You must have a strong math background," Nick said.

"It was always a subject I liked, but I always felt out of place being the only female in physics class."

"I bet you got a lot of attention from the boys," said Jane.

"Well, I think they may have felt I was intruding into a man's world."

"Hopefully, you'll find more acceptance in college," Nick said.

"Caroline, would you and Zoë care to join us in a game of Spades tonight after dinner?" Jane asked.

"I would love to, but Mother doesn't play cards much. Give her a good book and she's happy," Zoe said.

"Do you usually read in French or English, Caroline?" asked Jane.

"Either. Do you have some new American novels?"

"A couple. I'll get them for you later."

Their food arrived, and they were treated to ice water and Coca-Colas. Nick and Zoe talked incessantly, and Jane and Caroline smiled at the obvious attraction developing between the young couple.

After lunch, Jane and Caroline went to their rooms. Zoe and Nick took their Coca-Colas outside where they found some deck chairs to continue their conversation. Turner came by almost an hour later after standing guard on the roof, and the two were still talking. He introduced himself and learned he would be playing cards with Zoë later.

Turner found Jane in their room sitting in the small bathtub trying to cool down.

"Hello, playmate. What did you do to Nick to get him all fired up about that girl?"

"Just introduced them, and he was off to the races."

"Do you think he'll talk her to death and scare her off?" Turner asked.

"Hey, they either find out they like each other, or they don't. She's pretty and has had more experience than him, I feel sure."

"By that, you mean she's not a virgin like he is?" Turner said.

"Maybe. I didn't probe, but they will get around to that, I'm sure."

"You never asked me about my love life before you came along."

"Didn't care and don't care now. I love you even if you had slept with most of the girls in Belgium."

"By the time most people get out of high school, they have had at least one long-term relationship. That, I'm going to guess, is Zoe's story," Turner said.

"Did you have to write a letter back home to a girl when you met me?"

"Yes."

"I'm sorry if she got hurt."

"Love and war—you know. We weren't engaged—just a steady girlfriend. My parents felt comfortable around her and just assumed she would be the one."

"Your parents are wonderful and will love being grandparents.

Your sisters will probably have kids before we do, don't you think?"

"They have to finish college—but yes, I think so since we have pre-med, medical school, and residency plus any specialty we might choose."

While Turner had been talking, he had locked the door to their state room and undressed. He helped Jane from the tub and wet a towel, so she could wet him down. They then aimed the fan toward their bed and lay next to each other, staring into each other's eyes.

"Do we deserve to have this much fun?" Jane asked.

"We must have done something right."

They kissed lightly and used their fingers to trace each other's face. As Jane moved her finger over Turner's lip, he bit it gently.

"Oh, I'm sorry. I meant to wash that finger," Jane said and laughed.

The fan felt cool, and Turner moved down so they could enjoy oral sex while the air blew across their bodies. This position was enough to satisfy them both. In a few days, they would be in the jungle. There would be no fan, no bed, and no privacy. For now, they would make use of all these luxuries.

Chapter Seventeen

Bumba and Lifanga

Jane found two of the novels she had brought from the comfort house and went to Caroline's state room to deliver them. Caroline looked at the copies of *The Good Earth* and *Cimarron* and was thrilled to get them. In return, she gave Jane recent copies of the *London Times* that had been mailed to her by relatives in England. Jane asked about Zoë and found she was with Nick.

Caroline smiled and sighed, "I've never seen her so interested in a guy before. She dated a lot in Brussels and was fairly serious over a star football player, but I think it was more of a physical attraction. But this is different. She's mapping out her life with this guy."

"Nick's a virgin, so she'll have to take it easy on him. I mean—you know what I mean," Jane said, blushing.

"Zoë will hopefully let him take the lead in that department," Caroline laughed. "He's a doctor, you know."

"Yes. That's what worries me—that he'll get all scientific on her. I'll see you shortly for dinner. Thanks for the papers."

Jane stopped by the pilot house and said hello to Rudy, who was steering behind an intense stare.

"Expecting trouble, Rudy?"

"Hope not, but we have a few spots where we need to be on our toes."

"When will we be in Bumba?"

"Tomorrow—late morning—short stop," Rudy replied. "We'll take on wood and a few passengers. After that, the main channel runs near the east shore, and there's a lot of jungle. Tell your crew to be ready then. We need to check papers on everyone that comes onboard and watch the boats that tie up alongside."

"I'll tell them. Sorry you're having such a dangerous trip."

"Hope the troops do their job, but don't think they can stop all of them. I worry about your group going into the jungle in a few days."

"Hopefully, we won't meet up with them. See you later, and let us know if we can help you check people coming on the boat tomorrow," Jane said.

"May need your help. Thanks!"

Jane found Turner on the roof sitting next to Alan.

"Look what I have, guys! A few copies of the *London Times*."

"Wow! Let me see that!" Turner said.

He read the national news and then went to the movie section.

"*King Kong* is playing in London! I really want to see that movie. Fay Wray in the hands of a giant gorilla!"

"They won't get it in Leopoldville for a year or two. But when we go to the States in a few months we can see it there, if it's still playing," Jane said.

"Is it time for dinner?" asked Alan.

"Almost. I talked with Rudy, and he may need help checking people getting on the boat in Bumba. It's right in the middle of Manyema land. He also said the boat comes in close to the jungle right after leaving there."

"Busy day tomorrow. See you at dinner," Alan said as Turner and Jane climbed down a ladder from the roof.

Jane and Turner sat with Caroline and Alan for dinner as Zoë and Nick had taken snacks back in his room.

"Alan, I apologize for Zoe and Nick taking over your room for a while. Those two are inseparable right now," Caroline said.

"Ma'am, I was young once. I'm just a little jealous of them right now," Alan said.

Jane whispered in Caroline's ear. "Do they have any protection?"

"Yes, Zoë has them. I made sure," Caroline whispered back to Jane.

"Great! My mother demonstrated their use on a banana," Jane spoke softly, but the two men at the table overheard and laughed. Soon, the whole table erupted.

After dinner, Alan suggested that they get another partner and play a few hands of Spades. They recruited Max and extended the game as long as they could.

In a couple hours, Nick returned to the dining room and delivered Zoë to her mom, who was reading Pearl Buck's book at one of the back tables. He kissed Zoë goodnight and suggested they have breakfast together.

Alan smiled and asked Nick if it was safe to go back to the room. Nick nodded his head and sat down at the table. Alan and Max had finished their game and retired for the night. Jane looked at the beaming young doctor and had to inquire.

"Nick, you're moving pretty fast for an inexperienced newcomer to the ways of love."

"Yes, yes, I am. Something just clicked. All these years of living with my face in a book. I've been missing out on the best part of life. No more! Don't worry about us. We'll be a bit more methodical starting tomorrow. I hope we didn't act too weird."

"You're just fine. She's going to let you go in the jungle?" Jane asked.

"Yes, she knows I have to. Nothing is changing. She's going to her college, and I'm going to the same hospital for my residency in Brussels. We'll see each other there—may eventually stay together. I still need to decide on the specialty for me, and she'll support what I choose. Later—who knows—she can be an architect anywhere. I can be a doctor anywhere. For now, we'll just enjoy each other."

"Sounds like you guys are approaching it with maturity. Maybe you should just tell her to get naked and jump into your luggage!" Jane said, breaking everyone up with laughter.

They played one more round of Spades and turned in for the night.

~~~~~~

It was late morning, and the *Lapsley* pulled up to the crude, sloping, concrete dock at Bumba. Behind the dock were a few nice whitewashed government buildings—beyond that, huts and shacks. During the trip to Bumba and after the last attack, Rudy had ordered that armor would be placed by the railings, so shooters could be protected against another attack. His crew had constructed four half-inch steel shields four-feet square and had them welded to the deck railings. Behind them on each deck were armed men and one woman.

Jane and Turner took one of the lower deck shields and assisted as new passengers came onboard to have their papers checked. Some were bandaged from wounds received as they were caught in the crossfire of battles. Many had to be turned away because they didn't have money for the fare. Most were frightened natives. Many had moved their dugouts to the boat and tied them. They were told by the crew that they would be cut loose once the boat departed. Most looked desperate.

From the outside of the group of people, three natives wearing robes stood up in their canoe. Alan spotted them from his position on the upper deck.

"Turner, keep an eye on those three—might have guns under the robes!"

As they approached, they waved at the boat and yelled in French that they were good people. As they drew closer, they reached behind their backs and pulled out shotguns. Before they could position their guns to fire, Alan shot the first one in the chest and blew him over the side. Turner and Jane fired their pistols on semi-automatic, finding their marks in the head and chest of the other two, causing them to slump motionless into the dugout.

General panic ensued as natives scrambled aboard and hid wherever they could find shelter. Rudy declared the passenger list full and had his crew go about having everyone hold up their paid tickets. Those who didn't have them were ushered off the boat. Once the wood, water, and supplies were loaded, Rudy moved the big vessel out into the channel. Ordinarily, a squad of Belgian military came down to the docks for security, but they were now deployed inland.

The small town of Bumba was barely visible behind them when four natives in a dugout hidden behind a fallen tree at the edge of the river rushed out and started firing shotgun pellets at the boat. From the upper deck, a blast shook the entire boat. The dugout was blown in half and two of the natives were killed instantly. The two remaining ones fought to hold on to the remains of the boat when Alan picked them off. The first shot had come from Yambo with the 4-bore elephant gun. The cartridge resembled an artillery shell and did almost as much damage.

Rudy walked back next to where Alan and Yambo were standing by a steel shield. Max and Lutz walked over from their positions, and Turner and Jane ran up the gangway to meet with them.

"Boys, in about a day and a half, we'll be pulled next to the jungle—no way to avoid it. I'll have the crew build some more shields, and I'll have one hell of a head of steam when we blow through. My guess is if they attack, it could last about twenty minutes before the channel pushes us out of range of their guns. Make all your shots count because they will outnumber us. They'll probably paddle and swim out to board us. Can't let that happen. They'll kill everyone. Rape the women and slit their throats."

"Rudy, how well is your crew armed?" Alan asked.

"We have four Enfield thirty-eight pistols with maybe three or four crates of Ammo. Two 12-gauge shotguns with about forty or fifty rounds of double aught buckshot," Rudy said. He knew his was an impotent arsenal.

"Our approximate speed as we pass through the gauntlet?" asked Alan.

"Maybe twelve to fifteen knots if we don't blow up a boiler," Rudy said.

"They can't catch us, but I'm going to guess they will be in the water ahead of us, so they can grab on when we go by. We can put the elephant gun and shotguns on the bow along with some good pistol shooters. We don't have enough weapons. Is there any place where we can buy any before we get to the attack zone?" Max asked.

"Not really. The only village we pass on the west side of the river is Lifanga, and it's on a road that parallels the river. They do have a general store on the river used mainly by the natives. It's possible they have some ammunition for shotguns. There isn't a dock for us so we'll have to wait until their dugouts come to us or put one of our lifeboats in the water. I'll have the crew get one that has a small outboard motor ready. We will be there at about sunup, and our problem area will then be another four hours upriver," Rudy explained.

"Maybe we'd better start a war chest tonight, in case we can buy some weapons from them. I'll go around and collect money from everyone to buy arms and ammo," Jane said.

"The ship has a little cash from receipts. Personally, I think we'll be lucky to get some shotgun shells, but it's worth a try," Rudy said.

Dinner was a rushed affair consisting of fish bought from the villagers at Bumba. There was fresh fruit and some sweet potatoes. Rushed or not, it turned out to be a good meal.

The crew was up most of the night welding steel pieces to the bow and on the front railings. Nick recruited some native ladies to help with the wounded, and Zoë insisted on helping. No one onboard slept much.

The men with military experience checked the position of the sun for battle. If they had passed the spot in the early morning, the sun would have blasted them from the east. Now it looked like it would be midday and the sun wouldn't be a factor. The boat would be like a moving hill, giving the shooters a high vantage point, but when they found themselves outnumbered a hundred to one, it wouldn't matter much.

Morning dawned without the sun. It was raining—hard. The enemy would be exposed with water splashing in their eyes and the banks muddy and slippery. Their dugouts would fill with water and slow them down. They discussed this during a quick breakfast. Rudy recalled that there were crocodiles and hippos in this area because it was secluded with gentle, sloping shorelines. The natives would adapt easily. They lived in the Congo. Rain, mud, hippos, and crocodiles were their everyday world.

Jane and Turner could see dugouts on the shore and a large shack with an old black truck parked to the side. It must be the Lifanga store. They got in the lifeboat that was lowered from the roof, along with Alan, Max, and two of Rudy's crew members. Jane had a rain suit with a hat, but the rest only had head covers and were getting drenched. As soon as the boat hit the shore, it was pulled up a ways on land and everyone ran through the smelly mud to the store. As they stormed through the front door of the old Congo building, they were transported into another world. It wasn't a store for proper Belgian citizens, or tourists, or white people in general. It was a native store. It carried what natives needed to survive in one of the wildest, most unhospitable places on earth. Much of the trades that took place there were by barter as few natives had hard currency. Everything seemed used, from fishing nets, gigging spears, rope, cloth, shirts, pants, shoes, hats, and pots and pans blackened by heat. The smells from the dried fish, cut bush meat, and palm oil in open vats filled their nostrils. Above the counter was a rock python skin over twenty feet long. Behind it stood a man and woman of mixed ethnicity in their early fifties. They held their mouths agape and sported large, wide-open eyes. Jane spoke to them in French. No response. She tried Swahili and got a few grunts and moans. She knew enough basic Bantu of their dialect to communicate, and that did the trick. One of the native crew members with them also spoke Bantu and assisted Jane.

"Do you have guns and shells we can buy?"

"Shells—no guns," came the reply.

"We will give fifty dollars US for any used pump shotguns," Jane said, with the crew member's help.

"People very poor here—need guns to hunt," the man from behind the counter said.

"We'll give them one hundred dollars each and they can have them back in a few weeks when the steamer comes back through. Have the natives put their marks on them. On our return, we will leave the guns with you to return to their owners. Shells must come with the guns—need every one we can get. We will give you ten dollars a gun for your help. Can you please help us?" Jane pleaded but knew better than to say they would be fighting the Manyemas since she was sure that the outfitter traded with them. He probably had figured that out anyway.

The man looked at his female companion. Then he reached under the counter and pulled up two model 1897 Winchester pump shotguns. One was a 16-gauge, the other a 12-gauge. He also placed two boxes of shells for each gun on the counter. Jane paid him for the guns and $10 a box for the shells. The store owner said he could maybe get four more guns and some shells. Jane said the $100 was for guns and shells. He nodded and took $400 and got into his truck.

He came back in about thirty minutes with four shotguns, all twelve gauges. In the middle of one of the world's greatest depressions, the store owner had just made a few natives the equivalent of instant millionaires. Some shells came with them but only thirty or fifty buckshot shells. Jane gave him another $40 for the trouble of acquiring the guns. All were "slam fire" shotguns, which meant the trigger could be held down, and the pumping action would fire a round as fast as it could be pumped. The Germans in WWI asked for them to be outlawed since the British and Americans were so effective at cleaning out personnel in the trenches.

"Ask them if they have any Mauser ammo, would you?" Alan said.

Jane and the crew member struggled with the translation. The store owner pulled a large metal box from under his counter. Although it was old, the box was full of 7.92 x 57mm German Mauser ammunition. It was exactly what Alan needed for his BAR. Jane asked them for a price and he signaled they could have them. It was likely they had been stolen from a Belgian military patrol, so he would suffer no loss on the gift.

Alan was thrilled, and the boat loaded with guns and ammo headed quickly back to the steamer. Once back onboard Rudy, Alan, Max, and Lutz looked at the map to decide the placement of the men. They would need to canvass the passengers to see who had firearm experience, who might help assist at reloading, and who might have knives or spears to use as weapons in case they were boarded.

It appeared that the bow and port side would be major points of attack. There were only fourteen rounds left for the elephant gun, so Yambo would need great accuracy to take out entire dugouts with one shot. Alan had the ability to fire automatic bursts from his Browning Automatic Rifle but wanted to choose his shots and not waste ammunition. The slamfire capacity of the shotguns would help in case several Manyemas tried to climb aboard, yet the shells needed to be conserved. The big .577 big game gun used by Lutz would also wreak havoc, along with the .375 that Max brought along. Plans were discussed, and guns were distributed until everyone felt they knew their jobs. Considering the fire power the *Lapsley* was bringing to the fight, many Manyemas would be floating down the Congo this afternoon. Now there was nothing to do but wait.

Rudy made sure he would have a huge head of steam as he approached the area and was fully aware dugouts would be blocking the river. He pictured in his mind how he would strike them, so they would sink and not roll under the boat to disable one of his props. One of the steel shields had been placed over part of his wheelhouse on the port side and another forward so that lead pellets would be deflected. Rudy remembered that the river widened about three quarters of the way into the gauntlet, creating a big pool of water on the port side. That is where a large pod of hippos and crocs occupied the area. He couldn't imagine the natives taking their dugouts in those waters with so many violent bulls and protective mothers with young calves. If dugouts were there, the steamer would push them down the throats of the waiting hippos.

Sandwiches and beer made for a good pre-battle lunch. Guns were carried to the dining room, and the men laid them across their laps as they ate. There were repeated discussions about their placement for the upcoming fight. There seemed to be a ship-wide resolve to defeat this threat. Then they heard shouting from the leading edge of the roof.

"There they are, hundreds of them—maybe thousands!"

Chapter Eighteen

Blood Stains

From a mile away, Rudy could see many dugouts; it appeared one could walk across the entire Congo River by stepping in them. He headed straight for a few that had some separation. His instruments read sixteen knots—an unheard of speed for Rudy and his steamer. All the gauges in the busy boiler room were in the red, yet more wood was shoved in to be burned. On the shoreline were hundreds of warriors dressed up in feathers and shields. Many appeared to have only bows and arrows, others had spears, but some had modern weapons. Most of the natives in the boats had shotguns aimed at what they considered kill zones.

Alan was in charge of the upper deck and Max took the role of commander for the lower level.

"Fire when they are in range and see how many you can take out with one shot!" Alan shouted.

Most of the fire power was up front and on the side facing the shoreline. One shotgun had been deployed on the rear of the boat and only two shields had been welded on the starboard lower deck. Depending on how many dugouts Rudy displaced with his initial ramming, there would be several little boats left to attack the weak side of the boat.

"Keep an eye open for natives sneaking around to the starboard side of the ship," Max said as he walked along the deck on the back side.

Jane and Turner stood on the lower deck of the ship. They knew that once the big steamer hit the dugouts, chaos would ensue. A crewman with a shotgun stood next to them. He was a veteran of the

Great War and had used the '97 Winchester in battle with the Belgians against the Germans. His name was Arlo and he, unlike Turner and Jane, had been shot at before—and hit.

"Back in 1917, the Germans overran my position and wounded me in the arm and shoulder. I played dead. There was a counterattack almost immediately with tanks, so the Germans didn't stay around to check to see if anyone was left alive. They would have finished me off if I was discovered. Got lucky that day, I did."

The couple felt safer having someone battle-tested with them. They had no idea how crazy and disorganized a battle could be, but they were about to find out.

Several hundred yards from the line of boats, Rudy saw the natives raise their weapons. The river generated a considerable current through this area, and it was obvious members of the greeting party were having trouble aiming and standing at the same time. It became worse when a two-story,-200-ton boat sliced through their ranks. With remarkable accuracy, Alan squeezed the trigger twice and took out three boat people from almost four hundred yards using the big BAR.

"That deck rail makes a damn good gun rest. Not much up and down movement to deal with."

There were more shots from Max's .375 and finally, from two hundred yards, Lutz's Nitro .577 let loose almost cutting four men in half with a single shot.

"Few men get shot with an elephant gun. A little bit of overkill, but it's the only weapon I have," Lutz said to Max, standing next to him.

At one hundred yards the Manyemas started firing shotguns and although they were poorly aimed the pellets began hitting both decks and against the pilot house. Rudy's windows began blowing out glass in every direction. He always wore sunglasses and this habit kept him from being blinded. He was now bearing down on about fifty dugouts at almost twenty knots.

Something has to give, he thought

From the shoreline, a bevy of arrows filled the sky. As they struck the steamer, many bounced off and others stuck in everything imaginable.

The pygmies in the compound had sought shelter behind new welded metal plates but also had their own shields. They had asked Jane if they could help. Jane told them to stand by in case they were boarded by the Manyemas. Nestor said he would protect her if any of the natives came onboard.

Arrows penetrated the wheelhouse, but none struck Rudy as he ducked behind the shields. Alan and Yambo were exposed from the side and used Yambo's native shield as protection. It caught three arrows, which had a suspicious smell on the tips. Jane and Turner pushed their bodies against the welded metal and watched as arrows dropped behind them.

"The natives sound like they're right on us, Turner!" Jane said. She took a quick peek from the side of the armored railing. She could see them trying to climb on the boat. An arrow whizzed by, almost touching her hair. Turner pulled her back to safety.

Now they could hear the natives yelling and talking from behind their metal barrier. They were really close.

Rudy turned the big steamer a little towards the shore to maneuver in between about twenty or thirty dugouts and quickly turned back in the opposite direction.

"That should sink a few," Rudy muttered to himself.

Most of the little boats were upended and sunk. Some could be heard scraping the bottom of the steamer. Natives drowned and were chopped to pieces by the propellers. The water running out the boat's stern was now a maroon color. The maneuver left almost a hundred natives still in the water, some drowning but many were swimming towards the fast-moving giant. There were dugouts out front that headed directly for the sides of the boat on a trajectory that would allow them to throw ropes and to grab on to the behemoth. In a well-coordinated effort, arrows and several shotgun blasts were directed from shore towards the boat, which, because of the river channel, they were approaching rapidly. As the people on the steamer had to deal with the incoming rounds, the Manyemas' naval efforts were stepping up the attack.

"Jane, about twenty of them are trying to climb aboard. Start firing!"

Jane and Turner blasted away at those natives who had found something to hang onto and were trying to climb aboard. The shotgun blasts from the shore were relentless as the natives tried to give their water-based troops a chance to climb aboard.

Arlo rose during the shotgun barrage and slam fired his shotgun into eight natives hanging on ropes. It appeared they all were killed. One of the native's shotgun pellets caught him in the shoulder just above his scar from the Great War.

"Goddamn it! That fucking shoulder is a bullet magnet!" Arlo exclaimed.

"Medic! Medic!" Jane yelled. Nick and Zoe were there in an instant. The pellet went clear through. Nick slapped a salve and bandage on it since it didn't appear to be serious.

On the starboard side of the boat, a couple of dugouts with a total of ten natives grabbed on and were pulling themselves against the speed of the steamer to get onboard. Lutz saw them.

"Max, watch the bow. I've got natives coming in." He ran down and grabbed a shotgun from a passenger who was reluctant to use it.

"Give me that shotgun." He then slam fired four rounds into the dugouts. All of them were eliminated. A crew member came back, took the shotgun and shells, and sent the passenger to his cabin.

A huge boom shook the ship as Yambo tore another dugout in half with the elephant gun. The dugout was overloaded with about ten men in it. Most of them died. Alan took it from him and took out two more loaded dugouts then handed it back to Yambo.

"A couple of those rounds will turn your shoulder into mush," Alan said. Yambo smiled and nodded his head and then reloaded it.

Next to Turner and Jane, several natives were attached to the ropes along the gunnel of the steamer and were pulling themselves aboard.

"I'm killing as many as I can, but I'm about to use up this clip. How are you on rounds?" Turner asked his wife.

"I've lost count but must be about out." She blew two natives into the water and as she pointed her pistol at a native who was clearly ready to come aboard she heard an audible click. Turner pointed and picked up the one she had been unable to shoot. One more native was pushing his leg over the railing and Turner aimed and got that same helpless click.

As they dodged incoming arrows and pellets, they dropped to reload. They were losing the battle as more came up the sides preparing to board.

"Put one in the chamber before you work on your clip," Jane said. She didn't want to be caught without some firepower. Turner was ahead of her, as he had already slid in a round.

Arlo had used all his shotgun shells and was asking for extra. Just as two natives swung their legs over the rail to board the boat, Turner and Jane realized they didn't have time to finish reloading. Three more began to climb the rail. The single rounds they had chambered wouldn't help.

"Turner, we're being overrun!" Jane realized they were out of time.

Five small, black bodies suddenly swarmed all around the couple and started thrusting spears into the sides of the Manyemas. Screaming in pain, they released the ropes and fell over the side. After the pygmies had fought off the Manyemas, Jane made the pygmies get down below the metal shields since shotgun fire was still coming in heavy. The pygmies had saved their lives, but the battle was far from over. Turner and Jane worked on reloading clips, while the natives sheltered them from all sides. The shotgun pellets came in around them, splattering small pieces of lead on all of them. Everyone was bleeding from the small wounds.

"Look at that native on the small hill, Turner. He's got to be a leader of some sort."

On a raised sand bank, the couple watched a lone warrior standing with his arms crossed. He wore an impressive leopard skin robe but was without a weapon. His hair, possibly a wig, was bright red with green feathers attached. Warriors would run to him for instructions. There was no doubt he was a chief who was in charge of the battle. In particular, he observed the pygmies and followed everything they did. Turner had recalled stories of the British fighting the Zulus whose chiefs had similar battle practices. The man never moved from his position during the entire battle. One of the deck hands saw Turner and Jane staring at the strange native, and yelled to them, "He is Amcuda, King of the Manyemas and King of the Congo."

~~~~~~

The inside of Rudy's bridge was shot to pieces, and his helmsman was wounded in one arm and hand. Now, in spite of glass cuts to his face that caused streams of blood to trickle into his eyes, he had an important maneuver to navigate. He had come to the wide place where the large hippo pod resided, and in front of the herd were twenty or forty dugouts full of natives with shotguns. Instead of swinging away from them, Rudy steered the big boat right toward them.

"Let me see if the hippos are happy with the natives being in their river," Rudy muttered to himself.

Many started fleeing right into the mouths of the hippos which were gladly crushing the natives with their huge jaws. It was the hippos' sanctuary, and they were proving it. As the bow was pointed at them, the .375 and the .577 big game guns and Alan's BAR took the natives the hippos didn't kill. The crocodiles would clean up the mess. Rudy swung the steamer around and found the channel. It was over. The *Lapsley II* looked like a pincushion, most of her windows were blown out, everyone had wounds, but nobody died on the riverboat this day.

Nick and Zoë had set up a makeshift triage in the dining room, and people were lined according to the severity of their wounds. Most were glass cuts, but there were shotgun wounds and a few arrow wounds. The arrow wounds were not from poisoned tips, but Nick cleaned them with great care. He also used an experimental antibiotic called prontosil, which Germany had developed a year earlier. It was a sulfa drug that held much promise.

He would say to the patients, "I know this new drug well since I participated in the trials for it in medical school." He was probably the only doctor in Africa to have a supply of it, and he could be reasonably certain most of the people he treated didn't care about its history.

Yangambi was the next stop for the steamer. It didn't have many facilities, but government buildings were under construction because the area was going to be used as an agricultural test station. They had discovered a small, sweet banana there for use as a dessert. It wasn't native to Africa but seemed to be doing well in this area.

Rudy wanted to stop, so he could wire in to Stanleyville for parts he needed. He would give them replacement glass sizes and a list of other damaged items needed. He would also wire in the details of the battle. They should be in Yangambi the next morning. They needed wood since so much was used to run the gauntlet. In a couple of days, they would arrive in Stanleyville and from there on it would progressively get harder for the group going to the pygmy village. Tonight, there would be drinking and card games again.

Chapter Nineteen

To Stanleyville

Nick looked around the room at dinner and noticed that most everyone wore some sort of bandage. There were lots of cuts from flying glass and pellet wounds from buckshot. The thick metal plates that had been welded to the deck railings had given the defenders of the *Lapsley* protection from the shotgun pellets and the native arrows. The crew of the steamer also had the advantage of firing down at an enemy who had to fire at an upward angle. Many of their rounds and arrows were deflected. No one expected another attack, which was good because there wasn't much ammo left. The expedition hoped a big town like Stanleyville would have just about any ammo they needed. Alan had four rounds left for the Holland and Holland 4-bore elephant gun. Most of the time he found it best to buy ammo from the manufacturer of the weapon to assure the rounds would chamber correctly. Discussions were going around about everything they needed for their trip inland.

Nick, Zoë, Turner, and Jane were having dinner together. Caroline was eating with another of the mothers who were evacuated, and both seemed to be enjoying each other's company. She had a few cuts from glass shards and lead splatter, as she had also gone to Zoë and Nick's side to help with the wounded.

Jane couldn't see anyone who wasn't drinking. Now that she had been shot at, she didn't know if it was some sort of rite of passage, but she felt a rush while it happened and a little scared when it was over. She and Turner had minor wounds.

Dinner for the Simpson-Pygmy Rescue expedition's people was steaks, which they had saved for one of their final meals on the steamer. Nick was sharing his with Zoë. Everyone remarked that they seemed like an old married couple since they were so comfortable around each other. Tonight, Zoë was playing Spades with the group for the first time.

Dinner was concluded and with plenty of ice in their glasses for their drinks, the card game began.

"Well, I'd just like to say—I'm glad to be alive and glad it's over," Jane said as she dealt the cards.

"I would like to say I saw some brave people on our boat, and I'm proud of all of them," Turner said.

"You do know that our natives saved our lives from those Manyemas climbing onboard," Jane said.

"How did they know when to show up?" Nick asked.

"They were watching you guys the whole time—I saw them," Zoe said.

"They seem to always be there when I need them—same thing with the black cat—right beside me," Jane said. Then she had to explain to the others who didn't know the story.

"Anybody getting off the boat tomorrow? I'm not even sure they have a little store there," Zoë said.

"Maybe, if there anything to see," Jane said, eyeing the cards in her hand.

"If the government building is far enough along, they will have a commissary," Zoë said as she trumped the hand of cards with an ace of spades.

"You learn quickly," Jane said.

'What town is your dad's mine in?" Turner asked Zoë.

"One is in Katanga, which is a considerable distance west of here. It's a huge mine and has been around a while, so there are a lot of government compounds and private homes there.

"We were at the new mine when this trouble started, and it's in a remote but beautiful area. The mine is in the Equateur Province near a small village called Boende, which is on the Tshuapu River. You can take the river all the way to the Congo, which is what Mom and I did. The mine is a newly discovered diamond mine—small and remote. So far, it has produced a few gem quality stones.

"The diamonds that come out of other regions in the Congo are ninety percent industrial diamonds. My dad's mine is very small and may not be worth the cost to develop or expand it. It's not a part of the Congo where a lot of mining goes on, so there isn't mining equipment around or miners who know their stuff. We were living in an old colonial house in Boende, which was okay, but there wasn't much to do there, and we were right on the equator. You wouldn't believe the heat. We were there for only a few weeks and had planned to go back to Belgium soon anyway. My semester of school is about to start, but I may delay starting until the spring semester."

They played cards for an hour or so and then returned to their rooms. No one realized that their experience during the day had exhausted them so much. It was time for sleep—a long-deserved deep sleep.

~~~~~~

Early morning mist hung over Yangambi, but it didn't dispel the heat. The same collection of dugouts selling a crazy assortment of items for buyers on the steamer tied up to the big boat. Fish, small pigs, and on this trip, a small chimpanzee that had been gutted. The famous small sweet bananas were on the list, and the cook bought some for one of the meals. These people were selling eggs from some sort of winged bird, and the cook bought them as well. Rudy went into the partly completed government house and found a place to wire in his messages and file a report about the attack. It would be forwarded to the army headquarters.

He yelled back to the boat, "The commissary is open!"

The flood gates opened for everyone to sample the wonders of a Belgian Congo government-sponsored store. Almost all the Europeans scurried off the boat like excited children. Turner and Jane found candy bars—the first they had since Kinshasa. Beer, liquor, and tobacco were for sale. Just about everyone on the expedition smoked, except for Jane. Turner only smoked a pipe that his dad gave him for his eighteenth birthday, so he really hadn't gotten into it much. Jane's parents had both smoked and so did her Uncle Basil. She had tried it, but it caused her to gag. Since so many people around her smoked, she resigned herself to putting up with it.

Turner bought a pouch of a cherry-blend tobacco since Jane liked the aroma. They bought soft drinks, beer, and liquor. Max, Lutz, and Alan suggested they might want to get some snacks for the trip to the village. So they bought nuts, small sweet breads, crackers, and other small non-perishables.

Cut wood had been loaded on the boat, and Rudy blew the whistle for everyone to get aboard. He felt he could make it to Stanleyville by the evening if things went well. It was about 120 miles, and at ten knots, the boat would be there in less than twelve hours, maybe before dark.

There was one large village called Yanonge on the opposite shore about halfway to Stanleyville, but Rudy had no plans to stop. The dugouts would pull alongside with their floating markets as they did at all villages of any size, but the steamer would continue on course. He was in a hurry to get his steamer repaired and back in service. Most of the windows except for the wheelhouse were the same size, so there was hope of getting some replaced for the trip back. He had wired in the dimensions, but Stanleyville only had a few small glass shops. It was unlikely that all or possibly any of his order would be filled. There was other damage where shotgun blasts had penetrated walls, busted pipes, and torn through the galley, broke glass and punched holes in cooking equipment. The cooks had plenty of iron skillets and pots, so the show would go on.

Turner and Jane found the solitude of their cabin, and each had a cold beer from the commissary's cooler. The Belgians ran generators most of the time in the village for all the government buildings, and people put up with the noise when the reward was something cold to drink. They had just finished an early breakfast before the stop, and they wanted something to do. There was plenty of water to take a bath, but their blinds had huge holes in them from the shotgun blasts. If they hung sheets over the windows they blocked all the air and it became unbearable. At night people couldn't see in the room if the lights were off. Daytime allowed anyone to observe their activities through the busted blinds and shattered windows.

One unexpected benefit of having all their windows shot out was that more air was forced in by the movement of the boat. Ten knots generated a nice breeze. Because of the abundance of air, cooled somewhat by flowing over a large river, they could leave their door completely open now since the lovemaking sanctuary had been breached. They decided to find deck chairs and something to read. Rudy had a small library where passengers deposited books after they read them. Most were in French, but English titles were popular. American movies were the best in the world, and so many of them were adaptations of popular novels.

Turner found a tattered copy of *The Sun Also Rises* by Ernest Hemingway, and Jane located *Show Boat* by Edna Ferber. They had brought Ferber's *Cimarron* with them and had loaned it to Caroline. Since Jane was on a boat, she thought, *Why not read about a boat?*

They found deck chairs full of bullet holes and a couple of arrows stuck in them. The arrows would have made great souvenirs, if they had any place to store them.

They might spend one night in a hotel there before they left on the trip if they could find a place for the natives to stay. They would likely have a meeting after dinner to discuss the next phase of their expedition.

They read until lunch, and then the walking wounded started meandering into the dining room. Bandages and strips of medical tape were still in place on most. Nick still looked after the more seriously wounded and changed and cleaned their wounds. A few would need surgery to remove lead pellets when they reached Stanleyville. Turner had tape on his forehead and Jane had a piece of tape on her chin and a bandage on her hand where a pellet had struck her when she was firing her pistol.

They had the usual for lunch—sandwiches with cold cuts, crisps, and a cookie. Both had a beer and shared a table with Alan and Caroline, who complimented the young couple for their bravery under fire. Turner complimented Alan on his consistent fire with the BAR, and his and Yambo's success using the elephant gun. Jane explained that she and Turner had gone by several times to thank the pygmies for saving them from the natives trying to board the boat.

Alan said that Max had suggested they stay over one night to get all the supplies they needed before they took off. Ammo would be the main priority and they may have to search several stores to get all the various rounds they needed.

There was concern that the trucks would not be available because of all the military activity, and Max was going to visit the army headquarters while everyone else did their shopping. A request was made for three trucks and five bearers or porters. Because of the unrest, the bearers might be hard to find.

During lunch, Max came by to tell everyone to be packed and ready to unload in Stanleyville by nightfall. They would stay in a hotel that would let the natives stay on their lawn. The hotel wasn't luxurious, but it had a small café, ceiling fans in every room, and was within walking distance from the where the steamer was docked. They could eat an early dinner on the boat and enjoy a couple of nights in relative comfort. Jane wanted to talk to a float plane pilot, Nick needed more medical supplies, and everyone seemed to have last-minute errands before they went into the bush.

While eating dinner at about seven o'clock that evening, they saw the lights of Stanleyville in the distance. A toast was raised a short time later as Rudy blew the whistle, signaling he was docking. Everyone in the dining room lifted his or her glass and saluted the captain for getting the group through some pretty rough water.

As she was leaving the boat, Jane ran into the wheelhouse amid the broken glass and steel protective shields and found Rudy smoking a cigar he bought at the commissary and wearing the same dirty hat. It had something printed on it but was so soiled, no one could read it. Jane went over and kissed him on the cheek and told him she loved him and wanted to meet his daughter when they were back in Brazzaville. As usual, he smiled and tipped his hat at her.

Jane thought it was a little sad leaving the *Lapsley* since it had been home for a few weeks. The five white men and one woman walked two abreast carrying knapsacks; behind them were five very short black men and one who towered over everybody.

In a short while, they saw the sign for the Victoria Hotel. It was small but well-lit and had a large yard for the natives. Across the street was a small bakery, a general store, and grocery store. They were still open, so Jane bought bread, fruit and a large piece of cooked meat. There was a water pump in the yard. The hotel kept a supply of old blankets and mats for the natives. They had hosted expeditions many times before and knew how to make the natives comfortable.

Jane checked everyone into the hotel. Max announced that he would see everyone for breakfast and they would discuss plans. Nick had said his goodbyes to Zoë for a few weeks, but both had bonded and seemed to be inseparable at this point.

Turner opened the door to their room and saw a huge ceiling fan and a large bathtub. They looked at each other, turned on the water, and started peeling off clothes. They had discovered heaven on earth.

Chapter Twenty

Jungle Readiness

The morning sun edged around the window shades and streamed across the room illuminating the nude bodies of Jane and Turner Simpson. The big-bladed ceiling fan hummed a lazy song and turned just fast enough to move some humid air ever so slightly. Turner kissed Jane on the neck and smelled the lavender bath soap she had used the night before. They slowly kissed and wrapped around each other like tired pythons. They wanted the lovemaking session to be slow and to last a long time, so they could enjoy all the fruits of sex without rushing through any wonderful part. Afterwards, they took a bath together and got ready for breakfast and all the errands waiting for them.

Max greeted them in the hotel restaurant and pointed them towards a buffet line where Nick and Alan stood staring blankly with plates in their hands. Everyone recognized the fruit and scrambled eggs, but beyond that, they weren't sure the food was from planet Earth.

"What in the fuck kind of animals gave up their lives for our breakfast?" Turner said.

"It could be anything from a monkey to an anteater. Natives don't care. Meat is meat," Alan replied.

Jane was looking at the first display of bush meat ever served for her enjoyment. She gagged and went instead for things she could identify such as toast, fruit, and eggs. No one at the table was brave enough to try the meat. Monkeys were treasured as a delicacy by the natives and as stomach-purgers by Europeans.

"What do you people have on your list of errands today?" Max asked, not in an effort to supervise their purchases but just to make conversation. Ammunition was on everyone's list, so Max inquired at the hotel which store had the best variety.

"The Stanleyville Hardware is your best bet," Max said.

Everyone decided to go there first before fanning out for other errands.

They finished breakfast and strangely enough, their favorite part was the coffee. Africa has always grown their own beans and roasted them in the hotels. It had come from Rwanda and other mountainous areas where coffee has always thrived.

"I'll try to get a good supply of that coffee for our trip," Max announced.

Jane and Alan checked on the natives and saw to it they got fed, and then the group went to the hardware store. Not only did they carry ammunition, but they also sold guns, knives, spears, and gunpowder. Most of the cartridges were the smokeless variety and had been around since the turn of the century. Max and Lutz found their shells quickly. The same for Turner and Jane's .45 caliber pistol ammo.

The 4-bore ammo was getting harder and harder to find, and the hardware store didn't have what Alan needed. His gun couldn't use the smokeless powder, even if it were loaded in his huge cartridges. The pressure buildup by the cordite, nitroglycerin, and other compounds used might cause his weapon to explode. Alan did find Mauser rounds and purchased a box for the BAR. As he was checking out, Alan asked, "Do you know where I might get some four-bore shells?"

"Yes, one of the best gunsmiths in Africa is not far from here." The owner gave him the address of the gunsmith who loaded his own shells. Alan broke off from the rest and found the gunsmith a couple of blocks away.

The gunsmith was British and had been around since Stanley went through over forty years ago. His name was Findley Harper, a pudgy man in his mid-seventies, who appeared delighted to see another Brit come in his shop. Alan had brought his gun with him since the shell had to be sized for the gun. He introduced himself and gave his name to the gunsmith.

"You have a fine weapon, Mr. Chambers. Holland made some of the greatest large bores on the planet. Need some shells for it?" Findley asked.

"Yes, and I brought along some empty brass in case you reload." Alan laid five spent cartridges on his counter.

"Thanks. I do reload because new ones are hard to find. Tell me, what do you know about the good and bad with this shell?" Findley asked as he turned around and took a large round from a shelf.

"Since the bullet or projectile from this weapon weighs a fourth of a pound, it will stop most all big game in its tracks. A side shot on a bull elephant will penetrate the skull and drop it. The front of the skull is too thick to allow penetration but will slow it down for a second shot. There's so much smoke, it's hard to see the images of the elephant for a short while. But loaded with modern powder, the gun will not hold up under the pressure of the heavy gas."

"Let's get a little more specific, Mr. Chambers. Full black powder load on your four bore will deliver the round to the skull at thirteen hundred and fifty feet per second and the lead will deform quickly and mushroom on contact. Hold this round." Findley handed Alan a cartridge that had a gray-colored jacket instead of brass, and the round tip was shiny instead of the normal dull color of a lead bullet.

"Tell me about this. Will it safely fire in my Holland and Holland?" Alan asked.

"Yes, you have one of the later model guns that were manufactured at the turn of the century as black powder was being phased out and smokeless was all the rage. Holland wasn't sure if the new propellant was ever going to be made for the old bore guns, so just in case, they made the barrel and chamber a little stronger—unfortunately, not strong enough for a full load with the new powder. The second problem was the round itself. A load with excess pressure from the gasses also would cause the brass to blow open as it also wasn't strong enough. Even if you made a faster round that didn't blow your damn barrel off, it needed to be harder to penetrate further."

Alan held the round and studied it carefully. He pulled out a live round he had brought with him and compared them. They were the same size and just about the same weight.

"Okay, tell me what you've done with this shell."

"The brass has been replaced with steel, the projectile has fifty cents worth of silver mixed with the lead, and you have a light load of smokeless powder. I designed it to give you over fifteen hundred feet per second safely using the weapon you have. It will penetrate a savanna bull elephant and have no problem with these smaller forest elephants in the Congo."

"Okay, how much?" Alan knew these would not be cheap.

"Normally, ten dollars US for each one, but if you will give me the old brass, I will credit you three dollars each for them," Findley said, clearly hoping to get US currency instead of the Belgian franc.

Alan gave him five spent rounds and bought three rounds. The new ones ended up being five dollars each. He had bought the old ones for two dollars each at a small gun shop in Leopoldville. He was pleased and felt lucky he had found a munitions expert in the middle of nowhere.

Jane and Turner were looking for a float plane, while Max was checking on the trucks for the ride to the river. Nick was looking for medical supplies and also went by to check on Zoe and the repairs to the *Lapsley*. Lutz struck out to do some window shopping and to explore the small town. As each finished, they found their way back to the hotel for lunch. Everyone had coffee and waited as the individuals filed in at the table. Anxious for everyone's report, they began to describe their day when Max finally sat down.

"Well, a bit of good luck sprinkled with a tad of bad luck," Max said. "Because of the war with the Manyemas, we were able to get only one military truck. I was, however, able to hire one civilian truck about the same size. They're all Ford trucks with four-wheel drive conversions done by a US firm called Marmon-Herrington. They are the best four-wheel drive vehicles in the world, and we'll need them. One small rain and the roads are impassable. They'll be ready for us, along with three porters I've hired at a dollar a day. This afternoon we will purchase food for the trip. Hope we can fish some to supplement, and I'll pack some gear for that. We load up at 6:30 a.m. in front of the hotel and it'll take all day to get to the Bunga river crossing. If it rains a lot—two days." Max spoke with the confidence of someone who had made these trips before.

A waitress came by and handed out menus for lunch. The featured item was an African stew that utilized goat as the meat of the day. It was common to Africa, so everyone was used to it for lunch. The natives outside were getting it as well. Everyone ordered stew, except Turner and Jane who had chicken soup, local bread, and Coca-Colas.

Jane recalled what she found out about the float planes. "We found two planes at the dock and got to chat with both pilots. One was a three passenger and the other was for five people. Expensive, but much faster than the steamer. The small one was seventy-five each for the trip to Brazzaville and included two nights at rest houses on the way. They fly inland, strangely enough, and land on rivers because it's more of a straight line. The bigger plane was one hundred US each and followed the same course. We gave both of them our information and told them to look for us in about a month. Both planes looked old and beat up because they have been flying in the Congo since 1925. Time for new planes, and we understand they're on order. Hope they're here before we come out of the jungle," she said.

"I think we're all taking the steamer back since the tickets are only twenty-five to share a cabin," Alan said, and the others nodded approval. "We'll need to load aboard some more food, of course. By the way, I found a gunsmith who had cartridges for the four-bore."

"I found a clinic and was able to get more medical supplies. Most of mine were exhausted after the battle," Nick said and handed Jane an invoice for the supplies. Jane dug out some money from her purse and told Nick to pick up and pay for the supplies after lunch. The invoice included expenses for latex condoms, but Nick didn't bring that up around the others.

"Lutz, what did you do this morning?" Jane asked.

"Found some new boots, leggings, and some rain gear. Got some snacks, jerky, and fishing gear. I fly fish in Austria sometimes. Love it. Here I just bought a small rod, reel, filet knife, and some local lures and bait for local fish. Catfish are easy to catch, using some smelly bait around hooks that are laid on bottom. The lures also catch fish, but they warned me about tiger fish—huge teeth that will take your fingers off. I have palm oil, meal, and a small skillet, so I hope to help feed us," Lutz said with a smile.

"I'm glad someone is looking out for my stomach," Turner said.

Jane remembered that Nick was going to check on Zoë. "Nick, what did you find out about the steamer and Zoë?"

"The boat is replacing windows and pipes. Should be fixed in a couple days. Zoë and her mom are staying at one of the government houses in town, I was told. I will check on her this afternoon. They may take a float plane back to Leopoldville but haven't decided yet," Nick said repeating a conversation Zoë had with Rudy.

After lunch, the assembly scattered in different directions and pledged to meet back for dinner. Jane displayed a devious smile and pulled Turner towards the hotel room. Once the door to the room was closed, she began undressing Turner and pushed him onto the bed.

"Do you mind if I'm a little aggressive at times?" Jane asked.

"Hey, I love it. I was never that fond of undressing myself—especially when body parts get kissed and licked during the process. You do tend to wrinkle some of my clothes, though," Turner said. He laughed and started to undress Jane while she was stripping him.

"When is the sex supposed to get boring? I can't ever see that happening—can you?" Jane asked.

"My guess is, when babies make you tired, and age grabs you and slaps you in the face. I think I will get a nanny to help you, so you have time for sex. The growing-old part we will delay as long as possible—but growing old with you should be fun."

"Turner, I love you, but as usual, you're so full of shit. I'll take the nanny, though."

The couple made love with intensity, covered in sweat, breathing hard and tasting every square inch of each other's bodies. They had made love enough at this point in their relationship to where they had favorite positions and went right to them. They experimented less and made love more efficiently. On this occasion, Jane had an orgasm first, then played with Turner—teasing him until she milked him with her mouth and looked at him, laughing and happy she had pleased him. After their bath they laid on the bed naked and stared in each other's eyes, talking and gently kissing each other.

In the back of their minds, they knew they were about to do

something so dangerous and so difficult that they might not return from the trip. They had made a commitment, and they were both too young and crazy to turn back. For this reason and others, they made love again.

Dinner was fish of some sort, but everyone liked it. A considerable amount of drinking took place as the crew made last minute plans. Nick had spent some time with Zoë and would not see her again until they met again in Brussels three months from then as Nick had clinic work to complete in Leopoldville after the jungle experience. Most of the crew had stayed at the hotel and rested in the afternoon since there would be precious little rest in the next few weeks. Turner and Jane sat in the bar after dinner to talk.

"Jane, if I were your father, I would advise you not to go tomorrow. I would say that you're only fourteen years old and haven't lived long enough to risk your life, even if it was to help save some natives," Turner said.

"Turner, if I were your mother, I would first tell you not to marry a fourteen-year-old girl—oops, too late! Next, I would say to talk her out of a trek from the ocean to Brazzaville—oops, too late for that, too. I would tell her to please not drag my son through the jungle kicking and screaming. So far, you have remained relatively quiet except when I torture you by moving up and down on you ever so slowly when you are ready to blow your wad. So, we are crazy. If we live through it, we'll look back as older adults and say, 'What were we thinking?' but we aren't older, and I don't have parents, and yours have already spoken. We'll watch each other's back so that we come back alive. Is that a deal?"

Jane stuck out her hand for Turner to shake. He did and kissed it, then kissed her. They drank a lot and still had the presence of mind to ask the front desk to call their room at 5:30 the next morning.

Everyone had their knapsacks, guns, and supplies in front of the hotel at 6:30 a.m. when the two trucks pulled up.

Chapter Twenty-one

The Simpson-Pygmy Rescue Mission Moves Out

Each truck had two rows of uncomfortable metal seats in the rear bed. Max got a comfortable seat in front with the driver in the first truck, which transported the entire expedition, except for the natives who rode in the second truck. Jane was offered the shotgun seat in the truck with the natives and took it since she could communicate with them.

Their first stop would be the village of Bengamisa. Most decided that they would give up rifles, food, and money for some sort of cushion to sit on to protect their behinds from rusty metal benches.

After the first couple of miles, they untied sleeping bags from the knapsacks and used them as cushions. The road was dirt and gravel with huge potholes and gullies created by frequent downpours. Ahead, after about an hour, they passed through the small village of Yasangi, which consisted of huts on each side of the Lindi River. A small mine was to the right of the road as the trucks crossed over a poorly constructed wooden bridge. Then it was back to jungle. As they were driving, a dust storm formed on the back side of the two trucks. The second truck hugged the back bumper of the lead vehicle to keep from getting covered in dust. Both trucks had metal water coolers and paper cups in the back and spares in between the passengers in the front cabs. All of them were being used constantly.

About two miles beyond Yasangi, the road disappeared. Now, a huge gully cut across their path. Nothing suggested a road had ever been there. A recent rain storm had pushed the road bed deep into the surrounding jungle. There were four shovels in the rear bed of each truck, and they were passed out with the assurance that everyone would do their share of digging.

Turner and Jane set a good example and worked as part of the first crew filling in the gash with loose gravel and dirt. One crew, including all the natives and bearers, worked on the opposite side of the damaged roadway. After about an hour, the gulley was still there, but the sides had been sloped in to allow the four-wheel-drive trucks to maneuver. The hubs for the front axle were locked in place, and the trucks nosed down into the giant gulley. The transmissions made a whining sound as energy was sent to all the big mud tires, causing some to slip and others to dig into the loose road material. Everyone held their breath as the trucks started the steep climb out of the small canyon, accompanied by more whining and grinding.

After the second truck blew gravel and dirt behind it, everyone cheered the successful climb. A short water break was in order, and then everyone was back in the truck hoping the road ahead would be gully-free. Most African back roads had to be rebuilt constantly, but the real task was repairing bridges that collapsed after every flood. There had been floods just two weeks before their expedition, so likely the repairs had been completed.

Max rode in the cab of the lead truck which was driven by a Belgian military officer named Pierre.

"Tell me about the battle you were in with the Manyemas. How many of them do you think were killed?" Pierre asked.

"I'm not sure. What did Rudy say when you interviewed him?" Max asked.

"He gave us a number, but remember, he was piloting the steamer while all the shooting was going on."

"We had a BAR, a three-seventy-five, and around six or seven shotguns, mostly twelve-gauge. A four bore and a five-seventy-seven elephant gun, along with two forty-five caliber automatic pistols were manned by Turner and Jane. We didn't miss much and used up over a hundred—maybe two-hundred rounds of ammo. The elephant guns would take out more than one person at a time as would the buckshot, which sometimes wounded but didn't always kill. Also the pygmies, along with the Watutsi, took out several natives using spears and knives when they tried to board while Jane and Turner were reloading their clips. My estimate would be between eighty and a hundred and fifty dead and wounded. What was Rudy's estimate?" Max asked.

"You were very close to his estimate. He estimated the shots going out and felt it was about two hundred rounds going out from the boat. Maybe more. Also, he ran over several with the steamer and forced even more into mouths of angry hippos. I think only an individual inventory of ammo would tell us how many rounds were expended. You guys with the big guns fired less but took out multiple targets. The BAR, I understand would also fire several rounds into the same native. Those natives didn't recover. We needed to know what effect you guys had on the total Manyema population, and now we have a good idea. Furthermore, you need to know it was a big help to us to have their numbers reduced," Pierre said.

"Do you think there will be further trouble?" Max asked.

"Oh, yes, you can count on it. You guys at least got them out in the open. We won't be that lucky. Our army will be attacked in the jungle, and we may never see them. I hope that they don't come over to where you guys will be. Where will you be, by the way?" Pierre asked.

"The pygmies have villages along the head waters of a small river called the Lulu and it spills into the Bunga River which is also small; both rivers flow into the Aruwimi," Max said. "Neither of these rivers appear on most maps, but I located them on an old topographic version taken from an airplane flyover. From what I have researched, no white man has ever been there. We'll cross the Bunga after we cross the Aruwimi and go through Banalia. I have wired an outfitter there to get us enough dugouts for the trip. We will go downstream to the branch of the Lulu and go upstream to where it Ys, and then take it south to the headwaters. If it gets too hard to paddle upstream, we'll pull the dugouts out and walk the rest of the way. All fucking jungle, and we only have the native pygmies to guide us. Any Manyemas crazy enough to follow us in there will be really goddamn desperate."

The next road washout was near a small nameless village. As the expedition started sharing shovels for the road repair, the villagers came up on the road with rakes, hoes, and shovels to assist. Jane spoke to them in Bantu and got short responses. She said they felt bad that their road had failed them. It only took about thirty minutes to prepare the gravel highway to where the four-wheel drive trucks could work their magic and cross over to a roadway, which everyone knew would continue to fail them over and over again.

Jane was sharing the cab of a truck with a native driver named Rolly. He was very happy to have a pretty girl in his cab. Jane was glad there was a metal water cooler wedged between them since Rolly was a little too friendly. He had the annoying habit of wanting to touch her hand or arm when he talked to her. Jane was prepared to shoot him, if necessary. He preferred Bantu as a first language, but knew a little English, Swahili, and a lot of poorly pronounced French. He told jokes that were really not appropriate or funny. As they traveled further, Jane became more convinced that she was going to shoot him and push him to the side of the road. With her hand on the butt of her pistol, the village of Bengamisa came into view, allowing Rolly to live a little longer.

They pulled the trucks up next to a native-operated service station. Two attendants ran to the dusty vehicles, found the fuel caps, started filling them, and then began wiping dust from the windshields. Everyone else took a break.

The Belgian government had a large, red brick house near the station, and Max thought a quick visit might be helpful. Once the trucks were serviced, the caravan pulled into the circular driveway. Since the doors were open, the entire white delegation made their entrance. They were greeted by a Belgian official named Oliver Vermeulen, who was excited to have white visitors since they were rare.

"Welcome, welcome my friends. Have a seat in the living room," he said. Turning to his native servant, he said, "Mo, please get some lemonade for our guests."

Oliver returned his attention to his guests. "Mo has a long name and I can't ever remember it so I shortened it. What brings you to this area?" he asked, as he watched carefully to make sure his servant headed in the direction of the kitchen.

"We're on a humanitarian mission to assist some pygmy villages where they have had a smallpox outbreak," explained Nick, who then introduced himself as the team doctor. "The expedition is being called the Simpson-Pygmy Rescue Mission and was filed with the government under that name."

"Jesus, not many people have ever seen where the pygmies live. Very dangerous trip for anyone but especially for such a beautiful young woman." Oliver reached for Jane's hand and kissed it. He was a short man, but handsome and well dressed. His hair was graying, thinning, and combed to cover the disappearing regions.

"Thank you, Mr. Vermeulen. I am Jane Simpson and this is my husband, Turner." Jane then introduced the others.

Once that was done, Oliver stated his position with the Belgian Government was as the territorial area administrator answering to the provincial governor in Stanleyville. He went on to explain that the Belgian Congo Governor General had demoted his vice governor general down to his present position since everything was restructured in the last year. Seeing that he was boring the group to tears, he got off that subject.

"Do you happen to be the group who fought off the Manyemas on the steamer a few days ago?" Oliver asked.

"Yes, we were," Max said. "Have you seen any activity from them in this area?"

"No, we are some distance away, but military patrols come through quite often. I wish you to know that you are the talk of the Congo and in Belgium since the story has reached them. One of the headlines in a Brussels paper read, 'Small force of Europeans hold off attack by thousands of Congo natives,' and it further stated the steamer was so damaged it almost sank." Oliver was beaming with excitement at having world-famous fighters sipping lemonade in his living room.

Suddenly, everyone rose as Mrs. Vermeulen entered the room. She was attractive and gracious. "Welcome to our home," she said. "We see so few Europeans, so forgive us if we fall all over you. I overheard while I was in the kitchen that you were the brave fighters on the steamer. We're so very proud of you, and I'm sorry you had such a ghastly encounter. Normally, the natives are much better behaved. By the way, I am DaLinda."

Max made all the introduction for the group and everyone was seated again.

"This may bore you, but I must explain to you our official policy in the Congo. We abide by what we call the 'Colonial Trinity,' and here is where your expedition fits into the structure. All activity in this country is either classified as state, missionary, or private. Your activity, even though you are not saving souls, would be classified as missionary. You have already reported that your expedition is filed with the government. I will note your visit in my reports. Is there anything you need from us?" Oliver asked.

"My father is the director of native affairs in Brussels and recently went back from a visit here. He knows about the trip and cleared it as the Simpson-Pygmy Rescue Mission with the governor general, who lent us a military truck. He had given us two more, but the Manyemas caused us to lose those."

"Very good, and again I will report your visit here. Where will you start inland?"

"Past Banalia a few miles. We will go downstream on the Bunga River to a branch of the Lulu River, then upstream until we reach the mouth of the river. Both are small rivers and, for the most part, are uncharted," Max said.

"How do you communicate with the pygmies?" DaLinda asked. "I understand they have a difficult language."

"I have learned their language. I traveled through the jungle with them for a couple weeks after I was shipwrecked and had time to work on their language," Jane said.

"My God in heaven! Are you the world-famous Jungle Jane?"

"Well, unfortunately, that name has been slapped on me, Mrs. Vermeulen."

"Girl, you have adventure after adventure, and you're only fourteen, if the papers were right."

"I am fourteen, and I guess a little big for my age," Jane said.

"Now that I know you are Jane Ann Goode, I must tell you I met your dad at a conference in London. He was a really nice man, and we are truly sorry for your loss," Oliver said.

"Thank you. You're very kind," Jane said.

Max stood, signaling it was time to go. "We must hit the road. Since we'll have to rebuild it every few miles, we would like to make it to Banalia before dark," he said.

Everyone thanked Oliver and DaLinda for their hospitality and said they would try to stop by on the way back.

After ten hours of repairing the road and fixing two bridges that were about to collapse, the group passed over the wide Aruwimi River, and a few miles further, pulled into the village of Banalia. There was a small filling station, café, medical clinic, clothing store, bar, and river outfitter—all in the same building. The structure appeared to have been made of scrap lumber and several shades of tin roofing.

A Coca-Cola-emblazoned screen door welcomed them at the entrance. Natives were permitted inside, so everyone came in and found seats at homemade tables. The meal offered for dinner was African stew with pork. A small pig had been butchered earlier in the morning, knowing the group was on the way. The meals were one dollar each and included tea, water, or local beer. There was a loaf of bread on each table. A glass of ice cost twenty-five cents, and it wasn't a particularly large glass. Everyone could hear a generator running in the rear of the store, so the old Belgian gentleman who owned the store must have had a refrigerator. Jane and Turner were the only ones to spend lavishly on the ice. She wasn't surprised they were also paying twice the normal fifty cents for a blue plate special meal. Jane was happy that food was available and that the owner let the natives and bearers sit inside at tables. Very few Belgians would ignore the country's segregation policies and allow natives to eat at inside tables with whites.

Nick wasn't only a doctor; his first love was science. He wanted to know how everything worked, and he was amazed that a backwoods shack in the middle of the Belgian Congo would be generating electricity. He asked the store owner if he could see his generator. Turner was curious as well, and the old Belgian man walked them through his kitchen, where he had an old monitor-top refrigerator humming peacefully next to the wall. Out the back door and in a metal shed with a large, open padlock hanging on a clasp was a cast iron Kohler generator. Nick had only seen one other and was fascinated by this little gasoline unit that would turn itself on and off by demand from a battery attached to it. It had first been invented in the US for farm use in about 1920, and now was shipped all over the world.

"Admiral Byrd used one on his expedition to the North Pole," Nick said and thanked the store owner for showing it. "I really doubt if electricity will be available to most of Africa ever—who will pay for it once the expensive power lines are strung out to rural areas? They're too poor for electricity and probably always will be," Nick said to no one in particular.

"You haven't been there yet, but the comfort house has one of the Kohlers as well," Turner said. "I believe those little generators are many years ahead of everyone else. However, it's limited in power, so they have a big generator as well."

After they returned to the table, Jane asked what they had seen and then seemed bored when the guys started talking about generators and electricity. She was, however, enjoying the ice in her Coca-Cola.

She clinked her glass against Turner's. "To a successful jungle trip," she said. The others at the table and nearby all joined the toast.

Jane was presented with the bill, and she promptly paid it with the US dollars she had received from a bank in Stanleyville, using a check from her Brazzaville bank. They would need cash for the dugouts, the bearers, and more supplies to be loaded on the boats.

After dinner, the task of loading the four big dugouts began. One dugout, or pirogue as the Belgians called them in French, was strapped to the frames on the top of the trucks. One dugout each was pushed into the center of each truck bed. Max had decided that the five pygmies would lead the way in one dugout. Next would be Max, Lutz, and Nick, followed by Alan, Turner, Yambo, and Jane. The last boat would carry the three bearers and most of the supplies, so it was a larger pirogue than the rest.

The size of the dugouts depended on the girth of the tree from which they were hacked and chiseled. All four dugouts were teak, which the natives said was the best wood and hard to find unless you go deep into the jungle. Most new dugouts in the area were made from the Kigelia trees, which are more numerous.

The pygmies would not be joining them on the way back, so there would be fewer in the canoes to paddle, but most of the trip would be downstream until they hit the slow-moving Bunga River. The exception was a large section of rapids and a waterfall. There, they would portage the boats to go around them.

For the night, everyone would sleep on cots in a campground behind the store. It was under a metal roof shed with open sides. Crude latrines were built with sticks, a metal roof, and boards with round holes. The smell was oppressive, and according to Jane, could bring a bull elephant to its knees.

Breakfast would be coffee, fruit and bread. They would leave early for the river, and as much as Jane tried to get the pygmies to describe what the area would be like, the natives just said, "Big jungle—many animals—much danger." Jane was concerned because the pygmies were rarely afraid of anything. These were the forests where they lived, yet they had great respect for the dense jungle that surrounded their home.

As soon as it was dark, most everyone lay on their cots trying to get some sleep. In the village, however, were drums, dancers, and singers who were up late celebrating the expedition. The word was out that the doctor was going to treat an outbreak of smallpox, and they were happy someone cared enough to risk their lives to help natives. The celebration was to honor the people on the expedition. Tomorrow, they would enter a jungle so hostile, no white man had ever attempted to traverse it. The mouth of the Lulu River had never been reported, probably because very few knew it existed. Jane placed some cotton in her ears, kissed Turner goodnight, and scrunched down in her sleeping bag. She was asleep immediately.

Chapter Twenty-two

The Bunga

After a breakfast of coffee, fruit, and sweet breads, the expedition loaded their backpacks and guns in the truck and drove onto the road. They had gone one mile when it started to rain. They had been blessed with good weather the day before, but now the weather was making up for going easy on them. The trucks were forced to stop and lock in their front hubs into four-wheel drive and travel at a crawl, sliding side to side as the dirt became liquid beneath their tires. Canvas covers in the truck beds were unfolded and tied down.

Ordinarily, it would have taken only twenty minutes to reach the river crossing, but with the downpour, it took over an hour. Since it was a small river, there was concern it would be running fast from the rains. Once at the crossing, the river looked tame. It wasn't big anyway and apparently wasn't fed by a lot of creeks or streams, or else there wasn't much rain upstream.

It was down a slope to the water's edge and took several men on each dugout to get them situated. Supplies came down next, along with personal gear and guns. Once everyone was in place, the drivers said they would be back to pick them up in thirty days. If they got there early, they were to walk to the camp area. If they were late, the trucks would wait two days. After that, they would be on their own.

With everyone settled, Max asked for their attention and he got it.

"You can die many ways on this trip. Listen to me, so it doesn't happen." He paused to let Jane translate. "Insects can kill you. They will bite you and use you to hatch out their larvae, which will eat your flesh. The tsetse fly will give you sleeping sickness and kill you. You have taken medicine for malaria, but some strains will still make you sick—kill you, even."

He gave Jane time to translate again before continuing. "Use the netting on your hats, and before you get in the boats, cover yourself with insect repellent. At night, we will build a fire and make lean-tos with the dugouts and cover them with netting.

"Now let's talk about the Bunga and the Lulu. We will undoubtedly encounter rapids. When we do, we will pull the boats out and carry them. We have extra paddles, but don't lose them."

Jane explained mainly in Bantu unless the pygmies had questions. They were busy coating themselves in river bank mud.

Max went on, "We will give wide berth to hippos, elephants, and crocs. While we are on land, there will be forest buffalo, leopards, snakes and wild boar. Any of these can kill you. Some of you will cut our trail, while our gun bearers and hunters protect you from attack."

Jane did her best to try not to scare the bearers and cause them to leave.

"Last, and unlikely, in case we run into the Manyemas, we will take cover and hopefully have them outgunned. If you're rubbing mud on yourself for insects, get it off the bank and not in the water—that mud contains leeches. Any questions?"

Turner was the only one to raise his hand.

"Yes, Turner, what is it?" Max asked.

"Can I go home?" Turner asked, and there was laughter, which Jane had to explain to the natives. They thought it was funny as well.

The pygmies pulled their boat in first. As they paddled to the middle of the river, Jane asked them to not get too far ahead of the rest of the dugouts. Nestor waved that he understood. Max, Nick, and Lutz were next, then Turner and Jane's boat carrying Yambo and Alan. Last were the bearers and supplies. Many times, the boats were abreast of each other, so conversation was easy.

Although everyone was excited about starting the trip, they communicated in whispers, for some reason.

At times, when the river allowed an unobstructed view, black Colobus monkeys could be seen high in the canopies of the rain forest. Other monkeys could be seen in the lower branches watching. They screeched an alarm as the dugouts slid by in the water. The rain had stopped before they put the boats in, but water still dripped from leaves and branches. The jungle was primeval, unchanging, teeming, growing, living, and dying from the smallest insect, animal, and vine, to the largest teak and mahogany tree.

Jane thought, *If there is a God, the jungle and rainforest is where he tested how many living organisms could be combined in a symbiotic relationship.*

"Yambo, have you ever seen jungle like this?" Jane asked. He said he had not since his people lived on the savanna.

"I've never seen anything like this either and get the feeling few white men have ever traveled this river. Did anyone bring a shotgun?" Alan asked, as he eyed a large snake swimming towards Max's dugout. It was floating on top of the water which suggested it might be poisonous, as poisonous snakes usually fill their bodies full of air before swimming.

Alan watched as Max took a long pole with a clip on one end that was controlled by a small rope at the opposite end. Max grabbed the snake with the plyer-like grip and slung into the thick green vegetation.

"Forest cobra, I think," Max said.

"Hey, we didn't get a snake catcher," Jane said.

"Nick has a shotgun—rented from the outfitter if you want it," Max said. "And, sorry, I just brought one snake stick." Their boat came alongside, and Nick handed the shotgun to Alan.

"You'll just have to catch them with your hands, Jane," Turner said.

Jane smiled and eyed the water and overhead foliage for snakes. She began to notice large quantities of snakes that sunned themselves in any area where bright light filtered through the canopy. It appeared they had no desire to drop down on the expedition unless they were disturbed.

"Be quiet and let them sunbathe in peace," Jane murmured.

The Bunga River didn't have much current and moved along at a sluggish pace. Looking forward to the trip back, it would be easy to paddle upstream; however, everyone now had to paddle a great deal to get much movement out of the dugouts.

As they rounded a bend, a family of warthogs grunted, squealed, and pawed the ground before they disappeared into the underbrush. The jungle didn't give up much cleared ground and carried itself out into the water and over the river. A huge date palm curved out over the water and greeted them around another turn of the waterway. Monkeys were picking the ripe dates and squawked at the flotilla, throwing dates at the boats as they passed under the tree. There was a commotion in the jungle, and they cleared out of the tree and found their way up towards the canopy. Shortly after they were gone, a leopard walked up to the base of the tree and growled at the group, then walked calmly back into the forest.

"I don't think I've ever seen such an abundance of wildlife, and they have little fear of man," Alan said. "Look ahead—there are chimps, or maybe bonobos. They're only found in the Congo."

"How do you know the difference, Alan?" Jane asked.

"I've only seen them in zoos and in pictures. The bonobos are more slender, lighter in color, nostrils are different, and this part you'll like, Jane—it's a female-dominated society."

"It's about time!" Jane laughed and studied the troop, checking everything that Alan mentioned. "I do believe those are bonobos. See how the females direct the rest back into the jungle? And they're all slim—don't look like chimps."

"This place is like a lost continent—expect a dinosaur any minute," Turner quipped.

"If King Kong comes out, I refuse to go to his nest with him," Jane said laughing.

"Man, I hate we're missing that movie—hope it's still playing when we get to the States," Turner said.

"All of us are in a movie now, but no one is filming, unless Nick is doing the honors," Jane said.

"Hey, Nick, are you filming this trip?" Turner asked.

Nick held his movie camera up in the air from the dugout in front of them, and he then turned and rolled some footage pointed at the two boats following them. Jane had received a camera as a wedding gift and had it with her in a small rubber bag. While it was on her mind, she pulled out the new toy and wound the key until it stopped and started filming the boats and river scenes.

The river was widening ahead of them with big banks sloping down to the water. The crocodiles occupying the muddy areas slid into the water on both sides of the river as they neared. A couple of them were at least twenty feet long and truly looked prehistoric. They weren't dinosaurs but close enough, and there must have been sixty to seventy of them headed to the waterway under the approaching dugouts. One person in every boat had a weapon pointed towards the water. For a while, everyone thought it was going to be a nonevent.

Suddenly, one of the twenty footers rose from the river and took the lead boat in his jaws. He was so large that his mouth stretched across the width of the dugout, barely missing Nestor. An explosion from Alan's BAR sent multiple rounds into the beast. He let go of the boat and headed towards the second boat. Before he could reach it, Lutz put a huge .577 bullet into his skull, sinking him with a violent roll and slap of his tail. A second large croc opened his mouth and headed for the last boat. Alan, Lutz, and Max shot at about the same time. The giant reptile rolled and slapped until finally, it floated lifeless, almost even with the boats.

The river took a sharp bend, and rocky banks were in view with the sound of crashing water coming from the white-capped water ahead of them. They had come to the first series of rapids and knew they would have to pull into the bank. The shore was covered in gravel and was about thirty feet wide before a giant jungle swallowed up the open space. The lead boat was inspected and although scarred and scraped from the attack, it was fine. Two teeth were embedded on the outside gunnel lip of the boat and the pygmies pried them loose. They told Jane they made good magic.

While all the boats were pulled over, everyone ate prepared sandwiches from the general store. Max walked up the bank a ways to see how difficult the portage would be. He came back after a while and said there was plenty of riverbank to walk on, but it was a good distance to carry heavy teak dugouts. He was tempted to suggest they take the rapids, as they were mild compared to those he had seen. He asked Alan and Lutz to inspect them for their opinions. They also thought it was possible but dangerous. They called for Jane to walk the pygmies up to it in order to find out if they had done it before or had seen it done. They were willing to take on the fast water because they could swim and because they had done rapids before.

After polling everyone, they learned that two of the bearers, along with Nick and Yambo, were non-swimmers. It was determined that if they tried it, Turner would need to ride with the three natives in the last boat. After a short while, they decided to go through the rapids. It would save time since the portage distance was three miles of rocky shoreline. It was possible and even probable that people would get injured walking on slippery rocks carrying heavy teak boats and supplies.

Jane explained to the natives what was about to occur. She told them about the rapids and said Turner was going to be added to the crew because he could swim and assist the two non-swimmers. They nodded. She asked for their names; there was no way to be prepared for the answers. The first said his name was "Blick," the second was "Flick," and the third, who was the swimmer, was "Snick."

"Who gave you these names?" Jane asked.

In Bantu, they explained that they had worked with an American expedition a few years back. The Americans couldn't pronounce their native names, so they gave them the new names. They then said something that sounded like "Sno-ite."

It all made sense to Jane, and she smiled as she remembered her parents taking her to see the play *Snow White and the Seven Dwarfs* in London a few years back. It was a local production of a play that had been popular in the US some fifteen years before. They were names taken from three of the seven dwarfs in the play, which had stolen its story line from an old European fairy tale.

Seeing her smile, the three natives asked Jane to tell them the story of their names. She agreed, and they all sat down like children to hear the story. The pygmies and Yambo came over and sat next to them. Now she would have to tell it in two different languages. As she told the story of the beautiful queen who had a daughter with snow-white skin, she realized the need for a word for "snow." She asked Yambo about Kilimanjaro, and the white-cold on top. He told her the word was "theluji." She said this word to the Bantu. They knew it and responded with "ighwa" that produced clicking sounds on the vowels. She asked the pygmies if they understood the cold, white snow word. They did, using the Swahili word, even though they had never seen snow. She explained it just meant "very or much white." She continued with the story.

Turner watched his wife be ever-so-patient as she became animated, explaining one of her favorite fairy tales to three different tribes of natives in languages college graduates learned for their doctorate degrees. They laughed at the dwarfs who made Snow White clean and cook for them. The pygmies were surprised that little people were famous a world away from the steaming jungles of the Congo. They were fascinated by the magic mirror and the mean stepmother who was trying to harm Snow White. Turner could see tears in their eyes as Snow White bit into the poisoned apple and fell into a deep sleep. He witnessed the great joy in their faces as the prince came to save her, and they lived happily ever after in a castle.

Turner fell deeper in love with Jane when he realized what a wonderful, loving, and caring person she was. After the story ended, all the natives clapped and cheered as did the rest of the expedition, who had probably just witnessed the first time these natives had ever heard a western fairy tale. The whole group had watched as she switched from one language to another, mixed in Swahili, and substituted "chief" for "king" and "son of chief" for "prince," when necessary. On the banks of a little-known river, deep in the Congo basin, one culture had shared a story that had been told many hundreds of times for hundreds of years. It was a story of evil and overcoming evil. All cultures could relate, and Jane had just proven it.

"Since Flick, Blick, and Snick sound so much alike," Jane said, "would you mind if I gave you new names?" At this moment in time, the bearers would have allowed Jane to name them after different kinds of animal excrement.

"I'll give you names of men who make people happy. Snick, your new name is Moe, Flick, since you have no hair, you will be Curly, and Blick, you will be known as Larry." She had them repeat it several times and also told the pygmies.

"You're naming them after the Three Stooges?" Turner asked.

"Do they make people happy?" Jane asked.

"Never heard of them," Max and Lutz said.

"They are big with the in-crowd in the US and England," Turner said.

"Not in Belgium, I don't think, but my head is always buried in a book," Nick said.

With the native pygmies in the lead, the other boats pointed their bows toward the churning water and protruding rocks.

Chapter Twenty-three

Fast Water

The first series of rapids were choppy and noisy as the big wooden boats slammed into rocks and slid over them, sometimes screeching as the friction intensified between stone and wood. The pygmies kept their boat straight and picked the wide chutes that tunneled between the rocks. Sometimes the small natives would stand up and paddle, so they could see the danger ahead of them, blazing a water path for all he boats behind. Errors made by the expedition in these furious waters would ensure a quick and unforgiving lesson learned. Either keep the craft going straight by adjusting the paddle thrust on the right and left or feel the bruising intensity of having your body slammed into boulders and dragged under a bubbling liquid unable to judge up from down. The minds of everyone in the boats were focused on keeping from capsizing. Everyone was filled with fear, even those who could swim. Not a single person had a desire to plunge into a huge washing machine filled with rocks.

The boats were traveling fast, and before them was a rock—a huge boulder maybe twenty-to-thirty-feet high. It appeared to block their path, except they could see boiling chutes on each side. A deafening and terrifying sound emitted from behind the huge monolith. Nestor was on his feet, preparing to make a decision that might mean life or death for the entire expedition. He chose to take the right chute. Max, Lutz, and Nick were directly behind the lead boat as they witnessed the pygmies' dugout disappear in front of their eyes. It was too late to make an adjustment as rapids this intense make no provisions for going back or skipping a violent section. Either take a chance and paddle into it or panic and go through sideways or upside down, guaranteeing a bad outcome.

The view from Turner's boat was unsettling. One by one, he watched as dugouts disappeared into greenish brown water that seemed to swallow his friends and his wife whole. Nevertheless, he and his natives paddled with all their strength to avoid being swallowed and chewed alive by the river. The boat lurched forward and came down with a force so strong that the very breath was taken from the occupants. The rushing, ferocious, and roaring water dropped the dugout at a steep, just short of vertical, angle as it plunged into a large pool of water that circled around a whirlpool. Even though the boat went under briefly, everyone was still aboard, and all they lost was a spare paddle. Turner yelled for everyone to paddle hard to avoid the whirlpool. Once past it, another chute lay ahead. At first, it appeared to be tamer than the vicious tunnel they just experienced, but they soon found out otherwise. As their canoe neared the chute, they realized that there was no slope—it was straight down—a ten-to-fifteen-foot waterfall.

Jane and the rest of her crew were in the water holding on to their dugout. Alan and Yambo were there to help her, but she popped up and swam to their boat. Nick had gone under and then was pulled to safety by Max and Lutz. Their supplies had been tied to eye rings in the boat and were still intact. The pygmies were okay as well, having lost a couple of paddles, which Nestor was currently swimming to retrieve. The water was fast below the waterfall but losing its intensity.

All the boats and crew were in the water and there to see Turner's craft turn to its side as it struck a rock before plunging upside down into the foaming waterfall. Jane gasped as she didn't see anyone surface at first. Turner and Moe came up first and grabbed the side of the dugout, frantically looking for Larry and Curly. They didn't reappear, so Turner and Moe dove under the tossing water to find them. They both came back up, but there was still no sign of Curly and Larry. They went under again and Turner surfaced with an unconscious Larry. At the same time, Moe found Curly, who was spitting up water and flailing to grab hold of Moe.

Turner yelled, "Don't let Curly get his hands on you, or he'll take you down and you'll both drown!"

By now, Alan had swum over to take the limp native from Turner and swim him to shore. Turner swam out to face Curly, who was in a panicked and dangerous state. Then he motioned for Moe to swim over and hold on to the side of their boat. Turner dove down under the native and approached him from the rear. He walked up the nearly-drowned African's body with his hands and then he slid an arm around his neck and shoulder, holding him tight under his armpit. Curly broke loose and wrapped his arms around Turner, taking him under. Turner positioned his legs and kicked Curly in the chest to make him release, and then repeated the approach from behind Curly. He moved again to slide his arm under and across his chest, and then swam with him on his hip toward Alan, who had placed Larry on the gravel shore.

Once the water was shallow enough to turn him loose, Turner let the native go and went to assist Alan, who had started compressions on the back of the unconscious bearer. Nick arrived almost at the same time to direct the attempt at artificial respiration. At first, he placed him face down and pressed on his back, while Turner pulled on his arms in between compressions. After a few moments of this, Nick was unable to get a response, so he turned him over and pressed directly on his chest, then placed his mouth on Larry's mouth and gave him a few breaths. Max and Lutz looked shocked as they had never seen this technique. Turner took turns as Nick tired. After twenty minutes and as both were about to give up, Larry began to vomit water and food and gasp for air. He was weak and sick, but alive.

Turner asked, "Where did you learn those methods?"

"Mouth-to-mouth has been around since the 1700s but falls in and out of favor," Nick said. "The pressure pulls on the back and arm have actually saved a lot of people, but for those not responding, the mouth-to-mouth seems to give them enough oxygen to keep them alive until their body responds. I developed the chest compressions after studying the same method used in the past. It's nothing new but I may have used it a little differently. Whatever, I'm glad it worked."

"Turner, you must have had a lifesaving class before. You really showed some skills on Curly."

"I was in the Boy Scouts in San Francisco—made it to Eagle rank before we moved back to Belgium. Took lifesaving from a Red Cross instructor. Our summer camps were up in the beautiful Sierras. I loved every minute of it."

"My husband is a King's Scout! What other secrets do you harbor?" Jane asked.

"It's Eagle in the States, even though you Brits started the organization."

Nick spoke up. "I think we should camp here for the night, if Max agrees, and let Larry get his strength back. I have some meds. He can breathe them in with a mask and get some of the liquid off his lungs. He should be fine tomorrow," he said.

"We're through the worst part of the rapids and about where we would have been had we spent several hours carrying all the equipment," Max said. "We do need to swim for anything that came loose from the boats. However, now I see the pygmies are already doing that, so let's set up camp on the smooth gravel shore behind us and start collecting fire wood."

All the boats were pulled on shore, and tents were set up for those who wanted them. The natives all slept under the dugouts that were leaned on their sides and against each other with a big mosquito net draped over them. Jane and Turner set up their tent, put their gear in it, and set out to get firewood. Nick came by to thank Jane for giving him her rubber pouch for his medicine and his movie camera. He went back to take care of his patient and those that earned cuts and bruises from the waterfall experience.

"No wonder your mom and dad didn't try to talk you out of going on this trip. They knew you had skills in the outdoors. If I gave you a pocket knife and a bottle of beer, could you go into the forest and build me a two-story house?" Jane asked Turner.

"Dear, I could only build a small cottage and it would require a case of beer."

"Turner, I really wanted two stories, so I could watch for you carrying dead water buffaloes home for dinner."

As Jane spoke, she thought she saw something move near a pile of wood that Turner was busy placing pieces on.

"Sweetheart, water buffaloes are tough. What if I brought you a nice antelope and made you a ladder so you could stand on the roof?" Turner said, throwing a big limb with branches on the pile.

"Honey, I'm not hard to please. Would you build two stories if I met you naked at the door every evening?" The object she saw now moved away from the woodpile directly in front of Turner, who was looking at the top of the woodpile.

"I expect that, even if we were living in a tent—and by-the-way, I believe we are living in a tent," Turner quipped, just as he turned around and saw Jane pointing her pistol in his direction.

"Don't move, Turner!" Five shots rang out, and Turner heard a thrashing sound on the ground. He looked down and saw a huge forest cobra writhing and vibrating in a death coil, its head separated from its main body.

Max and Lutz ran in their direction, and Turner yelled, "It was a snake, and Jane got it!" Most of the camp came by to look at the huge snake. The pygmies retrieved, skinned, and cooked it on a stick over their fire. Jane and Turner sampled a piece.

"Taste like fishy chicken," Jane said. "It took me five shots to kill it. Did you notice?"

"Tastes like cooked cobra to me," Turner said. "I think I prefer my snakes killed and buried. I don't care how many shots it took—you killed it fair and square."

Nick walked over to where the natives were cooking the cobra and Turner and Jane were standing. He took a piece for himself.

"What could you have done for me if that cobra had struck me?" Turner asked the doctor.

"Quite a bit I could try since it was a cobra, but there are no guarantees. India, the British, and the Belgians have worked on antivenoms for them since the turn of the century. I have powdered meds, and you'd get it in your veins after I mixed it with saline. I would try to give an amount equal to what you had been given by the snake. Sometimes, there are violent allergic reactions. You might have swelling, muscle loss, and infections around the wound. Same thing if you were bitten by a viper, but there I use a medicine that's good for most all vipers. Boomslang—I've got a new med, but it's not foolproof. However, South Africa has done a lot of work on it. Mambas and kraits—still working on something effective for them, so I might amputate a limb or arm to try and save the unlucky chap," Nick explained.

"We'll try to only get bitten by a proper snake. No off-brand snakes for us," Turner told Nick.

"Cobra isn't that bad to eat. Better than insects and grub worms. More protein, too," Nick said as he walked over to the other expedition fire where the bearers were preparing a stew in a large pot.

Max walked over and changed the subject. "I think we should take turns on guards tonight. Three hours on—two guards at a time, both with guns. Can the bearers or the pygmies shoot?" Max asked.

"All of them can use the shotgun. Maybe use one person to keep the other awake. We will use the folding chairs and someone can lend them a watch to use," Alan said.

"I'll make a schedule and walk it around," Lutz said. "I'll pair an expedition member with a native, if possible."

While dinner was being prepared, it was late afternoon with abundant daylight, so Turner had a suggestion. He asked Max if he could drown-proof the non-swimmers.

"I'm a Red Cross lifeguard and a swim instructor. Do you mind if I try?" Turner asked.

"Hell, if you can keep what happened today from repeating itself, I say go ahead," Max said.

Turner recruited four helpers who didn't mind getting wet. Jane found a pair of shorts and a T-shirt, Alan, Nick, and Lutz improvised swimsuits from shorts, and Moe just wrapped a cloth around to cover his genitals as did Curly, Larry, and Yambo.

Turner found four branches about three feet long in the firewood pile and had the swimmers stand facing the novices. He asked them to get in waist-deep water first with the trainers facing the learners, while clutching the sticks they held onto for support. Turner started with a slow pace of having them stick their faces in the water and blow bubbles. Jane was holding the stick for Yambo, who was having trouble with this exercise. Jane demonstrated, and he finally succeeded. Then they were asked to hold on and stretch out and kick their feet.

Turner then demonstrated the dog paddle and asked them to bend and try it in shallow water. Yambo had problems because of his long lanky legs. Nick caught on quickly. Turner moved them deeper and worked on the technique more and more. Yambo was the last to catch on, but once he got the long legs and arms in sync, he did fine, and Jane praised him.

"The dog paddle will save your life but will tire you out. I now will teach you to rest in the water and this will also save your life," Turner said, and Jane translated for him. "You may get water in your mouth or eyes, but don't panic—these things will not kill you." He told the learners to hold onto the sticks, then stretch out, hold their breath, and just float in the water. He called it the "dead man float." He explained it would rest them, but they had to raise their head and breathe often.

"Next exercise will be harder to master but will allow you to be in deep water for hours without drowning. Now, you will float on your back. I'll ask your assistants to place the natives and Nick on their backs and gradually let them float. Be patient as it will take trust and time to allow your body to relax."

Nick learned quickly and seemed to have a stout body with a little more body fat than he needed. The rest of the natives were all sinew and muscle, so it was difficult. There was a lot of sputtering and coughing as water drifted into their mouths and noses. Jane's student had a different problem.

Jane had been holding Yambo through all this process. He had rubbed up against her and felt her soft hands on his body. He had held things in check until she turned him over in the water and held him from underneath. To get a good grasp, she had moved her body next to his and her breasts were solidly wedged against his side. Suddenly outside of the loin cloth that covered his genitals, an erection snapped to attention almost in her face. There it was in its full, black glory. It was her childhood dream—the subject of her fantasies ever since she was ten years old and saw Watutsis in a *National Geographic* magazine—a long, hard penis—the longest she had ever seen. It was slender, erect, and a total embarrassment for Yambo, who quickly dropped in the water and covered up. Turner laughed. So did everyone else, except for Jane, who quickly told Yambo he didn't need to be ashamed. He was thoroughly embarrassed, though, and decided his lessons were done. Turner was about finished anyway, and everyone thanked him for the class. Some stayed and dog-paddled around. Turner came over and put his arm around Jane.

"Dear, should I worry you're going to leave me for Yambo? It was the longest one I've ever seen."

"Wasn't it magnificent? Maybe I can have one carved from wood and make a lamp out of it. Yours is still my favorite, but Yambo is a close second. Soon as you die of old age—it's me and Yambo."

Jane and Turner were laughing as they told Max what happened. Yambo kept to himself until dinner and then returned to his normal self. Lutz made sure that Yambo and Jane weren't on guard duty together.

Chapter Twenty-four

Hippo Attack

Alan and Nestor were on guard duty at around one o'clock in the morning when an old male lion hobbled out of the forest. Nestor threw rocks at the animal to scare it off, but he kept advancing toward the camp. With ribs protruding, breathing labored, and eyes glazed, he was on a death walk. The old beast sported several scars, most likely earned fighting for the right to mate in a pride. One eye was partly closed and didn't appear functional.

As he crossed an imaginary line that Alan determined to be the ultimate range of safety, the BAR coughed a couple of times and the aged beast slid down in the gravel. It was a merciful kill. The camp was now up. Nestor explained to Jane that lions weren't common in the jungle, and the ones that came around were the old males too slow to hunt or stay with a pride.

"There were very few open areas for lions to hunt in this area of the Congo, so he may have walked for hundreds of miles," Jane said.

Everyone speculated that since water was always plentiful in the jungle, he many have stolen some kills from a leopard, serval, or civet cat to keep going. It was time for him to die, and Alan had kept the once mighty beast from starving to death.

The pygmies, Nestor, Lamia, Beli, Padi, and Azima, prepared to skin the lion. It would be a great prize for the pygmies' village. They built a frame and scraped the flesh from the hide, rolled, tied, and loaded it in their dugout. Later, in their village, it would be soaked in a tanning solution. Until then, it would be a stinking hide carried blissfully in the pygmies' boat.

After breakfast, the group struck camp and headed back downstream. The next goal was to find where the Lulu flowed in the Bunga. Then they would go upstream as far as they could, leave the dugouts and walk the rest of the way if the Lulu was unnavigable.

The Lulu split at one point with a tributary running into the Bunga and the other tributary flowing into the Aruwimi River. Max's goal was to stick with the boats, at least until they reached that split. Going back, they would be going downstream on the Lulu and back upstream when they hit the Bunga. They would know exactly where they would have to carry boats and how far. There would be five fewer people to accomplish the task. If a dugout had to be abandoned, the pygmies could put together a small expedition and retrieve it later as a prize.

Expansive bank areas along the Bunga were rare, but where they existed, wildlife was abundant and varied. A rare sighting of Bili chimpanzees occurred just before noon. Alan and Max were the only ones besides the pygmies who were aware they even existed. A group of these giant chimps were feeding on an unrecognizable carcass as the group drifted by. A male Bili, taller than an average man, stood up and watched as the boat passed. Carnivorous, huge, fearless and unstudied, the chimpanzees were an extraordinary sight, and Nick took advantage with his camera.

"They say they build nests on the ground and have no fear of leopards or lions. I can see why—they're monsters," Alan said.

"There are stories from the natives of a water-dwelling prehistoric monster that still lurks deep in the Congo jungle," Max said. The dugouts were so close that conversation was easy between all the boats.

"I'll tell you guys again, if Kong comes after me, just shoot me. Not my idea of a romantic evening, being molested by a giant ape." Jane was laughing but inside, she wondered if Kong was possible in this wild place.

"You two would make a cute couple," Nick said.

The expedition was making good time until about noon when they heard a series of rapids ahead. Seeing the river narrowing into fast chutes, they decided to pull to the bank. As they did, several crocodiles slid off to make room for the boats.

Alan and Yambo scouted ahead to assess the distance of the portage. They walked the riverbank until they were out of sight of the other travelers.

Lunch was prepared with fruit and some dried meat and bread. The natives built a quick fire and heated water for coffee and tea. Jane and Alan enjoyed the tea, an inescapable part of their life in England. The rest of the crew preferred coffee, and Africa didn't disappoint with their coffee's bold taste.

Max discussed the methods of carrying the heavy dugouts through the portage. All awaited Alan's news.

Alan reached back and pulled Yambo up a steep ridge of slippery rock and held his gun during the process.

"Slow here and watch your step," Alan said.

Once on the high escarpment, they could view the river for over a mile. The good news was that the river was clear and wide after the rough spot. The bad news was that they would have to haul dugouts and cargo over a small cliff to avoid a twenty-foot waterfall over sharp, protruding rocks. On level ground, four people could carry the dugouts easily. Getting the entire crew up a hill made of wet rocks would take six or eight people carrying a dugout on each trip. Up ahead in the river, Alan could clearly see a pod of hippos, and he worried more about that than the big hill. They walked back to the group and gave their report.

"We'll try with six people on a dugout and add more if needed. Once we get back in the water the big guns need to be ready. Hippos are fearless in often traveled waters and they'll have no problem killing us just because we're there, especially the bulls," Max said.

With lunch finished, the first boat manned by the pygmies and two bearers started up the cliff. One person acted as a guide, and two more held onto the sides for stability. Ten people labored to get it over the huge hill and balanced on the downward slope. Everybody slipped at one point, but someone was always there to catch them and stabilize the dugouts.

The pygmies came back to help with the other boat. They had the strength of people twice their size. All they had ever known was hard work, and they never complained or shirked from helping when they were needed. They made all four trips, even though they had tired a great deal by the last trip.

After a considerably long rest, the boats were off and running again, hugging the right shoreline to avoid the hippos.

The boats with the big guns acted as shields for the other two boats when they reached the pod of hippos. It appeared to be a herd, with maybe ten females and two or three large bulls. Each bull had his females nearby and was prepared to fight to the death to protect them. One bull was very aggressive and submerged about fifty yards from the boats; his huge, three-or-four-thousand-pound body pointed towards the boats, which were edging closer to the main hippo pod. Alan saw the disturbance on the surface of the river about fifteen yards off. Suddenly, the hippo rose from the churning water with his jaws open, exposing a monstrous pink mouth with huge foot-long, tusk-like teeth. He was headed for Max and Lutz. Alan fired the 4-bore at the side of the hippo's head, and the beast shook as though it had been hit with a two-ton rock. It sank for a while then floated back to the surface, motionless.

A quarter pound of lead tore through his brain and pulverized it as the force of the projectile shook water, mud, and debris from all sides of the gigantic water pig. The force of the recoil had turned Alan's boat completely around and came close to throwing him overboard. The noise and vibration sent all of the hippos to the far shore away from the expedition.

"Nice shot, Alan," Jane said.

The rest of the day was uneventful, except for the appearance of a few snakes that swam for the boats. A shotgun blast took care of them.

The boat portage had taken a lot of energy, so the travelers set up camp for the night earlier than normal. A couple of fires were started and the natives baked some bread in a covered metal oven and cooked a stew with dried meat and vegetables. During the night, the guards fired over a leopard's head on two different shifts. Monkeys and birds were extremely noisy in this area, possibly because they were deeper in the jungle.

The next morning, Turner and Jane sat at the water's edge with a couple of fishing rigs. Nestor, who told Jane many times that he was a great fisherman, had placed worms on the hooks.

"Turner, dear, do you see the heron fishing by the edge of the water?"

"Yes, why?"

"I bet you a dollar I catch a fish before he does."

"You have a bet, Jane." Turner looked at her beautiful blue eyes that seemed to splash around in pools of ocean colored water when she was excited. She had no make-up on her face, except for a small amount of lipstick that she used to keep her lips moist, but she was still the loveliest creature he had ever seen. He put his hand on her cheeks, pulled her to his mouth and kissed her.

"What was that all about?" Jane asked. Although surprised to have such a passionate kiss while fishing, she turned and kissed Turner again.

"I love fishing with you, but don't distract me. I have money on this gig," Jane said.

The Goliath heron, as identified by Nick, their resident birder, was a gorgeous specimen. It was covered with slate gray feathers except for its upper body. Jane described the bird's head and neck feathers as the result of a botched red dye job. Nick had called the color chestnut, but Turner and Jane said it was dull red. The feathers stood out in a frizzy, wild manner.

Suddenly, the heron froze. His body turned to stone; he stared down at the water without a hint of motion in his body. At the same instant, Jane felt something tug on her line. Across the river, there was a flash of red and the heron struck hard and deep. Jane jerked on her line hard causing a reaction from whatever was on the other end, which almost pulled her into the water. Turner grabbed her around her waist while she fought the fish.

The heron held a large green frog up in the air and worked it down his throat. The bird's neck could be seen pulsating and protruding as the frog futilely kicked his way down.

Jane placed the butt of the fishing rod on her stomach and began to reel the large fish towards her. Now the entire camp was standing behind her as she labored. Advice on how to fight the fish came freely. Jane had never caught a fish with this tenacity. As she reeled and gained ground, the fish would run and take the line away from her.

Then, without warning, the fish came out of the water and ripped its mighty tooth-laden mouth side to side in an effort to dislodge the tri-hook. The hook held, and Jane was now determined to land this creature. From behind her there were gasps and she heard the word "tigerfish." After another ten minutes of battle, the thirty-pound fish tired and was pulled on the bank, where the pygmies clubbed it and started to clean it. Jane stopped them, so she could get her picture with the fish. Turner held it in front of her, exposing the rows of lethal teeth while Nick took the snapshots with Jane's camera. Pictures secured, the natives started the cleaning process. Fried tigerfish was a welcome treat for breakfast for the entire expedition.

Across the river, the heron looked on at the excitement for a few minutes, then slowly walked the riverbank, eyes down, looking for any movement in the shallows.

Turner called the contest a tie but paid Jane the dollar anyway.

Chapter Twenty-five

Amcuda, King of the Kongo

Rectangular shields covered in buffalo hides were propped against wooden huts. Next to them were a strange collection of weapons used recently to repel the Belgian soldiers: spears, both close-in thrusting and throwing varieties, bows and arrows with pounded iron tips, and pump shotguns. Their personal weapons, such as knives, machetes, pistols, and a few swords captured in battle were always in a belt or holster. They rarely were separated from the warriors.

These were Manyema soldiers trained from childhood to take lives. Members of this tribe were fierce when Henry Stanley stomped through the Congo in the late 1800s, and they were equally as dangerous in 1933, except most no longer filed their teeth to a sharp point. Rarely were they caught eating human flesh in these modern times, but if faced with the opportunity, it was not a dinner call they shied away from.

Amcuda Mankala was the recently crowned king of this tribe which gave him the privilege of taking a body part from Sango, the deceased king, to use as a sacred artifact. Some in the past had used skulls, jawbones, and ribs. Amcuda choose Sango's large femur bone, as it would give him a holy club to take to battle. Amcuda had to win the vote of the crown council, prove his royal lineage and must prove his bravery in battle. He had passed all of the requirements including having his lineage traced to Ntinu Nimi a Lukeni, the first king of the Kongo crowned in 1380.

He was taller than most of the Manyemas, with ugly facial scars from past battles. One scar left the side of his mouth and curved up like a strange crooked smile locked in place. Dead, sinister eyes lay back in his skull like hidden black snakes ready to strike. When he did smile and flash his yellow teeth, on the bottom row were two canine teeth filed to sharp points exactly like his cannibal ancestors.

The new king had witnessed the slaughter of his men by the steamer *Lapsley II*. The losses were severe, yet a large number of native warriors survived. One of his men blew a kudu horn sounding a call for council with the king. Surrounded by his faithful chiefs, Amcuda spoke of ways to obtain magic to carry into battle against the Belgian military. Relaying and amplifying the story of the struggle against the steamer, he pointed out the hand-to-hand combat on the portside of the boat by the pygmies.

"They are not of this world. In their hearts lives much magic. If we eat their magic hearts, we will be able to defeat anyone. Some of you know of their villages. They are far away on the beginning of the Lulu River. We will encounter the white soldiers on the journey and kill as many as we can. Once we have our stomachs full of magic hearts, we will come back and kill all the white soldiers of Belgium land."

Amcuda's speech was met with frenzied yells and dances. Captured maps were laid inside the king's hut, creating a focal point for the military chiefs, and a finger pointing exercise, replete with yelling and cursing. A path was eventually agreed on. Two hundred miles of jungle, rivers and Belgian military strongholds lay in their path. Some said ten days, others said twenty days, but none was stupid enough to say it couldn't be done at all. After all, these were forest people—born and raised in the jungle. They would live off the fruit and plants in the jungle, catch fish in the rivers, and shoot animals to eat—humans if it came to that.

~~~~~~

The Lulu tributary drained a thick, tree-lined jungle with streams coming from both sides of the waterway. Many times the flow was muddy from recent rains; sometimes, it ran crystal clear over rocks, and the Lulu took on a gorgeous blue color. Often there were small waterfalls about knee- or waist-high and the boats would be lifted over them and pulled free by the crew. Rarely were there deep pools. When the deep areas were encountered, the water appeared emerald green. Other than the millions of insects trying to feed on them and wild carnivorous creatures waiting to attack them constantly, the jungle river was a wonderland. Orchids, beautiful flowers of probably unnamed species bloomed anywhere sun penetrated the jungle canopy, and palm trees with feathered fronds filled the banks of the waterway the entire trip. If there was a lost continent, they had surely found it. However, the slow pace of the trip caused Max to reconsider the use of the dugouts.

Camp was on the bank near an animal trail. Once the tents were pitched, they were at the edge of the water on one side and pushed up against the jungle on the other. The water was shallow, so there wasn't much fear of crocodiles or hippos. The trail width suggested smaller animals. Once a fire was built near where the trail met the water, Max suggested that they try one more day with the dugouts, then commence hiking, if travel on the river continued to be shallow and rocky. Guards were placed in the dugouts to watch the camp. A few animals came down the trail during the night and were turned back when the fire blocked their path to the water. Sleep was instant after grueling lifting of dugouts and only short periods of water suitable for floating the boats.

Early morning in the jungle provided an alarm clock of sounds difficult to sleep through.

"Jane, can you slip on top of me? Nobody will hear us with all the racket," Turner said.

She obliged and checked their dwindling supply of condoms.

"We may have to cut down to once a week very soon, my dear," Jane said.

"Just shoot me!"

"Now, now. We can adjust to other pleasurable pursuits."

"If it comes to that. How many days are we from the village? Does Nestor know?"

"Two to three days on this part of the Lulu and maybe five to seven days on her main channel going south," she said as she increased her thrust on top of a very happy husband. "If we have to walk and cut our way through the jungle—maybe twelve to fifteen days."

"Jesus!" Turner said in response to her answer and his orgasm.

The entire camp packed, consumed breakfast, and piled their sore bodies into the dugouts. The river was deeper, greener, and much more floatable immediately after launching. However, foliage flowed over the banks and above them. The banks of the river disappeared and water was visible under the trees and plants deep into the forest. It was now swamp and marshes. Crocodiles were numerous, but they made no attempt to attack the dugouts. The water was changing to a brown color as the river widened and became harder to paddle against.

"There are muddy banks ahead. Pull over there and rest for a while," Max said.

The expedition headed inland for bathroom breaks after the dugouts were banked. Crocodile tracks filled the entire bank.

"I will never get used to the smell of mud in the Congo," Jane said as she peed in some tall grass near the mud flats. Her hand reached for Turner to help her up as he zipped his pants.

"We should be thankful for any kind of bank, smelly or not, in the middle of this swamp," Turner said.

As they turned towards the dugouts, a twenty-foot-long Nile crocodile stood in their path with his mouth open. He could have enveloped both of them with one slamming motion with jaws as long as their bodies. Both pulled their pistols but knew they would do little harm against this prehistoric creature. It must have been in the tall grass. Maybe they had peed on it.

"Alan, I hope you or Yambo can get a bead on this thing!" Turner yelled. He didn't know Alan was in a full squat position far into the bush while Yambo stood guard for him.

Most of the group was still on a bathroom break. From the tall weeds on their right, a small black figure emerged. He held Alan's 4-bore Holland and Holland. Turner took it as the big croc stepped closer, mouth still open, teeth as long as knives. Pointing the elephant gun directly at the monster's brain, Turner cocked and fired the weapon. The ground shook from the blast of the giant gun and the airborne flop and landing of the great crocodile. He was dead, and nothing short of a bullet the size of a small artillery shell would have brought him down. Another cartridge subtracted from Alan's small arsenal.

"What the hell happened?" Alan said as he fastened his pants.

Then he saw a crocodile longer than any one of them had ever seen. He was measured, photographed, and eaten. Everyone stood on his back and hammed it up for Nick's camera; then he set a timer and joined the group picture. It measured twenty-two feet and eight inches. Finally, they cut meat from the tail, smoked and ate it and packed the rest away. They had wasted too much time, and they needed to get back on the river.

For two days, the river was perfect for going against the mild current, and they made good time. At night, they had to sleep in the dugouts because the banks were either non-existent or too muddy to set up tents. Most meals consisted of coffee and fried crocodile tail. The powdered meals were being saved for leaner times.

As they loaded out for the next day's trip, Nestor said, "Jane, we are close to the split in the Lulu River."

Her hopes of a pleasant day turned sour. Rapids and large waterfalls blocked their passage to the upper Lulu. Dense jungle presented itself on one side of the river, but they could see a large clearing on the other bank.

Jane's smile soon vanished when Max told her, "The area is a forest elephant's bia, where they take mud baths and drink salt and minerals from the waterholes."

Smaller than savanna elephants, forest elephants made up for it by being fearless and aggressive.

"Great. We have to hike through the jungle because of rapids and waterfalls. When we finally find an open space, it's owned by elephants," Jane lamented to the entire crew.

"Jane, please ask Nestor if the main channel of the Lulu is navigable," Max said.

She asked the head pygmy a series of questions and then gave a summary.

"He says the water is fast at the headwaters near the village, rapids are frequent, small waterfalls, very rocky, but smooth, deep, and very navigable a few miles before the Lulu splits. If we carry the dugout past the waterfall and rapids, we could go maybe ten or fifteen miles upstream on the main Lulu channel. After, mostly rapids that he has taken down but never back up. The pygmies always carry their boats back from there. We would most likely leave the dugouts for the trip back."

All the boats were back in the water. Early afternoon they heard the unmistakable sound of water blasting through channels, slapping rocks, and speeding ahead at breakneck speed. As they neared, they could see a waterfall in the distance—huge with mist and foam below it. To the right and left of the large falls was nothing but thick jungle.

Jane looked at Turner. "Yuk!"

Chapter Twenty-six

The Lulu River

Two truckloads of Belgian soldiers sat in open beds, waiting on a road crew to repair a washed-out section of the gravel road. Most were trying to sleep on their weapons; others were slumped over knapsacks. There wasn't a guard posted. Suddenly, more than a hundred Manyemas sprang from the jungle and sent spears and shotgun blasts into the mass of soldiers in both trucks. The government troops were seasoned soldiers after experiencing repeated armed conflict, so they recovered quickly, returning fire. Several BARs came to life and tore through the warring natives, forcing their retreat. Amcuda watched from a distance as the warriors assembled behind him. Six soldiers were killed and ten wounded. The Manyemas lost four, with eight wounded. A narrow victory for the natives. The soldiers were in hot pursuit, fanning out in the jungle with automatic weapons and leash-held dogs. If the dogs ran free, the Manyemas would kill and eat them. The natives were much too fast for the Belgian troops.

The Manyema warriors had been making at least fifteen miles a day, exceeding some of their earlier calculations. This run-in with the Belgian troops was the second and probably would not be the last. Every time they crossed a road, it was an opportunity for an ambush for both sides of the conflict. The wounded were treated and left to find their way back to the village or die in the jungle. There was no fear of the soldiers ever catching up to them in the heavy jungle.

Amcuda was determined, "We fought bravely today. Move out swiftly towards the villages of the little men. The Belgians will be waiting for us at the next road."

Eighty weary natives began to pick their way easily through the heavy foliage of vines and bushes, heading toward a river and village that most had never seen.

~~~~~~

So far, incredible luck had kept the expedition from hacking their way through dense jungle entanglements as they carried heavy waterlogged boats. However, as they looked upstream at a large waterfall in the distance they sensed their luck evaporate. The foliage was so thick that teams of four attacked the vines, shoots, small trees, and brush with machetes on alternating shifts. Twenty to thirty feet of trail was cleared in an hour on a good shift—unfortunately, these were rare. Insects attacked as though they felt they were under siege; compelled by tiny pissed-off brains, they found ways to fight back the destruction of their homes.

After each shift, Nick and Max made everyone bathe in the river with soap, and check for ticks, leeches, and insects. They took extra care to locate and dislodge insects preparing to hatch their young in the flesh of humans. Jane stripped down and performed the monkey-like ritual of picking insects from Turner's body, and he in turn checked her, noting places for Nick to examine.

Seeing Jane bathe naked wasn't a new experience for the expedition as she took baths often. If there had ever been a natural-born nudist she was the prototype. Occasionally, the pygmies would get erections that they tried to conceal, and at night, they could be heard masturbating. It wasn't so much Jane they were attracted to, it was the idea of a female being near, and their wives and girlfriends were not. Besides, the pygmies preferred women with great patches of hair covering their genitals and even growing on their chest.

Before every bather got dressed, Nick inspected them and applied medicine to insect bites. If he suspected a burrowing, egg-laying demon had gone to work on anyone, he would coat the area with alcohol and probe around for egg deposits. He was amazed at how fast the insects completed this task even after lapping up insect repellent like it was fine wine. He bottled many insects to be taken to Amsterdam for further study. Although the resident doctor, Nick also assumed the roles of biologist, geologist, naturalist, botanist, and any other scientific expertise not covered by the rest of the expedition.

"Turner, you know Jane is the only person on this expedition that I really enjoy checking for insects," Nick said with a lecherous smile. Jane smiled but lightly slapped Nick on the back of his head, as he probed an area near her navel.

"Do what you need to do, Nick, but please don't be a pervert!" Turner wasn't jealous of Nick but got irritated if he seemed to linger too long inspecting Jane's private areas.

"It's tough being a doctor and pretending I don't enjoy looking at beautiful female bodies. You would think it would be a benefit for a physician; instead, we have to act as though we're inspecting a homely old hag with a great deal of dispassionate indifference. So, I have to pretend Jane isn't one of the most beautiful creatures on earth. As you see, Turner, the benefits of being a doctor have to remain a secret," Nick said laughing. "Even you, whom I consider a good friend, will get testy if I make light of your wife's insect bite inspections. Out here, in the middle of the Congo jungle, I must remember to be a professional. This will be in my notes for medical school."

He would then launch into stories about Zoe, how much he missed her, and the great life they were planning in Amsterdam. Jane reconstituted his desire for female contact and incited the desire in everyone else on the mission.

The trail construction took three days of exhausting work. The first dugout was carried up the trail and down to the placid waters above the waterfall on the fourth day. What they had created was an eight-foot-wide trail over a thousand feet long. They felt a satisfaction not unlike the folks that dug the Panama Canal. Once the boats were resting on the banks, loaded with supplies, the entire crew kept staring at the magnificent path they cut through the tropical forest, knowing full well the jungle would erase the wound in a matter of weeks.

They could see a stunning gravel bank ahead. It was flat, with a small, clear steam running through the small river stones. Sunlight had broken through a huge hole in the jungle canopy, affording an unprecedented burst of exotic flowers.

The water color in the Lulu River was an inviting bluish green. Rainbow-inspired flowers from the rainforest cascaded down on top of the green plants like cake icing. Hummingbirds, parrots, and butterflies crowded the air. The smells, colors, and gorgeous setting motivated Nick to break out his camera equipment. Jane dug her new camera from her knapsack as well. The area was the Garden of Eden, the Hanging Gardens of Babylon, heaven on earth—untouched, unexplored, and without question, the most beautiful place the crew had ever seen or might ever see.

Nestor explained to Jane that the Lulu River split would be only one full day's travel from this spot. She passed along the information to Alan, Lutz, and Max. She also informed them she wouldn't be going with them since she and Turner were going to stay in this lovely spot forever, raise children, and live off the land. It was good for a laugh, yet was certainly tempting.

A red river pig with several large piglets walked out from the edge of the foliage and scurried back into the forest. However, two of the sow's fat young pigs didn't join her. Picked off by Yambo's BAR, they spun on a spit over an open fire. The tender pork, wild berries, and biscuits made one of the best meals of the journey. Tomorrow, they would see the river leading to the natives' village. They all wondered how many of the pygmies would still be alive.

~~~~~~

Amcuda and his men had made it to the Lulu River with only forty men. The two battles they had while crossing the roads had proven to be deadly as they were forced into open country, exposing them to enemy fire. Most were shot in the back while running away. Taking advantage of some unarmed villagers along the river, the warriors had stolen dugouts and paddled hard against the current to a campsite on a large, sloping bank deep in the jungle. Feeling safe, they bedded down for two days to rest and lick their wounds.

The Belgian troops reaped the superior advantage of surprise and overwhelming manpower when they struck early one morning before daylight from government boats. Some warriors were killed, but most surrendered and were brought back for trial. The warrior king and ten of his subjects escaped into the jungle. A couple of days later, wandering in and out of the undergrowth, they found another village with dugouts. Most of the men were on hunting trips, leaving women, children, and elderly men. The Manyemas raped the women, killed anyone who interfered, and left with two large dugouts.

After three days, they were only a short distance from the tributary of the Lulu River, which ran all the way to the Bunga. Again, they camped in order to rest. This time, the Belgians would not come since they had reduced Amcuda's forces to a small ragtag element of wounded and exhausted warriors. The Belgians had posted a $1,000 bounty for the capture of Amcuda. They would sit back and wait for greed to do its work.

~~~~~~

Late afternoon the next day, the forest seemed to be pushed back from the river as it expanded and began to create islands of gravel and yellow sand. The main river channels were joined by smaller inlets of blue water cutting through large, smooth rocks worn by thousands of years of rolling, churning, and grinding under the power of the fast water. The lead boat picked a river channel which had formed canyon walls where the water sped through, giving the impression of a dark, emerald tunnel waiting to envelop the explorers.

Chapter Twenty-seven

Battle on the River

Nestor and his men often paddled so hard they lost sight of the rest of the Simson-Pygmy Rescue Mission crew. Home was nearby, and they had been away for many months. Even though they dreaded what they might find, they wondered—who had died? Who was sick? What about wives, children, brothers, sisters, and parents. Would their families be there to greet them, or would they find their graves?

This part of the journey would still take almost a week. They were going upstream for a few miles, then on foot for fifty or sixty miles. True, the natives knew all the trails and shortcuts, but distance is still distance, and not something to be overcome easily.

All the good, deep water was used up on the first day. They camped where the river turned to cataracts. The hike would resume the next day. Nestor gave descriptions of the trails ahead to Jane, and she relayed the information to Max. The deep jungle trails were created for pygmies, and some had little height to them. Being tall, Alan and Turner were not pleased.

"I can see us duck-walking for fifty miles. We'll be permanently bent in half afterwards," Alan said.

"We'll hack away at overhead stuff, but most of the trail will be already be there," Turner said.

"Hope so," Alan said. "But sometimes deep jungle trails are just the roots of huge trees since the rays of the sun don't penetrate and allow for plants to grow in the darkness below the canopy. I don't know if tripping over giant tree roots is any better than hacking through thick undergrowth."

They set up tents on the riverbank in an area nestled behind a tall, forested hill along the river above where the rapids began. The topography was changing to a series of foothills, with mountains forming a backdrop to the north. According to Nestor, the rapids continued within a couple miles of his village. The pygmies were in multiple villages and interspersed between them were Lese natives. The Lese were farmers and they had formed a relationship based on trade with the pygmies, who were primarily hunters. Nestor said in a few miles they would begin to see villages on both sides of the river. In many areas, it was possible to walk across the river but only after passing the rapids.

"There's something Nestor told me that I've never shared with anyone," Jane began while everyone sat around the fire.

"Way up on the mountainous slopes beyond their villages is a troop of gorillas. For the most part the pygmies have found peace with them. They don't hunt them for fear of the giant silverback that guards the others. Once, a baby gorilla came into the village. A female pygmy carried the baby up the mountain and held it until she saw a female gorilla approach. She put the baby down and backed away. The young gorilla ran to the mother and was scooped up, carried away, and never returned. Directly behind the female was the silverback patriarch. He beat his chest, did a mock charge, then retreated to the mountain slopes. Maybe it was his way of saying thank you." Jane wove the tale as a Boy Scout would tell a campfire ghost story.

"Wow, I hope we get to see them," Nick said.

"I doubt it," Turner said. "But right now, we have work to do. I packed saws, hammers, and nails so we could build outhouses for them. According to Doctor Nick here, their open latrines are a source of sickness for the tribes."

"Did you pack shovels and lime?" asked Max.

"Camp shovels and a small amount of lime. They will have to use sand or dirt when it runs out. We'll supply some soap, too, until it runs out," Nick said.

"Haven't they survived for thousands of years without these conveniences?" Lutz asked.

"They have, and they will continue to survive without them. Each year, they lose a certain number of villagers to sickness. Maybe they have for thousands of years. All these deaths are acceptable to them. But, throw in smallpox and other white man diseases, and the balance tips. Losses are more than gains. If we can tip it in their favor for a while with sanitation and vaccines, they may survive as a tribe a little longer," Nick said.

"Enough campfire fun," said Max. "We need guards posted tonight as usual. Two by the campfire. Lutz and I are going to walk up the big hill for a look around." He didn't really have a reason for the trek up the hill, except for being presented with an observation post for the first time on the mission.

As everyone but the guards entered their tents, the two leaders scaled the steep, rocky hill behind the campsite. Since the hill was in front of the camp area, it sheltered it from view downriver. Once on the hill, the two older men took a moment to catch their breath and began to adjust to the dark. It was a clear, star-filled night. They watched the twinkling sky and marveled at the clarity and intensity of the celestial fanfare.

Below the skyline, the two men noticed, at almost the same time, a twinkle out of place. A mile or so away, at the edge of the river was a campfire. It was unmistakable. Using his field glasses, Max could barely make out two dugouts by the river. Neither felt good about the camp. Max sent Lutz down to get Alan, Nestor, and Jane. Turner stayed at the camp on guard duty.

Max passed his binoculars over to Alan, then to Nestor and Jane. Nestor assured them that they were not natives from his tribe and no one lived on the river for almost fifty miles in that direction. Everyone's guess was that it was the Manyemas. Since the expedition's campfire was hidden from view of the other natives, they felt they weren't detected. Everyone was called to a fireside war council.

"If they are Manyemas, why are they here?" Max asked.

Jane relayed the question to Nestor, who informed her that many tribes believed the pygmies were magical and could kill witches and cast spells. He also said some tribes believed it was good luck and might allow magic properties to kill pygmies and eat them.

"Holy shit! We can't let that happen," Nick exclaimed.

"I suggest we set up a defense and attack them when they have to pull over for the rapids. We have three good, long-range guns and several close-in combat weapons. The boats should be pulled into the underbrush; otherwise we will be running from them in the jungle. We'll have backpacks and supplies—they will carry only weapons. We can't outrun them, even if we started tonight. It's best if we stand and fight," Alan said. His experience was appreciated as he had been a hero in WWI and had more military knowledge than anyone in the crew.

"How does everyone feel about this?" asked Max.

Hands went up. All agreed. Nestor suggested sending a runner to the village for help, but it was too far. No one slept much. The pygmies sought out trees hanging over the river, deep brush, and ambush cover. Rifles were positioned on the rocky hill. The fire was extinguished, so there wouldn't be any smoke in the morning. They decided that any animals that came around would be frightened away with noiseless spears, arrows, and rocks.

The natives in the last dugout turned it on its side and hid it in the jungle next to the river. It made a great bunker to fire from. Jane, Turner, and Nick also took positions behind the dugout. Everyone waited for the morning sun to sweep the Manyemas into their boats and into a battle they could not win.

~~~~~~

The Manyemas' fire had served them well through the night. A leopard came close but backed off at the sight of the big blazing fire. An evening meal of fresh fish wrapped in plantain leaves had been cooked on the coals. As the sun came up, they loaded what few supplies they had on the two boats and paddled upstream.

As they neared the tall hill and assessed the rapids, Amcuda smelled a faint scent of smoke in the air. He sniffed himself to see if the fire from last night had clung to his blanket. It had no smell of smoke. The king raked his eyes across the hill and saw the glint of metal shining from behind a rock.

"Turn around! It's a trap!" he yelled in Bantu. Immediately, gunfire burst from the hill and the adjacent forest. His men started firing their shotguns at the hill, the jungle, and into the trees where numerous arrows showered down on them. Most got off a few rounds before they were killed. Amcuda was one of the first hit, once in his upper left arm, and another bullet grazed his skull and took off most of his right ear. He fell into the water, pulled down by the weight of his shotgun and a heavy bone in his front belt.

As he tumbled and slammed on rocks, he was caught in the swift current and pushed to the far shore where tropical foliage hung off the river. Barely conscious, floating in a blue haze, he surfaced under an overhanging fern. He tore a piece of his clothing and used it as a compress for his arm. He wrapped another large section of cloth around his head. He would live, but first he had to escape.

Back at the battle scene, one of the Manyemas washed ashore, mortally wounded. Jane and Moe held him before he died. He spoke Bantu. Both asked him about his chief.

Coughing and in pain from numerous bullet wounds, he spoke. "My leader is Amcuda, King of the Manyemas. We are the last of warriors who fought the steamboat and against the Belgian troops." He then spotted Nestor standing nearby. "Please have the pygmy touch my forehead before I die." Nestor obliged. The warrior passed away silently with a smile. Nestor closed his dead eyes.

The expedition was not without casualties. Lutz had caught a buckshot pellet in his neck, barely missing an artery. Curly had also been hit with a pellet to his chest. A rib kept it from entering his lung. Two of the pygmies, Lamia and Azima had pellets in their legs from being shot while in the trees. Nick treated them but chose to wait until they were in camp to operate since there would be some recovery time. He believed that with bandages and some pain medication, they could make the trip.

They decided to burn the Manyemas' bodies on a huge stack of wood. The dead, stacked crisscross, slowly turned to ashes after the mighty flames engulfed their bodies. They realized that King Amcuda was not on the pile. The pygmies had found where he had crawled up the opposite bank, left a blood trail, and disappeared into the jungle. No one wanted to see him again.

Bandaged, patched, and doped-up, the expedition headed out with their packs in the early afternoon, anxious to make up for time lost fighting with the Manyemas. The native porters carried the heavy supplies, but everyone felt the strain. This was the first time boats were abandoned, and it felt strange to be without them. Max was pleased they had gone this far by water—much farther than he anticipated.

"Jane, how does your pack feel?" Turner asked.

"Like I'm carrying you on my back."

"You going to be able to carry it?"

"Yes, but I'll require a massage tonight—know where I can get one?"

"I believe Nestor's village has a full spa—pedicures—the whole works. However, we will have to erect the outhouse first," Turner said.

"You'll open up the Turner-Simpson Spa in our tent. Payment will be bartered with sexual favors," Jane laughed.

"Sounds like a brothel to me," Nick chimed in.

"Wow! That makes it exciting!" Turner said.

Nestor backed off the lead to drop back and talk to Jane.

"Jane, we will have elephants ahead. Maybe two—three hours ahead. There is a mud hole across the river, but if the big bulls see us they might charge. Tell everyone to be ready," Nestor said and walked back next to the other pygmies.

Jane walked to the side of the trail and waited for Max to catch up and relayed the news.

"The three big guns need to be ready, and Yambo can back us up with the BAR. I'm hoping we can get everyone by without disturbing them. The four guns can act as shields, while everyone walks through," Max said.

After about five miles on the jungle path that paralleled the river, they could hear bellowing in the distance. Nestor sent Padi ahead to scout the area. He came back to report two large males were crowding the right bank. One was standing on their path. He repeated this to

Jane who translated to the others.

"Can we go inland and avoid them?" asked Nick.

"Thousand-foot cliff to our right and river to the left. We have wounded people and need to get to the village. A big climb would really set us back. We'll try a warning shot to stampede them. If that doesn't work—well, Alan can take the big fellow out," Max said.

Jane remembered the first time the little man got up at dinner in the comfort house and could barely see over the back of his chair. She set him straight on Henry Stanley but now had a profound respect for the little man. He had proven himself to be courageous and an excellent leader. She considered him and Alan to be father figures for her.

A few hours later, the expedition neared the area of the herd of elephants. Yambo walked to the front and fired five rounds from the BAR. All the big beasts ran into the jungle across the river except for the large bull directly on the trail. He seemed to be in musk, highly irritated, and fearless. He charged the group, then stopped and bellowed.

"I need to hit him on the side of his skull to make sure it penetrates," Alan said.

Jane heard his request, dropped her pack, and ran to the water's edge in front of the agitated elephant. He charged her, turning his body broadside in front of Alan.

"Goddamn it, Jane! You're crazy!" Turner yelled as she dove into the river at the instant Alan pulled the trigger and placed a 4-bore round a few inches right of the elephant's eye, dropping him into the water, only a few feet from Jane.

"You've got to stop the Jungle Jane shit before you get killed," Turner said as he pulled her from the water and helped her to shore.

"I'm sorry, but it just seemed to be the thing to do."

"What if he had missed?" her husband asked.

"Max, Lutz, and Yambo had guns ready. If it had charged us directly, a lot of people would have died if the shot had bounced off the front skull. I just reacted."

"Promise me you will not do anything like that again, my dear."

"Okay—okay. Don't be mad at Jane. Jane much fun. Jane will love you long time."

"Your comic routine only helps a little," Turner said, smiling.

"Thanks for turning the elephant. If I had missed, do you think you could have out-swum the old boy?" Alan asked.

"I had confidence that if anyone in Africa could make that shot, it would be you, Alan."

"Let's make more time on the trail before dark," Max said.

"Nestor said our first village will be in three days. It isn't a pygmy village but a settlement of Lese natives. They are mainly farmers who trade sweet potatoes and other vegetables with the pygmies for meat," Jane said.

Jane changed into dry clothes standing on the trail while Alan stood on top of the dead elephant for a picture. Nick eventually got everyone to stand on the huge creature. The natives cut off some meat for dinner later.

In a matter of minutes, they were back on the trail. A few hours later, everyone was ready for rest. Nick treated wounds, changed dressings, and gave pain medication.

Everyone enjoyed the surprisingly tasty elephant meat. The carnivores and scavengers would also enjoy a feast on this night. Insects and worms would work the giant carcass down to the skeleton. The jungle creatures would take everything except the bones and tusks, which the tribes could take later and use for trade.

Later, Turner was overheard in the couple's tent.

"Jane needs to make Tarzan happy. Tarzan very lonely."

Chapter Twenty-eight

Villages

The next few days seemed to duplicate themselves, offering discomfort and miserable jungle conditions over and over. Ghostly early morning mist and fog, sticky oppressive heat at midday, hard, stinging rain in the afternoon, followed by attacks of blood-starved, dive-bombing insects. Camp was squared away with the smokiest fire possible to repel insects. Cooking pots filled with food that had either been speared, caught in the river by fishing line, or shot in the jungle or at the water's edge, hung above the fire.

It was time for the daily body checks. "Nick, if you don't mind, Jane and I will help you with the body checks," Turner said. "You get undressed first, and then Jane will have her way with you."

Nick laughed and handed Jane his medical journal and began to undress. Turner and Jane made notes on all his insect bites, cuts, and blisters. Turner applied medicine where it was needed, then took the journal from Jane, and she undressed for her inspection. Turner made notes and provided necessary treatments. The process was repeated as he removed his clothes.

"Okay, I'm going to let you guys record the journal today on everyone. If you see infections call me over." Nick walked through camp and asked everyone to line up for the daily inspections. This was the signal for everyone to bathe in the river and then line up. This had been done almost every day on this expedition, and it had undoubtedly kept the entire crew much healthier because of it.

Lutz asked to be excused from the inspection because he wasn't feeling well. Nick patted Lutz gently on his back and spoke to him.

"Lutz, as soon as we get to Nestor's village I will set up a field hospital and take that shotgun pellet out of your neck."

"My neck hurts but also I feel lethargic—got no energy and feel tired and sleepy all the time. Is that from the lead pellet?" Lutz asked.

"Maybe, but there might be something else going on. I'll try to run some blood tests with the limited equipment I have with me."

Nick suspected what was causing the problem but would not mention it to anyone. Lutz wasn't a large man, and he was in his late fifties, with a slender build. Nick had noticed he was losing weight and his skin was pale. He would watch Lutz closely.

While supervised by Nick, Turner and Jane learned a great deal about tropical medicine. On a daily basis, the team would see more tropical diseases, insect bites, and jungle infections that most mainland doctors would encounter in a lifetime.

"Here's your journal back," Jane said. The book contained medical notes on almost every detail of everyone on the mission.

"I noticed you even recorded my periods on this trip. What in the world is that about?" Jane asked.

"As long as they're timely, you're healthy. For a doctor, it's just a signpost. If you start spotting or having irregular periods, then it deviates from normal. It gets my attention," Nick explained.

"For God's sake, I don't want to get your attention!" Jane said, laughing.

Nick blushed, then changed the subject and asked Jane to bring Nestor over so they could come up with a plan to work the villages efficiently.

Nestor returned with Jane and Turner. Using Jane to translate, Nick asked, "Nestor, would you draw the locations of the villages we are about to encounter? I understand some of the villages are another tribe called the Lese, and I want to have those identified." Nick had heard about the other tribe from Jane's discussions with the pygmies.

Nick opened a page near the end of his medical journal and handed Nestor a pencil. He held the writing instrument awkwardly and carefully traced out the river, tapering down to a small stream. He then drew circles for the villages on both sides of the river.

"That's great, Nestor!" Nick said and took the pencil and asked about each village circle.

"Is this one a pygmy village or the Lese?" Nick asked and made notes next to each. He already knew that the Lese were farming natives that had a trading arrangement with the pygmies.

"How many natives in this village?" Nick would ask about all the villages. He was formulating a plan in his mind on how he would treat each one according to size. The third village they would visit was the largest and the home of the five pygmies who were a part of the expedition. He would have his field hospital constructed there. He drew plans for it and tore the page from his journal and gave it to Max and Alan to construct once they were in the village.

Mosquito nets were mandatory for everyone at night, and they were cut and stuffed under hats in the day time. In the mornings, Nick could be seen collecting insects that had become lodged in the nets for his growing collection. So far, thanks to either his demanding prophylactic efforts, or the immunizations given to everyone before and during the trip, not a single case of malaria had occurred. But Nick was painfully aware that the sickness might take hold even after the expedition had ended.

After the crew packed up, they walked on a well-worn trail near the river for several hours. It was so much easier traveling on an existing path, so they made good time.

"Wow! Can you guys smell that?" asked Jane.

The foul smell was the first signal they were near the Lese village. It was just where Nestor had placed it on the map. Nestor led the way into their village of about thirty tribespeople. None appeared to have smallpox now, but the village had lost about ten people in the last few months to the disease. Nestor got permission to have the village vaccinated for smallpox by calling it white man's magic. He showed them the magic scar on his arm, which the other crew members also displayed. They would do this many times in the next few days. Nick completed his vaccinations and treatment of other conditions he found among the villagers. He had a question concerning the pygmies in the village.

"Nestor, why are there pygmy women here?" Nick asked.

Nestor explained, "Pygmy women have lots of hair on their chest and between their legs. Lese men like women to be hairy. Many marry our women." Nestor pounded on his chest and pointed to a pygmy woman who had a large amount of hair growing on her sternum and an abundance of pubic hair. Jane smiled, remembering her first encounter with the pygmies and how inquisitive they were about her lack of chest hair.

They set up camp next to this village. The crew spent time building some crude latrines. They were still a full day from Nestor's village, so they would spend the night and leave early the next morning.

Late the next day, the scent of the first pygmy villages burned their nostrils. It wasn't the village of Nestor or the five pygmies, but they had relatives there. Nestor relayed the news of sickness caused by the bad witches.

He reported to Nick that more than half the villagers had died but none were still sick. Some of the villages on the other side of the river still had the sickness.

Nestor convinced the pygmies to get the vaccine by again showing his scar and the white people's scars. Nick did his job and made notes on some conditions that needed follow-up. He was anxious to get to Nestor's village, so he didn't waste any time and hurried the crew to get back on the trail.

A few hours later, they arrived at the village of the expedition's five pygmies. They had finally made it. These little African men had brought help for their village 3,000 miles away by following the instructions of their village elders—many of whom were now dead. The odds of finding someone at the ocean's edge who would help a pygmy tribe in an unexplored part of the Congo wasn't calculable, but here was a young doctor—a great doctor—who was persuaded by a fourteen-year-old girl to risk his life in the jungle to help some natives.

Nestor and the other pygmies who were sent on the trip were young. None of them, except for Padi, had taken wives and had children. That was the very reason the elders sent all teenagers on the trip. Nestor was the oldest at eighteen. He was seventeen when he left the village. Their village had been hit especially hard on two occasions and still had active cases. Jane saw the apprehension on the faces of her diminutive friends.

"Nestor, are any of your family members still alive?" Jane asked.

Before he could answer, there were screams in the village as they realized their young men had come home.

"My brother Nestor!" yelled a young boy who ran and jumped in Nestor's arms.

"Our mother is dead!" he cried as he hugged Nestor. Tears streamed down both their faces.

Fires were burning in the village, some inside huts, which sent choking smoke through the thatched roofs and pouring from the front entrances. Everyone understood it was their way of disinfecting the huts without burning them to the ground.

The other four pygmies ran to seek relatives and friends. Padi found that his wife had survived but had become sick within the last two days with symptoms of smallpox. It appeared to Nick that this secondary outbreak had just happened within the last week.

"Nestor, would you please have the village assemble as a group and we'll explain why we're here," Jane said. About fifty villagers walked to where Nestor and the other pygmies were standing. Some were sick and needed help standing. Jane spoke to them, translating Nick's words.

"Everyone in the village must get a vaccination against this disease that we call smallpox. Some of you say it was caused by bad witches. You will not get the disease once you have this scar." Almost as if they had rehearsed, the members of the expedition showed their scars.

"Some of you are already sick and it will help you too. Please let the sickest people get their vaccination first." With Turner and Jane assisting, they started the process and gave Padi's wife the first treatment. Nick had previously instructed Alan, Max, and the bearers on the type of field hospital he wanted constructed, so they began work on it as he prepared the doses for the tribe.

Max, Alan, and the porters began to construct a high, wooden bed so Nick could operate. They used a tarp for a roof, which was held up by long poles and shorter poles for the sides with guide ropes. Mosquito netting covered the sides with a cut made for a door. It looked like a field hospital and was large enough for several cots or beds. The dirt floor was a source for bacteria and had no drainage properties. Nick asked the natives who were healthy to heat sand to rid it of bugs and bacteria and spread it on the floor of the structure.

"Jane and Turner, you have watched me give the smallpox vaccination so many times, I know you can do it now," Nick said and turned the job over to them, while he helped to get the operating table ready for Lutz.

"Turner, can you believe we're giving vaccine to pygmies in Africa, and people in the United States haven't received it yet?" Jane said as the two took turns scraping the skin and applying the smallpox liquid.

When the field hospital was completed, the expedition began working on latrines. After that, it was ten chairs, and six more cot frames. Many of these designs had been worked on at each stop on the trip.

Nestor helped Jane and Turner enter the information for each native in Nick's journal.

"How old is the next one, Nestor?" Jane would ask Nestor. He would guess at their age, and it would be entered.

Lutz was first to try the hospital bed, which now featured some blankets and a cloth sheet that came from a supply of trade items the porters had carried in. He still had a shotgun pellet lodged at the back of his neck, narrowly missing critical arteries. He also had a general overall aching fever and was always sleepy. Nick had cleaned and applied a crude antibiotic on the entry wound each day, but Lutz's condition had not improved.

A blood infection in this place might not be treatable. Just in case, Nick asked for blood types from all except the natives. Turner, Jane, and Alan were type O, Lutz was AB, and Max was B. Nick was also AB. Everyone had a RH positive status. If the natives needed a blood transfusion, Nick had a method of typing blood by mixing some of their blood with known blood types to see if there was a reaction. His limited power microscope would be pushed to the limit.

"Can someone fix me a wash basin?" Nick asked when he was ready to operate on Lutz.

A large metal tub was placed on a newly constructed table next to the operating table. It was filled with water and latex gloves, powder, and soap were laid by it. The injection of an analgesia deadened the site and alcohol-soaked instruments appeared on his round table top now covered with clean cloth fabric. After making his incision, he took the forceps and pulled out two lead pellets. They clattered when it dropped them into a small metal bowl. The wound was cleaned, and a form of experimental penicillin was applied. Nick tied stitches and placed a small rubber hose to drain the infected area.

"Do you feel like moving to a cot?" Turner asked.

"Yes, I believe I could sleep for a bit," Lutz said. Turner helped him from the high table to a lower cot.

A shot of morphine knocked him out for a while. Next in line were Lamia and Azima who had easily-removable pellets in their legs. Nick was careful to clean the wounds and place the antibiotic on the areas. Dr. Nick Dubois was now caught up on his patients for a while and laid down for a nap on one of the cots. The noise of sawing and hammering as the crew built things in the village unsuccessfully competed with his world-class snoring.

Turner and Jane were sitting in one of the newly built chairs when a middle-aged villager came to Nestor to tell him an elderly villager had died. Turner put his journal aside. Nestor agreed to go with Jane to help with the strange burial custom.

He told Jane what would occur. "A grave will be dug using the new shovels brought by the expedition, and the old lady will be placed in a shallow grave and covered with dirt. A fire will be built on top of the grave and it will be kept burning for one month. Afterwards, they will dig the person up and smoke the body until it's preserved. Then it will be wrapped in cloth and stood up in the family's hut. Sometimes, it will be there for years until it deteriorates and then is incinerated."

"Can you show me some of the wrapped bodies in huts?" Jane asked. He said he would after the woman was buried.

"What's the ruckus?" Nick said when he woke from his nap.

Jane explained the burial rituals about to take place. Nick wanted to see the body and obtained permission. He reported that she had died of complications of smallpox and old age. Smallpox had a thirty to forty percent mortality rate among otherwise healthy adults. In this case, it had been deadly for an elderly person.

Nick, Turner, and Jane observed the burial, as did the rest of the expedition who were cutting timber for making latrines. After the hole was filled with dirt and the fire built on top of the grave, Nestor led the group to a large hut, owned by an older pygmy couple and their grown children.

"Is this person a chief?" Jane asked.

"Pygmies don't have chiefs—only elders," Nestor said in his language. "Lese have chiefs."

Nestor obtained permission to go inside. Since the natives always built their huts above the ground because of the torrential rains, first they had to step up about a foot. They crawled in on their knees to clear the top of the door. It smelled of dirt, body odor, and smoke. They smoked the huts often to clear out bugs, snakes and other creatures. Between the sleeping areas, one for the men and another for the women, were two mummified bodies standing upright and leaning against the walls of the hut. They were wrapped in cloth except for the faces which appeared shrunken and shriveled. Jane covered her mouth when she saw the macabre spectacle. Nick asked questions. Jane translated for a while and then asked if she could leave. They all headed to the hospital tent to check on Lutz. He was coming to after the morphine shot had knocked him out but wasn't coherent.

Everyone decided they would put their sleeping bags and equipment inside the tent and sleep there. It was like a big bunkhouse. Nick studied Nestor's drawing and planned how to work the villages for vaccinations the next few days.

"I think what I'll do is work the natives on this side of the river first. That may take a few days since we need to build latrines. Then we will hike to the farthest Lese village and work our way back," Nick said. There were no objections.

Just before dark, two pygmy hunting parties came into the village.

One had a small forest antelope and the others had a large, red river hog. Nick took care of the vaccine for the hunters, and the natives began to cook a feast for the entire village and the crew. A well-earned meal, and it would give them the energy to call on a lot of villages in the next few days.

Chapter Twenty-nine

Sickness

The next morning, Jane sat in a chair near one of the fires drinking coffee with Nestor. He reported on the grim numbers of his friends and relatives affected by the sickness. Nick poured himself a cup of coffee and joined them.

"Each of the five pygmies have lost family members. Four have lost at least one parent. Most of our expedition pygmies have lost aunts, uncles, cousins, sisters, and brothers. Some, like Padi's wife, are still sick. We would have lost many more if you had not come here."

"I wish I had good news on Lutz," Nick said. "He has more wrong with him than the bullet wound. I took blood and looked under my microscope. He has a case of Trypanosomiasis from a tsetse fly bite. I have drugs to treat the first stage of African sleeping sickness, but if he progresses to the second stage, he'll need to get treatment back in Germany. Sometimes it is many years before the second stage kicks in. They're always working on new drugs, so maybe he'll find one a little more surefire than the ones we have now."

"Do you think he's still at risk for blood poisoning?" Jane asked.

"Yes. If I had a good injectable antibiotic, it would probably save him. If he gets a blood disorder coupled with the Trypanosomiasis— well, he might not make it at his age."

"We need to go across the river and start working the villages. Maybe you, Turner, Nestor, Alan, and I can go. We can leave Max to keep Lutz company," Jane said.

"Sounds good. We'll leave after breakfast, but we need to get back as soon as possible for Lutz. Maybe spend one night out and be back late tomorrow. I have enough vaccine for about one hundred doses—should be enough. We may not get all the latrines built but we are leaving saws, hammers, and nails for Nestor's people to build them for all the villages," Nick said.

After the morning meal of biscuits and smoked meat from the feast the night before, the group slung their packs over their shoulders, and Nestor took the lead with Alan as rear guard. They were in the next pygmy village in an hour, treated the sickest first, and vaccinated the rest. Nestor had organized a work crew to stay behind and build latrines and then move on to the next village. Dugouts awaited them after they worked the settlement and took them to the farthest Lese village to begin work there. Each Lese Village had a chief who had to make the decision for vaccination. Nestor convinced him after considerable arguing.

They showed their scars at each village. As expected, there were more active cases on that side of the river. After a day and a half, they had finished their work and headed back to Nestor's village. When their dugout pulled up on the shore, everyone could tell something was wrong. No one meeting them was smiling.

They were greeted with the news that Lutz had died during the night. Max had been in the tent with him, and there was no sign of distress. Max awoke and found him unresponsive. Nick examined the body and declared that the combination of infection and the African sleeping sickness had defeated his fifty-eight-year-old body. Most likely it had caused a heart attack.

Jane thought about her verbal attack on his support for Hitler. She wouldn't take back anything she had said, but he had been a kind and helpful man on the trip and never again let his beliefs in German supremacy surface—not once. Turner and Nick consoled her as she cried.

"I wish there was something else I could have done for him," Nick said.

The burial was Christian style. There wasn't a fire placed on his grave, there wasn't a smoking that took place, just a grave with a cross and a few kind words spoken over the site. Jane had picked a few flowers and laid them on the grave with loving care.

Jane felt the pygmies were disappointed by such a bland and final ceremony. White people were a strange lot to them and "cared very little about their friend" was the sentiment relayed by Nestor later.

The next day, Lutz's personal effects were packed for the return trip and would be forwarded to his relatives in Germany. Max suggested that he could personally deliver them on his next trip home. The group was not ready to leave yet as they had more latrines to build. Medical treatment was ongoing, not only for smallpox, but many other disorders that Nick encountered for the first time in his medical career.

Even though there was much to do, a calm and restful atmosphere settled in for the expedition. They found themselves enjoying village life by playing cards at night, laughing, and relaxing. For a while, they weren't battling new cases of smallpox, slashing through jungles, running rapids, shooting at cannibals, and wild animals. Everyone had earned some fun and peace.

"Alan and Max, I just wanted to thank you for building us a card table," Jane said, and dealt hands of Spades on the new table, which was just the right height for the chairs they had built previously.

"No problem, girl. Just let us win a few times," Alan laughed.

Later, Jane and Turner slept in their tent instead of the hospital compound, so they could resume their lovemaking. Village kids sneaked up and listened to their moaning and heavy breathing, then ran laughing back towards the village.

Nick learned that many of the elderly women among the pygmies and the Lese knew remedies for certain disorders. They shared the plants, roots, berries, and tubers with him and explained their purposes. Many medicines had already come from the jungles, so he took their homemade medicines seriously, bottling them with samples and instructions. He had a treasure trove of jungle items to take back to Brussels.

What was most gratifying to Nick was the stabilization of these African tribes along the Lulu River. The declining population would most surely have led to the extinction of both these tribes in time. He had certainly reversed the trend. If they followed some of the sanitizing instructions, an even more satisfying outcome might be possible. No one wanted to change or interfere with their way of life. After all, they had survived in these jungles for fifty-to-ninety-thousand years. Smallpox was a disease introduced recently by Europeans and not at all a part of their long history.

Max called a meeting about a week after all the vaccinations were completed. "I would like to congratulate everyone for a successful mission. We have made a difference here. Nick wasn't able to save everyone, but few have passed away since he started the treatments. Nick, thank you for what you have done for these natives, and thanks for keeping us healthy on the trip.

"It's time to pack up. The work has been done, and we'll take the knowledge learned here back to Europe and the United States. We leave in two days," Max said.

Once Nestor and his four traveling companions saw that the expedition was preparing to leave, they pulled Jane aside and spoke to her in their language with a few English words interspersed here and there.

"Jane, we have special gift for you and Turner. We told you at your wedding we wanted to give you gift. You will travel for two days there—two days back. Please ask no questions. You can no bring cameras, and only you and Turner can go. We leave in morning. You bring your weapons—can be dangerous," Nestor said.

"Okay, we'll go with you. Thank you for a wedding present; however, it isn't necessary."

Turner walked up shortly after the exchange. "What's up?"

"We're going to be given a gift but have to travel two days to get it—no cameras."

"Intriguing—exciting."

Later, as the expedition members had dinner, Jane explained as best she could.

"We are being given a wedding gift. Apparently, we will travel two days to get it and cannot take cameras—guns are okay," Jane explained.

"Do you need me to go with you?" Alan asked.

"Only Turner and I can go. Sorry. And we can't talk about what we see, so don't ask us any questions when we get back, or we'll have to lie to you." Jane smiled but was serious. "Also, we can't take pictures."

"A secret place. Very interesting," Max said.

"My God—what a great mystery. I bet you two are about to piss in your pants," Nick said.

"I'm beyond excited just with the expectation of what kind of place it might be. I won't be able to sleep tonight," Jane said.

The evening card game was filled with conversations about lost cities, gold mines, and of course the great book, *King Solomon's Mines*. One thing led to another and the subject of Edgar Rice Burroughs' *Tarzan* surfaced for much discussion.

"I hated the ending," said Jane, who received nods from the others. "Greystoke worked so hard to win over Jane, even came to her home and saved her life again only to be rejected as she chose an old friend to be her intended husband. Why would he do that to us?" Jane asked.

"I think it speaks to classes in society at the time. He could never have been a part of the European social scene because he would have been treated as a freak—raised by apes and all," Max said.

"Maybe, but I think Burroughs just didn't want a fairy tale ending," Turner said.

"I really believe the Manyemas were the cannibals portrayed in the book. The filed sharp teeth and all. He might have picked up the information from Henry Stanley's books," Nick said.

It was a conversation between educated Europeans in a makeshift hospital tent deep in the rain forest of Africa. Their words filtered through the pygmy village of tiny aborigines where a book had never been read, a movie never watched, and school was taught by families who learned skills from natives who were relatively unchanged for thousands of years. It was comforting for the group that missionaries would never be able to penetrate this far into the jungle to change a group of people who were doing just fine on their own.

Before the sun rose the next morning, Turner and Jane were rousted out of their tent. They were told to only bring their sleeping bags; their tents wouldn't be needed. When they asked why, they received no answer.

Some biscuits and dried meat were taken for the trip, along with plenty of purified water.

The original five pygmies led them upriver, first by dugouts, then along jungle trails. Even though the rain forest was typical, with great teak and mahogany trees reaching over a hundred feet tall, there was room to walk in the dark green underworld. Massive roots crossed their path, but few plants grew in the dull light under the canopies. Color was muted, and except for a few orchids, there was little color or flowering plants. It was evident they were following the river upstream probably to its source; the river was not often seen.

The couple was glad they had rested for a few days and had hiked a lot on the trip. It was good training for this trek, which was all uphill, in damp air, thick sucking heat, and they were behind pygmies who were the finest forest humans on earth. The pygmies would stop occasionally to let the large white people rest. The little people observed them trying to catch their breath with a strange curiosity—it wasn't pity—more like amusement. By late afternoon, they merged with a trail that paralleled the now small, trickling stream posing as a river. The thick forest gave way to a grassy slope, and they could see a black ridge of rocks high above them.

Suddenly, there were grunts and howls on the other side of the river. A giant silverback gorilla neared the river, stopped, and pounded his chest. He emitted a ferocious scream that was a conversation understood by everyone in earshot.

Nestor bowed his head. "Look down and don't look in his eyes," he said.

Jane told Turner what Nestor had said, but he had already figured out what they were doing.

Soon the huge beast walked over to where a couple of female gorillas held young babies. The humans took that opportunity to continue their hike on the trail.

It was late afternoon when Jane noticed a structure on a ridge above them with two guards posted at the entrance. As they got closer, it took Jane's breath away. It was an ancient building with twisted Solomonic columns. Some parts were lava blocks; there was also some granite with carvings. Jane and Turner ran until they were touching the outside of the structure. Her hand ran along the carvings on the side of the wall. With her forefinger, she traced the series of side-laying triangles; some pointed to the left and others to the right with slashes crossing them diagonally. Boxes and rectangles were carved next to the arrow-like images.

"Turner, this language could be Sumerian…uhhh…cuneiform… what the…? They're possibly two thousand, three thousand BC!" If Jane had a hobby, it was the study of languages, both written and spoken, and she particularly enjoyed the ancient forms.

"Where in the hell are we?" Turner asked.

Chapter Thirty

Ancient City

"Very old city. Our tribes fought these people for many years and never let any escape to tell of this place. Most of them died of sickness after they built the city. You are the first white people to see this place. It is great honor, but you must never tell anyone. Great secret," Nestor said in his native tongue.

"We will honor that request, Nestor. How did these people come to find this place?" Turner asked and Jane translated.

"They came up Lulu River. Many boats. While they built city, we stole boats and hid them. If any tried to leave, we killed them. They stayed many years, and all finally died. We attacked the city many times. Now we guard city."

Nestor explained to Jane that they would spend the night at this outpost building and go on to the jungle city the next day. Jane and Turner were fascinated by the building, which had remained remarkably unchanged for some four-to-five-thousand years. The roof had been replaced many times, but the natives had kept weeds and vines from overtaking the structure. More writing was found on the interior of the building.

"Turner, you know it's possible much of this writing could be only understood by the person who carved it. Much of it might have been like a personal journal only translatable by the person who carved it."

"You're the linguist in the group, but many of the symbols repeat themselves. If we could copy phrases and take them to a university that has a great antiquities department we might learn part of it."

"Great idea, Turner! Let me ask Nestor if I can copy the symbols," Jane said.

Nestor understood she wanted to try to see what the symbols said. He conferred with the others and they approved it with the provision that neither she nor Turner could tell anyone where she got the symbols.

For hours, the two amateur archeologists poked around every inch of the ancient outpost. The pygmies prepared dinner. They had killed a small antelope and cooked it outside the building next to a stone wall that was the perfect height for sitting and having a meal.

The guards worked shifts. Jane had seen them in the villages and noticed they still had their bandages covering their smallpox vaccinations. Nestor said there were more guards ahead on the trail, never out of sight from the next set of guards.

"As I recall, some forms of very old writings were called proto-writing," Jane said to Turner as she copied more of the ancient script into her journal after dinner. "Mnemonic symbols were used that conveyed some information but were devoid of any real linguistic content. Drawings of hunters stalking animals were told as stories on cave walls going back many thousands of years. Maybe that became like a collection of symbols, such as wavy lines for water and feather-like drawings for wheat or barley. I think our symbols here may have been the shift to something more linguistic."

"What makes you think that, Professor Jane?"

"Well, butt face, the mixture of those common symbols and the arrangement of many other ones in complex combinations suggest more than simple inventories or daily counts. It just looks like conversations to me."

"I'm sure someone at Stanford would love to look at all this," Turner said.

"That'll be great until they ask, 'Where in the hell did you get this?'"

"We will honor Nestor's request," Turner said.

"Absolutely, and that goes for Max, Alan, and Nick," Jane said. "Because if we don't, the word will get out, and people will start poking around here."

They slept in the outpost building with their sleeping bags pulled together. They talked quietly but excitedly with their lips almost touching for much of the night, anticipating what the city would look like. They had been through so much on this expedition, and this side trip seemed to be the ultimate reward. A fourteen-year-old girl and an eighteen-year-old boy had grown to full maturity on this journey. Both were highly intelligent but had lacked the real-world experiences of facing danger and overcoming them until this jaunt. The couple had scars, both emotional and physical, from gun battles, jungle treks, capsizing in rapids, and the loss of people around them. They hoped no one else would be lost on the way out. Their love for each other had grown with the struggles they both shared. It was a honeymoon coming to a close like no other newly married couple in the world had ever experienced. Life should pose lesser problems and obstacles after this adventure.

The morning found the natives cooking native biscuits made from flour given to them by the crew. Normally, they would grind up cassava into flour, but the taste left something to be desired. The leaves of the manioc tree which produced the cassava tubers could also be cooked to add in stews. The Portuguese had brought the plant to Africa five hundred years ago, and it had spread from bird and animal droppings and along waterways where seeds floated.

"How far to the city?" Jane asked Nestor.

"Half day. We will have lunch there. Very beautiful in city."

"Can't wait."

"Do you realize we will be the first people outside his village to see this place in maybe five thousand years? It's incomprehensible!" Turner blurted.

"Well, they don't get a lot of visitors, and my guess is they kill the ones that just stop by for tea."

Nestor led the way to a tree line above a rocky escarpment. From the outpost to the trees were large open grasslands with an unobstructed view. Perched on rocks by the tree line were two more guards. Nestor waved at them as they passed climbing rock by rock on the ridge then upwards taking a well-worn trail next to the now diminutive Lulu River.

"Why would anyone, including a lost civilization or race of people, follow this river to its source?" Turner asked.

"I believe people thought it was like finding the end of a rainbow. Magical things might be there. Some people made it a quest, like finding the source of the Nile," Jane said.

"It's possible they found precious metals in the river and followed that trail upriver," Turner said.

"You're probably right. Let's say it's gold. They may have tried several small rivers until they sampled the Lulu and found small traces of gold farther downstream," Jane said.

"Jane, do you notice how much volcanic rock is strewn around in the river bed?"

"Yes, and the outpost was built with much of it. So, can we assume that on top of this mountain we are climbing is an extinct volcano?

"The very ground we are walking on is part of it as well," Jane said.

"Try not to anger the volcano gods, my dear."

"Little old me? Never."

Four hours and twenty guards later, a huge wall became visible. The walls were black lava stones cut perfectly and capped with a yellowish stone which appeared from a distance to be sandstone. The gigantic doors stood twenty-feet tall, made from native teak and mahogany, with ironwood placed in areas of stress. The hinges were metallic, possibly bronze or an iron alloy. The shape of the entrance and the doors was a slanted triangle with a flat top. Above the door, the wall was decorated by a statue of a man with a beehive headdress, his beard squared at the bottom and top, and wearing a pleated skirt. If this was one of their gods, he had huge protruding eyes to watch over his followers. His beard was shaped like the door, an architectural style reflected in all the doors and windows throughout the many buildings.

As they entered the walled city, they saw a monstrous, flat-topped pyramid structure made of granite and limestone in the center. It was tall and wide, made entirely of light-colored stones, and featured a long ramp going directly center with two other ramps parallel to it and reaching a height equal to a four-story building. On top was a temple like structure which featured rows of twisted columns identical to the ones at the outpost.

"Holy crap!" Jane said, her mouth open in amazement.

"Jesus Christ! It looks like it was built yesterday. Looks new," Turner blurted.

As they walked towards the large ceremonial pyramid, they noticed the streets were porous stone bricks cut from lava, worn in areas where people and carts had moved about. From that evidence alone, Jane and Turner assumed these people occupied this city for many years.

"Let's go on top and see the temple," Jane said.

They walked the steps on the center ramp until they reached the top level and crossed to the temple structure. There was the same oddly shaped door except this one was covered in sheets of thick hammered gold. Turner opened it and examined the hinges which appeared to be solid gold. Both stepped through the door to a dimly lit interior where slices of light illuminated the room from small rectangular windows. Particles of dust floated through the sunlight which was focused on an altar, also covered in a sheet of gold. No chairs, tables, or other furniture were there, only the golden altar. It was obvious that the room had been swept and the altar dusted. The natives kept it as they found it. As they walked out and looked across the roof of the pyramid, their eyes suddenly locked on the huge, black mountain at the rear of the city and noticed for the first time a cave so large it could have swallowed the city.

Chapter Thirty-one

Unspeakable Treasure

Two buildings stood on each side of the cave. Native guards were stationed holding spears and bow and arrows acting as primitive sentries placed to protect the cave from intruders. Jane and Turner rushed down from the pyramid and joined Nestor and the others who were already heading in the direction of the behemoth-sized opening in the mountain. The group walked through well-worn, lava-brick streets, through what appeared to be business districts of large buildings with twisted columns on the front porticos, and finally the smaller stone houses sitting with doors open waiting for occupants who would never come home. Occasionally, erect penises were carved into the sidewalks, pointing to buildings that served as bordellos in ancient times.

"I've seen these penis carvings when I studied Pompeii in school," Jane said.

"You probably studied the penises more than Pompeii, didn't you?"

"Hey, I'm an inquisitive student."

As they neared the cave entrance, the street became a boulevard surrounded by tall rock walls peppered every few yards with guard boxes perched along the outside rim. On each side of the street were channels of fast-moving water running directly from the mouth of the cave and diverted underground to holding areas for drinking, bathing, cleaning, and perhaps even to flush out the sewage and waste of the city. Nearing the cave entrance, the lava bricks gave way to a smooth road surface which led into the cave and also to their right side through a tunnel dipping below the surface of the city.

"Whatever was brought out of the cave must go through that tunnel to be processed," Turner said. "And I'm guessing gold since the door, hinges, and altar were made from it."

"The pygmies don't wear any gold jewelry, but it could be they don't want anyone asking where it came from," Jane said.

The natives split up after being handed torches at the entrance to provide light in front of and behind the group. The smooth surface continued into the darkness. After about a quarter of a mile, the waterway became a single, small river after passing a series of waterfalls on each side that drained through the big mountain from sources high above them. The river was much more placid now, with increasing black sandbanks on each side. The path split and dipped down towards the banks on both sides. Nestor and the pygmies led them off the path and across the sandy banks along the right side. The ceiling of the cave was less imposing than before, yet still some thirty or forty feet above them. They could see a dark area on the wall nearest to them. As they closed the distance, they could see it was obviously a room, not a natural room, but carved by someone. Nestor walked up a series of steps into the chiseled room first. Padi and the others followed with their burning and smoky torches.

At first, Jane was gazing at the marks on the ceiling, which looked like flint used to make primitive arrowheads. Her eyes drifted down at the same time as Nestor lowered his torch over a large waist-high, golden container. The contents exploded with sparkles and dancing reflections of light. Thousands—no, millions of white diamonds filled the golden trunk. Quickly, Nestor walked to another trunk and dipped the burning light, exposing another treasury of pink diamonds, and then another with green, brown, blue, and yellow diamonds. It seemed that someone knew how to grade the industrial stones from the gem-quality diamonds.

At the rear of the room, Padi dipped his torch over the largest of the trunks full of large, irregularly-rounded pieces of placer gold, smoothed from rolling for centuries in the fast-moving waters. As the smoke collected in the room Jane coughed and stuck her head out to grab some fresh air. Nestor followed her out. A wonderful, cool breeze flowed through the cavern and blew her blonde hair into her face. She pulled it back and noticed Nestor standing in front of here.

"I told you back at comfort house we wished to give you wedding present. It is also for saving my people. Here are two sacks for you and Turner. Please fill them but tell no one where they came from. I am glad the other people came with you. Dr. Nick has saved many lives. Give him and the others money after you sell our gifts. Do not let them know you received diamonds and gold. They will tell others, and we will kill them if they come here. Then, many white people will come and kill us to get the diamonds. You hold a great secret. Keep it the greatest secret of your life—forever. You and Turner are much loved by my people."

Jane took the leather sacks made from crocodile skins and wiped the tears from below her eyes. She hugged Nestor and kissed him on his forehead and noticed he had once again produced his often-present erection. She smiled and told Turner about the secrets to be kept and handed him his bag.

"I don't know where to start. Maybe a little gold first—only enough to fill the bottom. So heavy," Turner said. "Oh, yes, tell Nestor I said thanks."

Jane and Turner only put enough gold in their new pouches that they could carry comfortably when they hiked out of the jungle. Then they approached the clear white diamonds and began to fill the bags. The sizes ranged from tiny pieces to stones as large as bird eggs. Next, they filled most of the remaining space with the valuable pink-and rose-colored stones. They only took a handful of the other colored stones, which both believed were industrial-grade gems. They pulled the drawstrings taut, stuffed the bag into their packs, and followed Nestor out of the gigantic cave.

The sunlight seemed different and especially warm on their skin. Jane and Turner looked at each other. Turner looked at Jane's beautiful face and saw her with eyes that now looked way into the future. He was the luckiest man in the world. Each of them would have helped Nestor's people without receiving a dime. Now they were rich beyond what they knew of fortunes. Both their families had wealth but not like this. They had millions of dollars in precious gems, more money than they could ever spend, given to them as a total surprise.

"Please don't let this change us, Jane," Turner said. "I love you without this fortune we just received. Can we use it to help other people?"

"Turner, I love your heart, your kindness, and—your sexy body. We will use enough to get us through medical school and then start a fund to help people who need it. The Goode Foundation. How does that sound?"

"How about the Jungle Jane Foundation for Natives with Uncontrollable Erections?" Turner said, laughing. He too had seen Nestor's reaction to Jane's hug.

"Funny guy. We have to make sure no one finds where these diamonds came from. Can't mention who gave them to us. Can't mention the area where we found them. Can't even say they came from Africa."

They walked with the pygmies out the front gate of the city and on to the trail towards the outpost, which was several hours away. They wanted to get there before dark. Walking down the steep trail, their leg muscles were cramping because different ones were strained.

Other than leg pains, the group was making good time. Every mile or so, they would pass guards stationed on large rocks. After several hours, they encountered the last set of guards before the outpost building. They called Nestor over to express their concern since they had not seen the guards below them in an hour. Nestor asked them to hurry so they could check on the outpost natives. The group hurried down the treeless slope. To the right, at some distance, a silverback gorilla announced his territory. Jane strained to see him, but he was too far off.

A strong breeze blew up from the valley carrying scents of grass, smoke, and something that set the pygmies on edge. As they approached the back patio of the ancient building, a figure walked out on the light-colored stone. His eyes were lifeless, sunken, dull, the color of black slate—void of anything remotely human. He held a bleeding human heart in his right hand, and in the other, he held tightly to wet, greasy hair attached to the severed head of one of the guards. Amcuda's sharpened teeth bit into the heart, chewed it, and swallowed. He let the fresh blood flow down his chin, cheeks, and through the corners of his satanical, grinning mouth onto his naked chest and protruding brown belly, finally sloshing and splattering on his bare feet. Since no weapon was in sight, invincibility and magic powers must have surged through his body. He was prepared to test his imperviousness to being killed.

Chapter Thirty-two

Congo Kingdom Ends

Turner and Jane started to draw their pistols, but Nestor stopped them. This was their fight. Two pygmies had been killed and violated by this Manyema vampire. He would find justice at the hands of the tribe of the victims. In unison, the five pygmies attacked the bloated Amcuda. He fought against them for only a short time, holding out hope his new magic would overcome anything. But there were too many pygmies and too little magic.

The pygmies eventually pushed him down on the stone floor and tied his hands behind his back, with rope supplied by Jane. He seemed to be totally void of the charmed state of immunity he traveled so far to possess. The Europeans knew his death would be slow, excruciating, and enjoyed by all the tribes in the area. Snacking on the heart of a pygmy was high on the capital punishment list of offenses of the natives' justice system. A slow, entertaining, torturous death would be advertised by drums and runners to all the villages.

Jane wanted no part of it and planned to be on the trail home before the festivities began. Instead of spending the night at the outpost, they walked through the jungle and along the river, taking advantage of as much of the remaining daylight as possible. Stretchers were made from tarps from Turner and Jane's packs to carry the two dead guards. One of the guards at the level above the outpost came down and agreed to be a runner to summon help carrying the dismembered corpses.

By the time they had reached the first village, swarms of villagers were marching beside them, jeering and poking at the Manyeman

King. It was long after dark when they reached Nestor's village, but they had learned from runners Amcuda was on his way. They inserted a huge pole in the center of the village, and on his arrival, Amcuda was securely strapped and bound in this place of dishonor. He was welcomed with the removal of his loin cloth, and honey was placed on his scrotum and penis. His screams rattled through the village as the contents of an anthill were poured onto his honey-laden groin. However, a more lethal creature would soon be unleashed on him, as the pygmies brought a greenish yellow snake into the village from the forest.

"Boomslang!" Turner said.

"It will be a slow, excruciating, horrifying death," Nick said as he joined Turner and Jane in the hospital tent.

One of the pygmies dangled the poisonous reptile near Amcuda's calf muscle, pressed and opened the snake's mouth, exposing two sets of triplicate rear fangs. With the precision of an accomplished herpetologist, the native turned the boomslang's head at an angle, allowing only fangs on one side to inject one of the world's most insidious venoms.

"He is limiting the amount of poison so it will take him longer to die," Nick explained. "The poison breaks down the blood's ability to clot, and in about 24 hours, he will start bleeding to death from all of his orifices."

"Yuck! I wish they would just kill him already and go on about their lives," Jane said.

"This is their life," Max said. "Tell us about your trip and how all this started."

Jane and Turner had rehearsed their explanation of the trip. Lying always requires practice and repetition to make it believable, but it was no less a distasteful act to subject on their friends.

Turner chose to lie first. "They took us to one of their sacred places where the water for the Lulu River comes out of the mountain or volcano, I guess you would call it. They had built a few stone walls and guarded the place for probably thousands of years. It was beautiful, and we both hope no one will ever disturb its pristine beauty. It was a great gift for us to see it. On the way back, there were two guards by a lower wall who had been killed by Amcuda. He had cut out their hearts and severed their heads. When we approached the wall on the way down, he showed himself and bit into one of the hearts and ate part of it in front of us."

"Don't ever try to go up there as they have orders to kill anyone that sets foot on the sacred grounds. We were the first white people to go there, and it is considered a great honor," Jane said.

"I've got no desire to go there and risk my ass," Max said.

Nick and Alan also shook their heads in disapproval.

No one seemed suspicious as to what else was found on the trip, so they had no reason to question them further. Turner and Jane both felt badly about concealing the marvelous discovery. One word or slip-up about the incredible treasure might cause hordes of adventurers to overrun the villages. It would be as though they had murdered all the people in every village.

Jane and Turner would convert some of the bounty over to cash and pay the other members a handsome bonus which would dilute their guilt a great deal.

"What are they doing now?" Jane asked as she saw several natives carrying something in a piece of cloth.

"My God!" stammered Nick.

The natives had fashioned a diaper from cloth and filled it with leeches, then tied it securely around Amcuda's groin area. They could see the leeches crawling out of the diaper and attaching to his thigh and stomach area. The creatures inside the wrap were heading for the tender areas. Amcuda's now-hoarse screams were unsettling for the Europeans, but they knew better than to interfere.

It was late. Turner and Jane were wasted from the trip and decided to turn in. To dampen the sound from Amcuda's agony, they stuffed cotton balls in their ears and buried up in their sleeping bags. After an hour or so, Amcuda fainted from the pain, allowing the couple to get some much needed sleep.

Their sleep was deep. Beyond the realm of abysmal slumber, they didn't hear the disturbing noises outside their tent. At three o'clock in the morning, four Manyeman warriors held shotguns on the five explorers in the hospital tent. Alan, Nick, and Max were standing in their underwear, while the Manyema natives poked the barrels of their guns over and over into the rib cages of the exhausted couple.

Finally, they woke, groggy, disoriented, and pissed. Yambo, Nestor, and the other members of the expedition had found girlfriends in the village and were sleeping soundly. The tall Watutsi could easily be spotted, as his feet protruded from the hut of a young pygmy girl. There were many widows after the smallpox epidemic, and they believed all the members of the expedition were heroes and should be rewarded. None of the men complained.

As the Manyemas quietly marched the group from the tent to the waterfront, it became clear that Amcuda had been cut loose from the pole and had been moved. Two pygmies lay dead near the pole, their throats cut, and body parts removed. Jane played the grogginess to her advantage. Staggering around, she grabbed at her pants and gun belt but was asked to drop them both by the natives. She was in her underwear, as were the others, and protested.

"Let me have my pants. I only have panties on," she said in their language.

She held her pants and gun belt in her shaking hands. One large warrior grabbed them from her and pointed her towards the door of the tent. She stumbled going out the door and fell near a perpetually burning fire pit. Turner reached down to help her up and blocked her body from the nearest native as he watched her toss something in the fire. The bullet bounced off a fiery log and directly into the red hot coals out of view. She had pulled it from her ammunition belt while fumbling with her pants.

There were only three Manyeman dugouts docked at the river's edge, one colorfully decorated to accommodate their king. All the pygmies' boats had been pushed out into the darkness of the Lulu River. Although it was very dark, Alan counted eight warriors, four with Amcuda, and two in each of the dugouts with the expedition members. They silently moved out into the stream under a dark night sky, where fast-moving clouds had temporarily masked a full moon.

They had not gone far when the sound of a small explosion rattled and bounced across the water and startled everyone in the boats, except for a couple of smiling perpetrators. Paddles then dug deep into the water and panicked expressions stuck to the faces of the kidnappers.

Nestor was the first to respond to the bullet exploding, followed by Yambo, who quickly retrieved his BAR and an extra drum of ammunition. Once the two dead and mutilated guards were found it was like a kicked-over anthill throughout the village. Those villagers who could swim headed into the river to capture some runaway boats. Nestor, Padi, and the other expedition natives headed downriver on a well-known pygmy trail. Beli, Azima and Lamia all found guns in the tent. Beli had been given the responsibility of learning to use and care for Lutz's big game rifle, while Azima and Lamia had pump 12-gauge shotguns, one part of the village's collection of fine arms. Nestor and Padi had found Jane and Turner's .45 automatics. Both had fired them while on the trip when there was downtime and scored tin cans and big logs with circles drawn with charcoal from fire pits. All the natives had their bows and arrows strapped to their back in hopes that they could takes the lives of the intruders with traditional methods. Even though it was pitch dark, Nestor and his band of soldiers were running at full speed along the narrow trail.

Jane punched Turner, while trying not to look at the sky.

"In an hour or so, the clouds will blow over and expose a full moon. If Yambo has the BAR, he can take most of them out. Also, we'll have to stop for the rapids and walk the boats around them," Jane said.

"They won't stop," Turner said. "It will be do or die. But I don't know what they expect to do with us."

The Manyemas yelled at the couple in Bantu to shut up. The air had cooled flowing over the fast-moving water, and Jane was wearing only a light sleep shirt and underwear so she clung to Turner for warmth. Turner wore only boxer shorts, but Max, being old-fashioned, was wearing full pajamas. He quickly pulled off his pants and passed them back to Jane, who would have married him at that point, except she remembered she was taken.

"They plan to eat us!" Max said, looking at his boxers to see if anything had escaped from the front flap. "If the pygmies didn't have the magic the Manyemas had hoped for, then maybe white people have a little magic. The truth is, they like white human meat."

"What part of me would they eat first?" Jane asked with a smile. She was making conversation to keep from being scared.

"Your ass. It's beautiful, plenty of meat, and tender," Turner said.

"Maybe your breasts. Tender, and I've been told they're made mostly of fat. So maybe they're flavorful," Max said.

"I always figured you for a boob man," Turner said.

"I love breasts, but the truth is they go for internal organs first since there is no skin to remove, and they figure the liver, kidneys, and heart hold all the magic and power," Max said.

"I'll refrain from ever telling any of you to 'bite my ass' since you just might do it. Do you think they will cook me first? It seems like an 'ass' steak should be grilled and seasoned. Maybe they could carve a rump roast out of me?" Jane chuckled, causing the native to bump her with the butt of his shotgun as he told her to be quiet. They heard laughter from Alan and Nick in a nearby dugout; the two men had been monitoring their conversation.

After what seemed like hours, they heard something in the distance. Unmistakably, it was monstrous rapids—rapids that no sane person would try to attempt in daylight, let alone on a dark night. The moon had yet to escape the flow of charcoal clouds, even though it looked like it would any minute.

The Manyemas looked up as though they were also waiting for the moon. They pulled to the bank and continued to wait. Finally, the sky cleared, and a beautiful golden moon burst out into the heavens and lit up the river. A yell—then rapid conversation could be heard from the royal dugout. Jane translated the natives' excited words.

"Amcuda is bleeding from his eyes, mouth, nose, ears— everywhere! It appears the aristocracy of the Manyema nation is going to need a new monarch," she said.

A clamor above the boat overpowered the roar of the approaching rapids. At first, it sounded like the flutter of a huge flock of birds. The sky was dark above them as arrows flew over, swarmed, and dove into the royal canoe. Hundreds of these primitive shafts covered every inch of the vessel and the bodies and heads of the Manyemas, killing all of them in the boat.

The head of the native standing by Jane disappeared before she heard the gunshot. The native at the bow of their dugout turned and fired his shotgun just as he was hit multiple times by the BAR manned by Yambo. The two paddlers in Alan and Nick's boat were both blown from the boat by the elephant gun of Lutz, manned by Beli, and another barrage of bullets from Yambo's BAR. The captives were fortunate that Yambo and Beli had been trained to use the weapons that took out the Manyemas and didn't strike any of the captives.

Swimmers dove in and pulled the dugouts and Amcuda's vessel to the shore. The expedition didn't want to know what hideous ritual would accompany the disposition of those bodies—especially the native king's snake-bitten and arrow-riddled carcass. Regardless, they would know soon enough.

A huge pyre was constructed on the river bank from wood found along the bank, in the jungle, and cut from nearby trees. While Jane sat on the edge of one of the dugouts, she saw the pygmies cut the heads from the Manyema warriors and bury them in a hole dug in deep sand and gravel. Dismembered bodies were stacked on the giant bonfire as it was ignited from torches brought by tribal members. They now wouldn't be able to find their way to the afterlife since their heads were missing.

Amcuda was a different matter. It was clear he was royalty, and the evil king of the Manyemas deserved attention unlike any enemy faced by the pygmies. Nestor approached Jane with the description of the disposition of Amcuda's remains.

"We will smoke his head and cure it—decorate it—and put it on a tall pole. Each village will have it for equal times. A special honor to have a king's head to celebrate. His bones will be taken from him and divided among the villages. They will carve fish hooks—much magic. Knives, arrow and spear points will help with the hunt. Every bone will have a purpose, even for the Lese, who will make hoes for farming. Great medicine for everyone."

Turner and Jane were not too shocked by the recycling of body parts. It was well known that many tribes took great pleasure in using their enemy's carcasses in many ways. Had the pygmies been the defeated foes of the Manyemas, their bodies would have been cut in small pieces and shared with their tribal members as a special meal.

While the bodies were still burning, the expedition was taken upstream to Nestor's village. It had been a traumatic night, but Jane was still going to get some sleep because the plans were to pack up and head back later that day. She gave Max his pajamas and thanked him with a hug.

Turner walked out of the tent to the latrine before getting in his sleeping bag. Across from the latrine, a new fire was burning. The wood was mostly green, causing a tremendous amount of smoke. As he watched, Amcuda's head was placed in the center, mounted on a large green bamboo pole. His eyes had been sewn shut and the brains removed and placed somewhere. Turner didn't want to know where. He wanted to pee, to sleep, and leave, in that order, as soon as possible.

Chapter Thirty-three

The Way Back

Nick made his rounds with the natives after getting up around noon. There had been no new smallpox cases in any of the villages. Boils, cysts, tumors, and other ailments had been treated by Nick's competent hands. The rest of the expedition was packing and loading the dugouts.

Nestor appeared at the front of the hospital tent, accompanied by a young female. Jane came outside and Nestor introduced her to his wife. Jane took her hand and wished her well in her language. Nestor felt compelled to tell her the story of their marriage.

"I asked her father if I could marry his daughter and gave him an antelope I had killed. She screamed and ran into the forest, but I chased her and brought her back. She did this three times before she agreed to be my wife. Her father said it was done, and we are married. We don't have ceremonies."

Jane congratulated him and his wife. Before she left, she would meet all the new wives. The original five pygmies accompanied them out of the village and went with the crew of nine upriver as far as they could in the pygmies' dugouts. The expedition had hiked in but would cut off two to three days travel by taking advantage of the downstream current.

They took the first series of rapids without a problem and found good water for most of the day. They passed all the villages they had stopped at before and waved as they went by. Late in the afternoon, the group passed by the elephant bia. No elephants could be seen anywhere.

The crew was put ashore at the base of some unnavigable rapids. Nestor and his friends said their goodbyes and posed for pictures. It was not said, but everyone thought it—they would never see each other again. They waved as they paddled their dugouts against the current on their way back to their village. Jane wiped her eyes and watched until the pygmies were out of sight. They set up camp next to the well-worn jungle trail. Starting the next morning, everyone would know what to expect on the way back.

The group followed the trail for two days and found the four dugouts just where they had left them. Now they only needed three. Yambo joined Nick and Max and took Lutz's place in the boat. The three porters had a canoe to themselves, and Jane, Turner, and Alan were together. A smaller assemblage than when they started, but experience and knowledge of the river and its surrounding geography made travel easy. Now they were going downstream and would soon meet the tributary that would take them along the Lulu until they merged with the Bunga. It would be upstream from there until they came to the road crossing.

In less than two weeks, they had completed the journey back to Stanleyville. A military truck had been waiting for them when they reached the road. They stopped along the way at the general store to turn in the canoes and pay for the one they left by the river, and briefly at the government house to report on their mission. Here, they received information on the Manyemas and their fight with the Belgians.

"The fighting is over between the natives and the Belgian troops. Since there was no king to lead them they laid down their arms and went back to their villages. The soldiers also went home. Peace for now, but before long, they will get another king and start all over again," Oliver Vermeulen said.

Turner and Jane found the hotel in Stanleyville to be their private cloud nine. They contacted the float plane owner and learned he would be there the next day. The rest of the group was taking the boat back, and it was already docked. Jane went aboard and spoke to captain Rudy, who couldn't believe they were still alive. He promised to stop and give the shotguns up at the Congo general store since they had only rented them. He claimed he forgot to stop on his trip back. Arrangements were made for Rudy to bring his daughter by the comfort house to have her picture made with Jane.

Jane paid the expedition members twice what she had promised from her branch bank in Stanleyville and took down their addresses and account numbers of their banks, so she could send them even more bonuses later. Sending money to other countries was tricky because of the Depression, but postal orders were simple to use for small transfers. Large European banks could do wire transfers in certain conditions. The US had passed a banking stabilization act earlier that year, but it didn't solve all the problems of the economy—just kept it from getting worse. Part of the act stated that individuals and companies could not possess monetary gold. Jane and Turner's gold was the placer nugget variety, but it probably would have to be sold in Great Britain or another European country where no restrictions existed.

Once everyone was in place onboard the *Lapsley*, Turner and Jane found the solitude of their hotel room.

"Turner, can we take a bath together?"

"Oh, I guess so. Do I get my back washed?"

"Dear, you get everything washed!"

"Okay then."

Jane drew the bath with water heated in the hotel's boiler. All their clothes were filthy, and they would have to hand-wash them after their bath. Even though the hotel had a laundry service, they wouldn't get them back in time for their flight. Outside their hotel window was a small balcony—perfect for draping clothes out to dry.

"You first, dear," said Turner. He helped her step over into the large, claw-foot porcelain bathtub and then slid in with his back against her front.

"Turner, we did it!"

"I know. We're damn lucky to be alive."

"Thanks for going with me—thanks for being my husband."

"It's not a hard job. Well, maybe when you play the part of Jungle Jane."

"They know we're back. The hotel clerk said a reporter will be here to interview us at breakfast," Jane said.

"Had better make it quick. We have a plane to catch."

"Wow! I believe someone around front is happy to see me." She reached between Turner's legs and soaped him until he released.

"Happy guy?"

"Of course, but let's hope he comes back to life for you later."

"I'll take my chances."

"Do you have any idea what we're going to do with the diamonds and gold?" Turner asked.

"We can leave some in the safety deposit box in Brazzaville—take the rest to London. As we need money, we go to Amsterdam or Brussels and sell some diamonds," Jane said.

"Too simple. You forget about Customs. We need luggage with a false bottom, secret compartments, a lining that unzips. Can we find luggage like that or have it made?" Turner asked. "If we bring diamonds in without paying Customs and get caught, it's jail time."

"If we leave most of the gold and a lot of the diamonds at my bank, we can come here to visit every few years and retrieve some. What we take with us will be worth millions so there is no hurry to come back. All our problems are good ones, my dear," Jane said. "Also, if we fly all the way to a small airport in England, there will be very little security—maybe not any. Just a passport check and the question, 'Do you have anything to declare?'"

They took their bath and dried each other off, washed a change of clothes, then hung them on the balcony. Their lovemaking was intense since it had been a couple of weeks since they had had sex. Their depleted supply of condoms was remedied thanks to a local drug store.

The next morning, they packed and carried their backpacks with them to the hotel café for breakfast. While they were eating eggs, biscuits, and bacon and drinking great African coffee, a newsman came by their table to interview the great Jungle Jane.

"Jane, were you attacked by cannibals when you went to the pygmies' village? How did you survive? Were you taken captive? How many did you personally shoot? Do the pygmies really have poisoned arrows? Did you really have an elephant chase you, so your big game hunter could get a shot?" The reporter had obviously talked with other members of the expedition.

Jane played down her part and gave most of the credit to the pygmies for their brave attack on the Manyemas. The reporter would have no part of it and continued to paint the picture of Jungle Jane, the hero. He finally left with a story destined to be embellished and enhanced. The truth would be the victim of a growing need to build a legend.

After quizzing the front desk clerk, they learned there was a luggage store close to the street that led to the float planes. There they bought crocodile luggage that contained secret compartments with zippers hidden behind flaps, pockets, and liners. They were smiling when they loaded their gear on the old float plane.

The trip to Brazzaville was exciting and beautiful as the plane sputtered along for hours over green jungles and muddy rivers. Late the next day, they arrived in Brazzaville after several stops for fuel, meals, and bathroom breaks. Jane used the payphone at the docks and got Francis on the line.

"Hey, can you guys pick us up at the docks?"

"Be there in ten minutes. Both of you alive?"

"Of course—you forget—I'm Jungle Jane."

"My God! You crazy kids made it!" Francis said, as he threw their luggage in the back of his old truck. Hattie was waiting in the yard to greet them when they pulled to a stop.

"God was looking out for your asses—that's for damn sure! Come here and let me hug you both," Hattie said. She ran to them and squeezed the air from their lungs.

The entire complement of luggage and backpacks were pitched in the same room Jane occupied the day she first arrived. Drinks were prepared and guests all got up to greet them. Jane and Turner didn't recognize anyone, except Roger Janssen. Jane shook his hand.

"Thank you again for buying the stone. It helped finance the expedition and saved many lives," Jane said. She would have loved to ask him how to smuggle millions of dollars of diamonds into England without spending the rest of her life in jail.

Repeatedly, Jane and Turner told of their adventure, as guests hung on every word. It wasn't long before a local reporter came by and got his interview. It would be in all the papers, a compelling reason for the couple to be asked to fly by charter to small airports to avoid the onslaught of camera and reporters. Africa didn't have great air service anyway, so charters were quite common.

When Hattie finally got Turner and Jane alone, she said, "Stanford sent you a big package."

"Where is it?" Jane asked.

Hattie disappeared into the kitchen where she kept her desk and came out with a bulky manila envelope. The couple tore into it and found their official acceptance letters from Stanford, a study guide, college handbook, and biology textbook. Even though they had received a wire message before their trip, this package contained everything they needed for completing prerequisite courses.

Inside the envelope was an itemized bill of $1,265 each for the first year at Stanford, including room and board for married students, starting with the summer term. Their scholarships were pending approval. There was a strange item listed as a health fee for $10. A welcome letter was signed by the newly appointed Dean of Medicine, Dr. Loren "Yank" Chandler.

They could take all courses at Oxford in time for the trip to America. Jane had high school courses, and both needed a special biology course. That one they would take together and share the book sent to them. It would be finished while they waited for the crew to arrive on the steamer. From the information in the packet, they found that Stanford's medical campus was actually in San Francisco at the site of the old Cooper Medical School—now they would be that much closer to Turner's friend Jim.

Jane and Turner stayed at the comfort house until Rudy's boat arrived. The whole crew came by to stay a couple of days, which was a good excuse for a party. It was planned for the night that Rudy brought his daughter over. The girl was very excited to meet Jane. Mr. Z took her picture with Jane, thanks to her dad hiring the professional photographer. Max, Alan, Nick, and Yambo had pictures made with the entire expedition holding up drinks. Max offered a toast to the memory of Lutz Holtzman, and many kind words were spoken about him. The next day, Jane and Turner started their long journey back home.

The couple flew to Cape Town on float planes in order to catch the Imperial Airlines AW Artemis plane, which covered much of their flight home. Most planes could only go a few hundred miles, if that far, and then, while it was still daylight, the pilot would have to find a small airfield that had a small hotel or rooms to rent, and meals.

After a week of landing at small airstrips requiring overnight accommodations in small African towns, Jane and Turner Simpson boarded a private charter and landed at a small regional airport in Reading, England. Their passports were stamped by a Customs official who had been given a bonus by Basil to make an appearance at this obscure landing strip.

The young couple was whisked away after their entire luggage was pitched unceremoniously into the spacious trunk of Basil's Bentley. Sitting in the back seat, Jane and Turner smelled the fine leather, ran their hands over the polished walnut trim, and listened to Jane's Aunt Abbie rattle on about having Jungle Jane captured in her car.

In unison, Jane and Turner turned and stared toward the trunk where their fortune rode in luxury and smiled.

The End

Charles L. (Chap) Harper

Chap Harper is the author of five published books. His most recent, Shortcut, is a thriller which begins with investigations by Interpol agents into strange satellite phone chatter in Lyon, France. At the same time, a former law enforcement officer, Lester McFarlin, questions strange occurrences on a cruise ship where he is enjoying his honeymoon. As the inquiries continue, a far-reaching and complex plot is uncovered concerning Islamic terrorists who plan to blow up the Panama Canal and all the ships in the locks.

Harper's first book Once Upon a Reef was published by Green King Publishing in 2012. He followed up that novel with Once Upon the Congo in 2015, Beer, Bait, and Ammo in 2016, Under Cuba in 2017, and Shortcut in 2018, all through Smoking Gun Publishing. Chap attended the University of Arkansas and retired as an officer with the CNA Insurance Companies. He and his wife Susan live on Lake Hamilton in Hot Springs, Arkansas.